• CUBE KID •

DIARY OF AN 8-BIT WARRIOR

GRAPHIC NOVEL

AN OP ALLIANCE

STORY ADAPTED BY
PIRATE SOURCIL

ILLUSTRATED BY
JEZ ⬡ COLORED BY
ODONE

Andrews McMeel
PUBLISHING®

Thank you, Jez and Joël, for taking my ideas and
expressing them perfectly in art and color!
Thanks also to my family, Marion, and to
Anne-Charlotte for her steady support!
THOMAS

Thanks to my loved ones, Maite and Meryl, for their support.
Thanks also to the dream team, Thomas, Joël, and
Anne-Charlotte. It was great working with you!
And thank you, Cube Kid, for letting us play in your universe!
JEZ

This edition © 2021 by Andrews McMeel Publishing.

All rights reserved. Printed in China. No part of this book may be used
or reproduced in any manner whatsoever without written permission
except in the case of reprints in the context of reviews.

Translated and based on the series of novels originally created
by Cube Kid © 404 éditions, a department of Édi8. Text by Pirate
Sourcil and illustrations by Jez © 2019 Editions Jungle/ Édi8.

Minecraft is a Notch Development AB registered trademark. This book
is a work of fiction and not an official Minecraft product, nor approved
by or associated with Mojang. The other names, characters, places,
and plots are either imagined by the author or used fictitiously.

Andrews McMeel Publishing
a division of Andrews McMeel Universal
1130 Walnut Street, Kansas City, Missouri 64106
www.andrewsmcmeel.com

21 22 23 24 25 SDB 10 9 8 7 6 5 4 3 2 1

ISBN: 978-1-5248-6316-6 (Paperback)
ISBN: 978-1-5248-6757-7 (Hardback)

Library of Congress Control Number: 2020945405

Made by:
King Yip (Dongguan) Printing & Packaging Factory Ltd.
Address and location of manufacturer:
Daning Administrative District, Humen Town
Dongguan Guangdong, China 523930
1st printing—11/23/20

ATTENTION: SCHOOLS AND BUSINESSES
Andrews McMeel books are available at quantity discounts with
bulk purchase for educational, business, or sales promotional use.
For information, please e-mail the Andrews McMeel Publishing
Special Sales Department: specialsales@amuniversal.com.

PART ONE

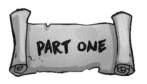

A NEW WARRIOR

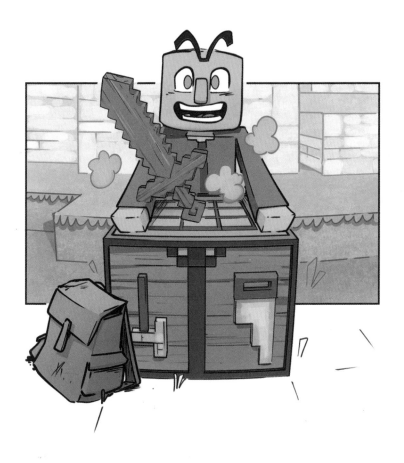

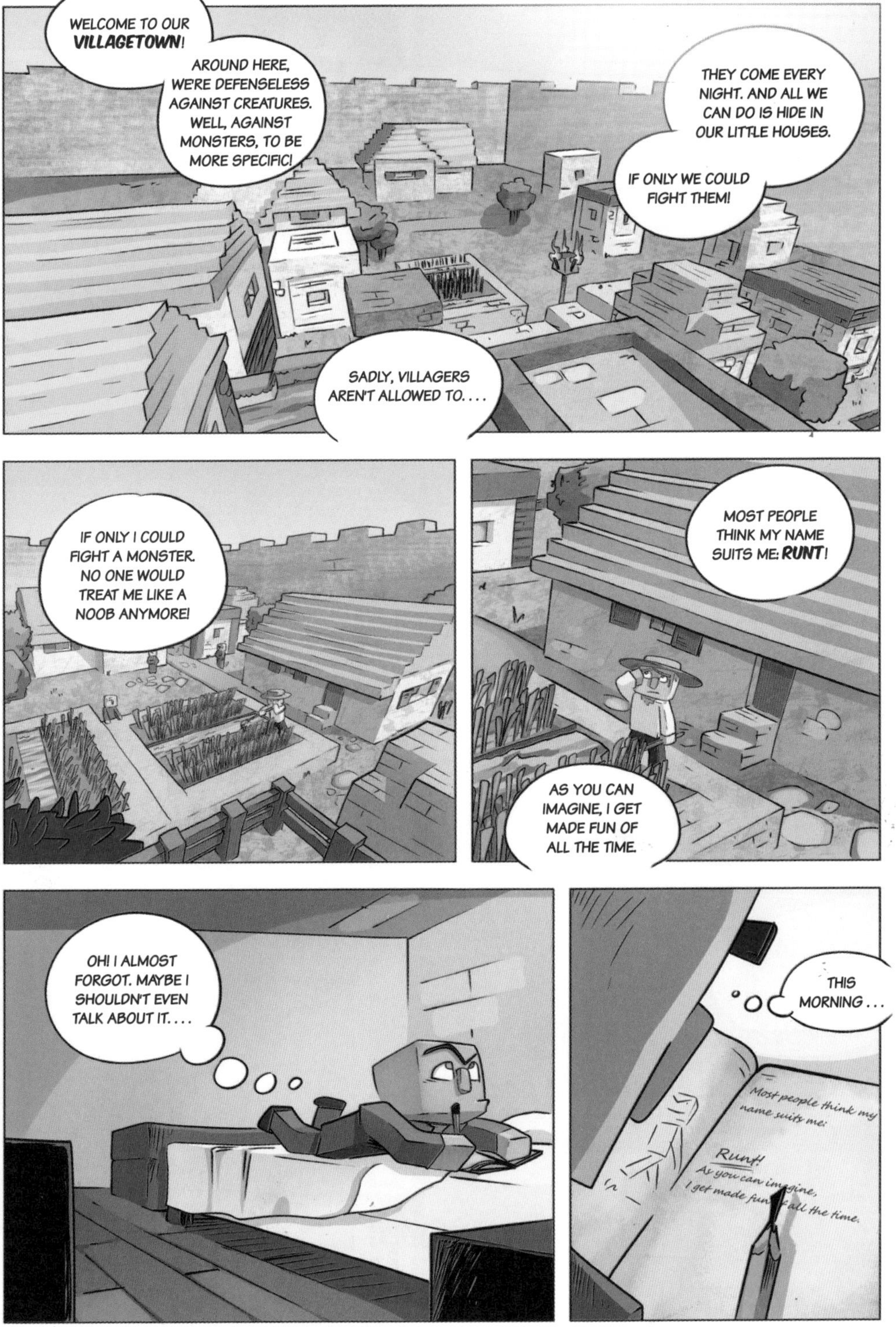

WELCOME TO OUR **VILLAGETOWN**!
AROUND HERE, WE'RE DEFENSELESS AGAINST CREATURES. WELL, AGAINST MONSTERS, TO BE MORE SPECIFIC!
THEY COME EVERY NIGHT. AND ALL WE CAN DO IS HIDE IN OUR LITTLE HOUSES.
IF ONLY WE COULD FIGHT THEM!
SADLY, VILLAGERS AREN'T ALLOWED TO. . . .
IF ONLY I COULD FIGHT A MONSTER. NO ONE WOULD TREAT ME LIKE A NOOB ANYMORE!
MOST PEOPLE THINK MY NAME SUITS ME: **RUNT**!
AS YOU CAN IMAGINE, I GET MADE FUN OF ALL THE TIME.
OH! I ALMOST FORGOT. MAYBE I SHOULDN'T EVEN TALK ABOUT IT. . . .
THIS MORNING . . .
Most people think my name suits me:
Runt!
As you can imagine,
all the time.

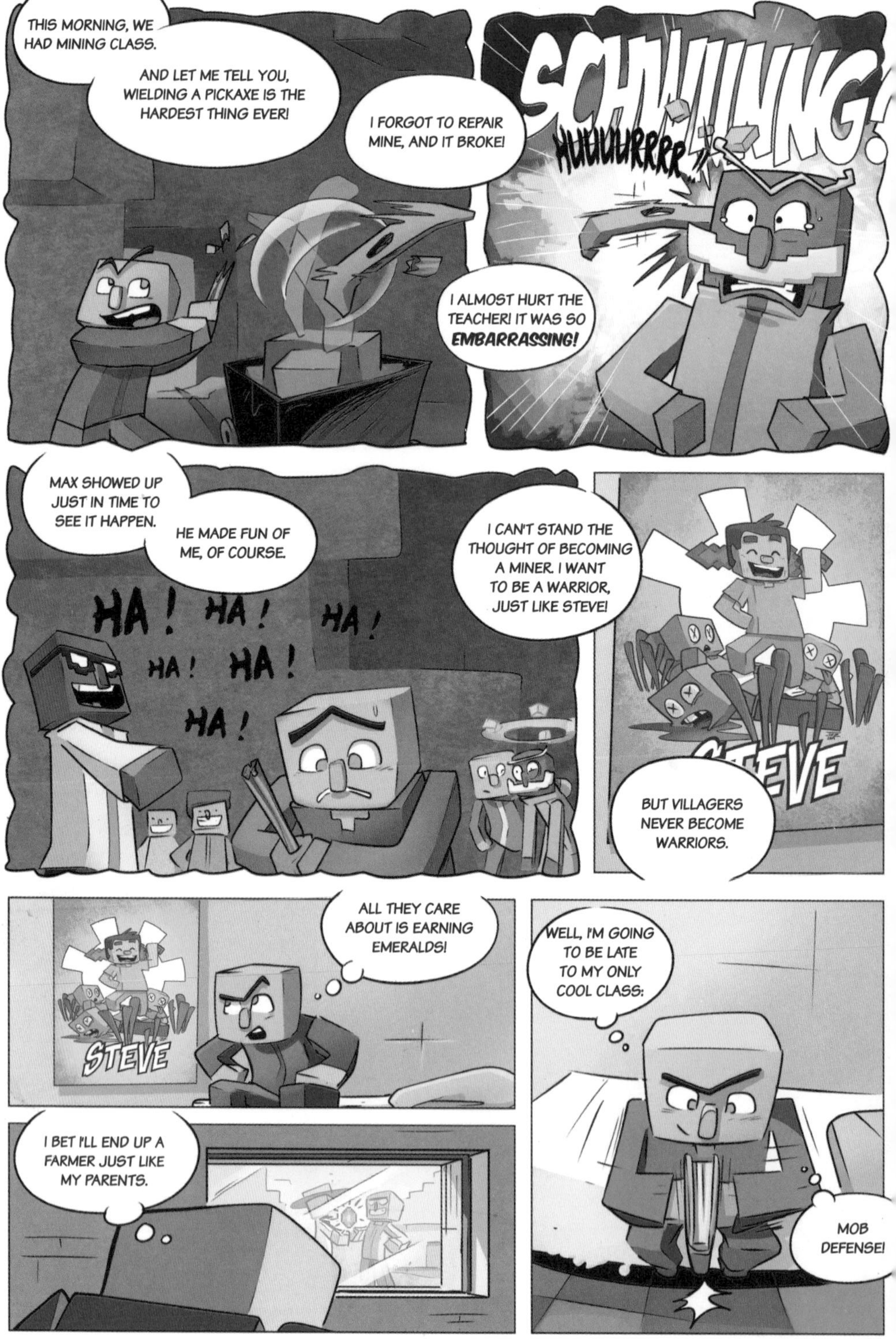
THIS MORNING, WE HAD MINING CLASS.
AND LET ME TELL YOU, WIELDING A PICKAXE IS THE HARDEST THING EVER!
I FORGOT TO REPAIR MINE, AND IT BROKE!
SCHWIIING!
HUUUURRRR!!
I ALMOST HURT THE TEACHER! IT WAS SO **EMBARRASSING!**
MAX SHOWED UP JUST IN TIME TO SEE IT HAPPEN.
HE MADE FUN OF ME, OF COURSE.
HA! HA! HA! HA! HA! HA!
I CAN'T STAND THE THOUGHT OF BECOMING A MINER. I WANT TO BE A WARRIOR, JUST LIKE STEVE!
STEVE
BUT VILLAGERS NEVER BECOME WARRIORS.
ALL THEY CARE ABOUT IS EARNING EMERALDS!
STEVE
WELL, I'M GOING TO BE LATE TO MY ONLY COOL CLASS:
I BET I'LL END UP A FARMER JUST LIKE MY PARENTS.
MOB DEFENSE!

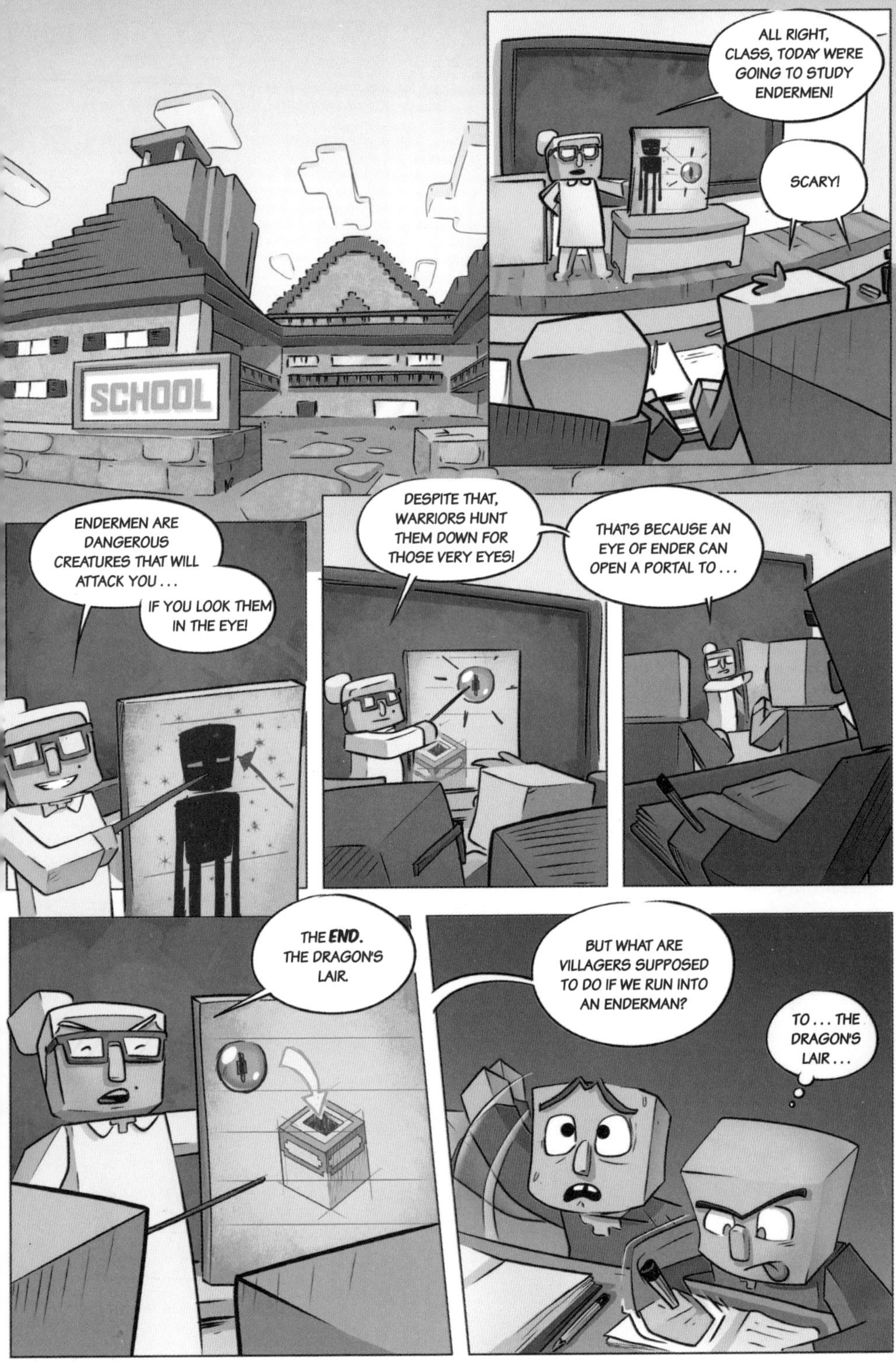
SCHOOL
ALL RIGHT, CLASS, TODAY WE'RE GOING TO STUDY ENDERMEN!
SCARY!
ENDERMEN ARE DANGEROUS CREATURES THAT WILL ATTACK YOU . . .
IF YOU LOOK THEM IN THE EYE!
DESPITE THAT, WARRIORS HUNT THEM DOWN FOR THOSE VERY EYES!
THAT'S BECAUSE AN EYE OF ENDER CAN OPEN A PORTAL TO . . .
THE **END.** THE DRAGON'S LAIR.
BUT WHAT ARE VILLAGERS SUPPOSED TO DO IF WE RUN INTO AN ENDERMAN?
TO . . . THE DRAGON'S LAIR . . .

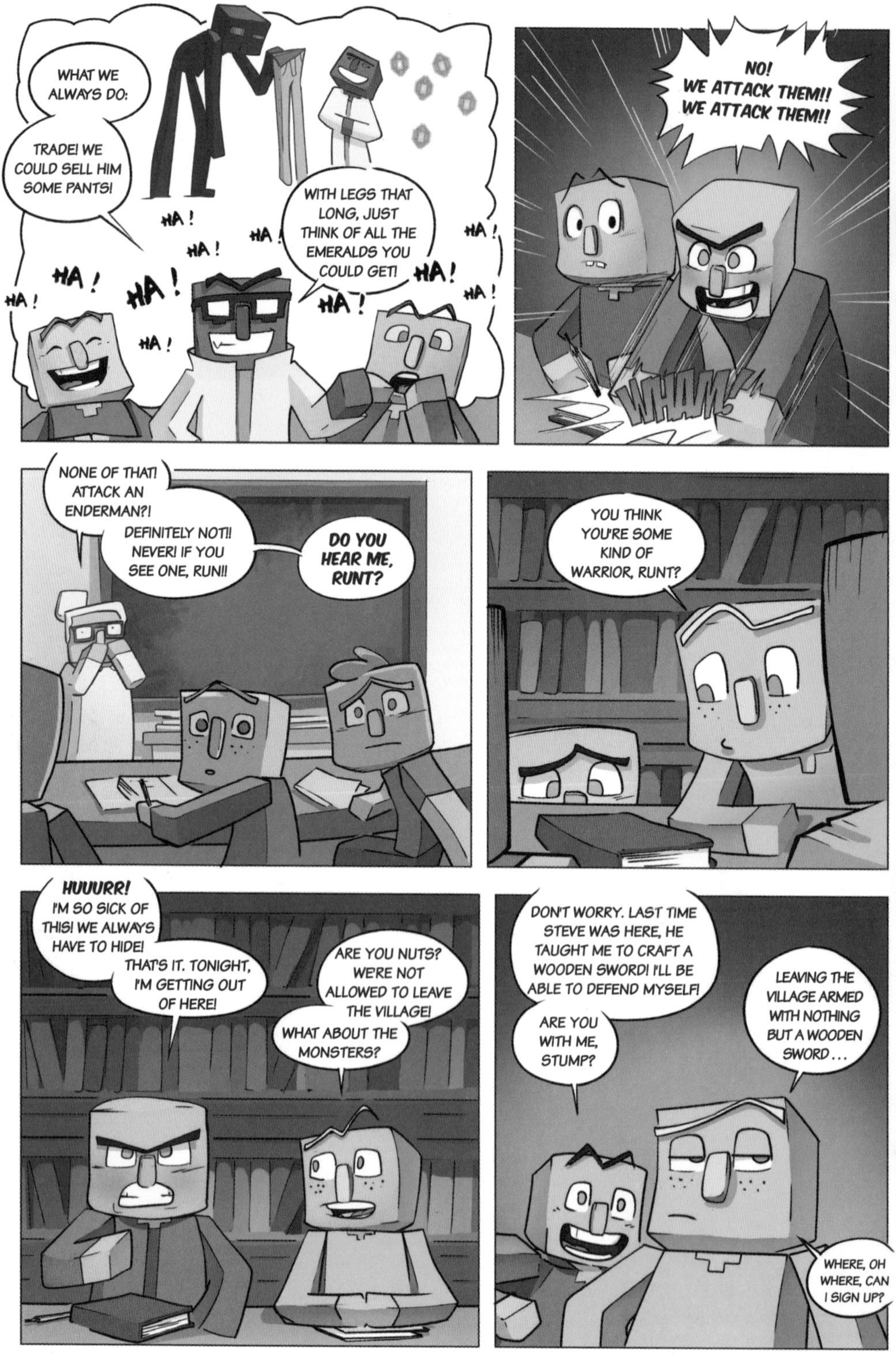
WHAT WE ALWAYS DO:
TRADE! WE COULD SELL HIM SOME PANTS!
WITH LEGS THAT LONG, JUST THINK OF ALL THE EMERALDS YOU COULD GET!
HA! HA! HA! HA! HA! HA! HA! HA! HA! HA! HA! HA!
NO! WE ATTACK THEM!! WE ATTACK THEM!!
WHAM!
NONE OF THAT! ATTACK AN ENDERMAN?!
DEFINITELY NOT!! NEVER! IF YOU SEE ONE, RUN!!
DO YOU HEAR ME, RUNT?
YOU THINK YOU'RE SOME KIND OF WARRIOR, RUNT?
HUUURR! I'M SO SICK OF THIS! WE ALWAYS HAVE TO HIDE!
THAT'S IT. TONIGHT, I'M GETTING OUT OF HERE!
ARE YOU NUTS? WE'RE NOT ALLOWED TO LEAVE THE VILLAGE!
WHAT ABOUT THE MONSTERS?
DON'T WORRY. LAST TIME STEVE WAS HERE, HE TAUGHT ME TO CRAFT A WOODEN SWORD! I'LL BE ABLE TO DEFEND MYSELF!
ARE YOU WITH ME, STUMP?
LEAVING THE VILLAGE ARMED WITH NOTHING BUT A WOODEN SWORD . . .
WHERE, OH WHERE, CAN I SIGN UP?

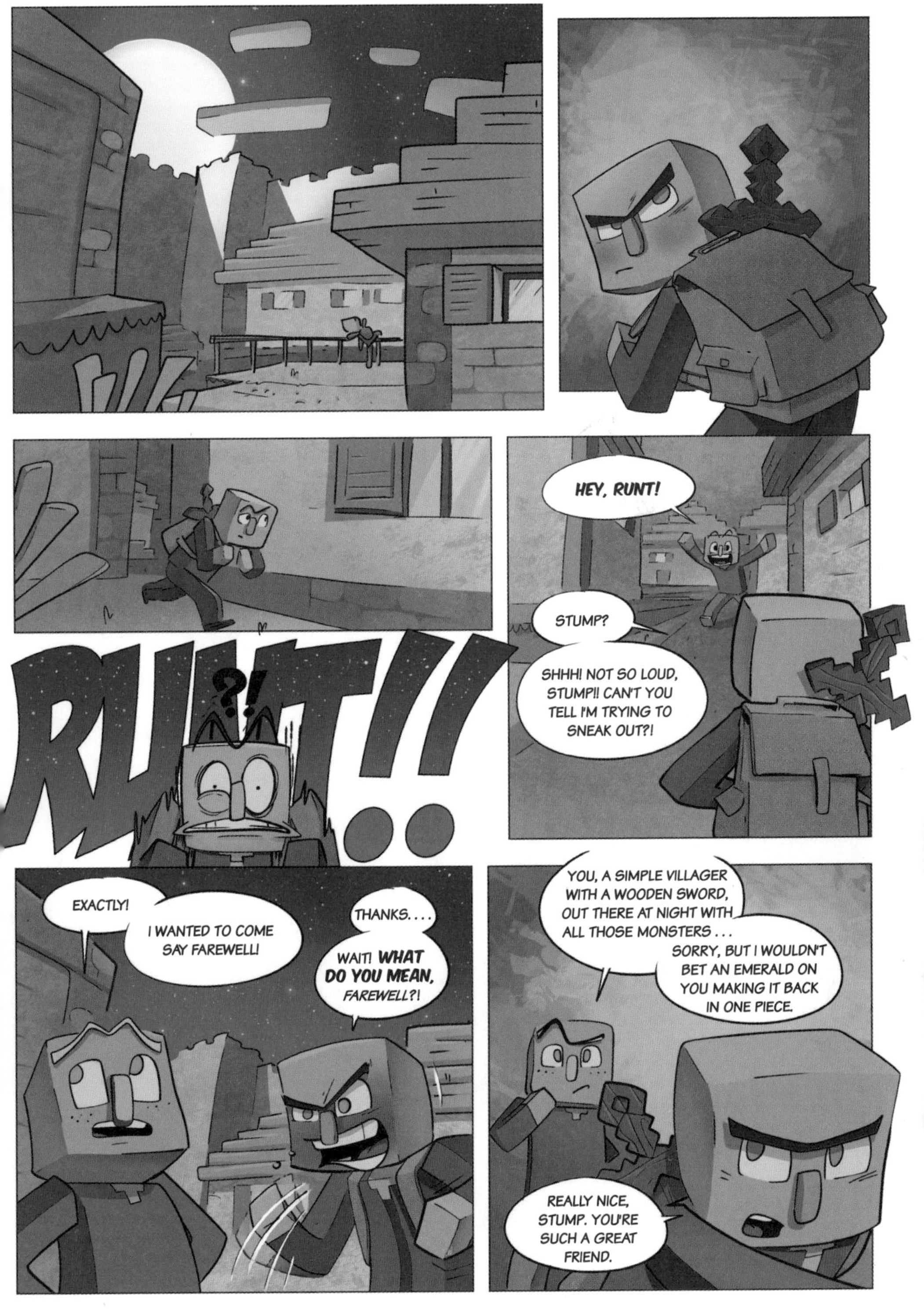
HEY, RUNT!
STUMP?
SHHH! NOT SO LOUD, STUMP!! CAN'T YOU TELL I'M TRYING TO SNEAK OUT?!
RUNT!!
?!
EXACTLY!
I WANTED TO COME SAY FAREWELL!
THANKS. . . .
WAIT! WHAT DO YOU MEAN, FAREWELL?!
YOU, A SIMPLE VILLAGER WITH A WOODEN SWORD, OUT THERE AT NIGHT WITH ALL THOSE MONSTERS . . .
SORRY, BUT I WOULDN'T BET AN EMERALD ON YOU MAKING IT BACK IN ONE PIECE.
REALLY NICE, STUMP. YOU'RE SUCH A GREAT FRIEND.

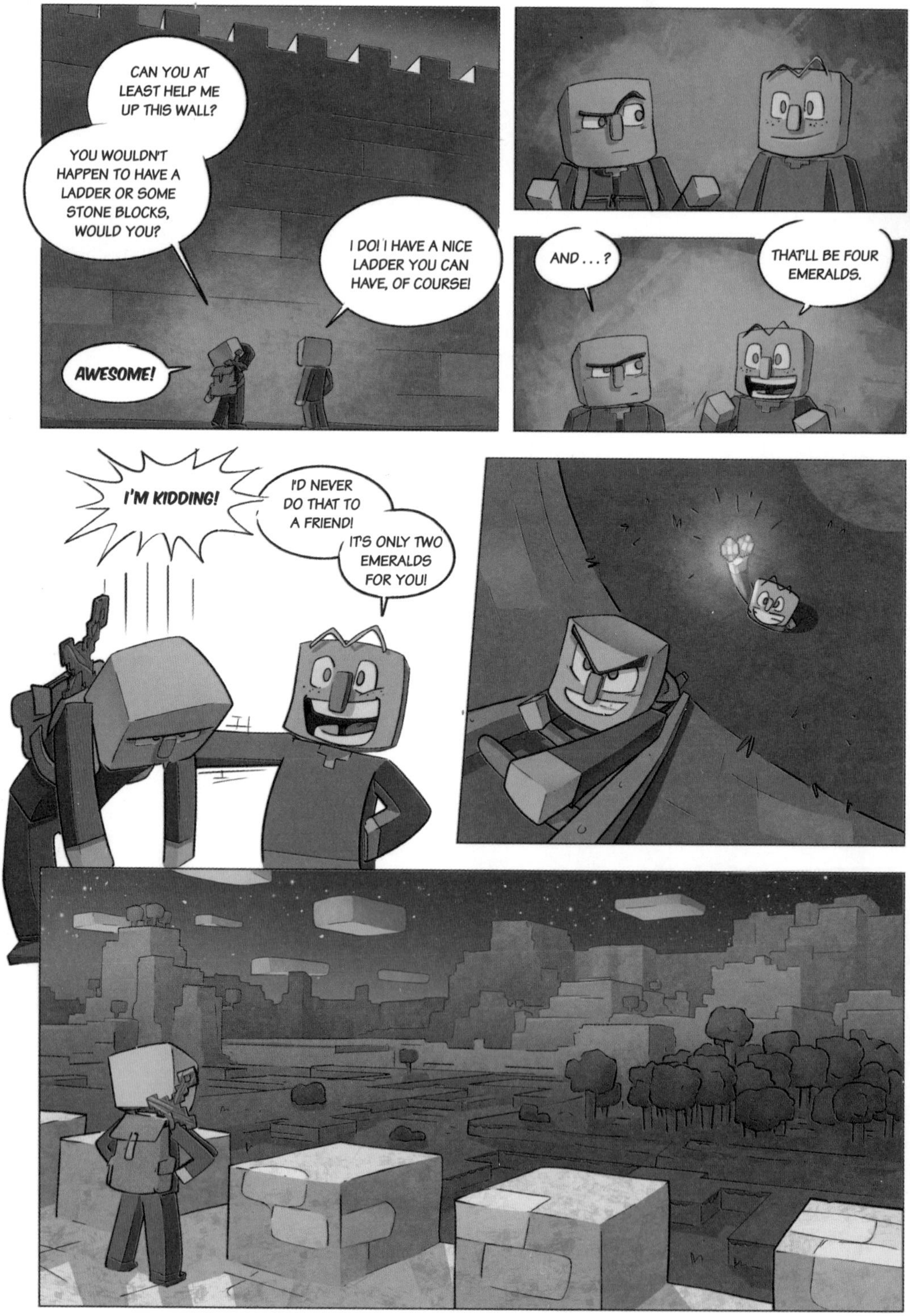
CAN YOU AT LEAST HELP ME UP THIS WALL?
YOU WOULDN'T HAPPEN TO HAVE A LADDER OR SOME STONE BLOCKS, WOULD YOU?
I DO! I HAVE A NICE LADDER YOU CAN HAVE, OF COURSE!
AWESOME!
AND . . . ?
THAT'LL BE FOUR EMERALDS.
I'M KIDDING!
I'D NEVER DO THAT TO A FRIEND!
IT'S ONLY TWO EMERALDS FOR YOU!

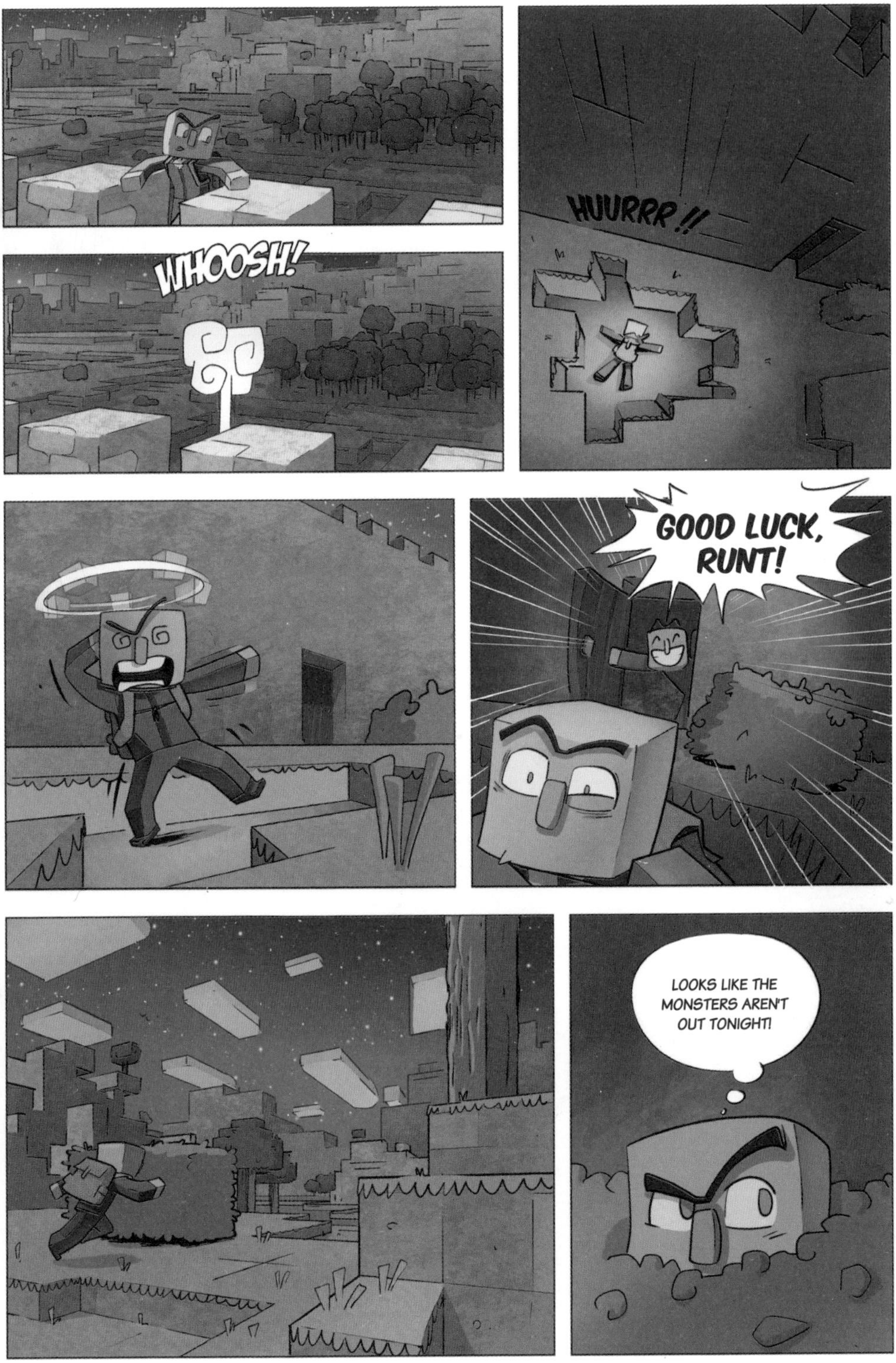
WHOOSH!
HUURRR!!
GOOD LUCK, RUNT!
LOOKS LIKE THE MONSTERS AREN'T OUT TONIGHT!

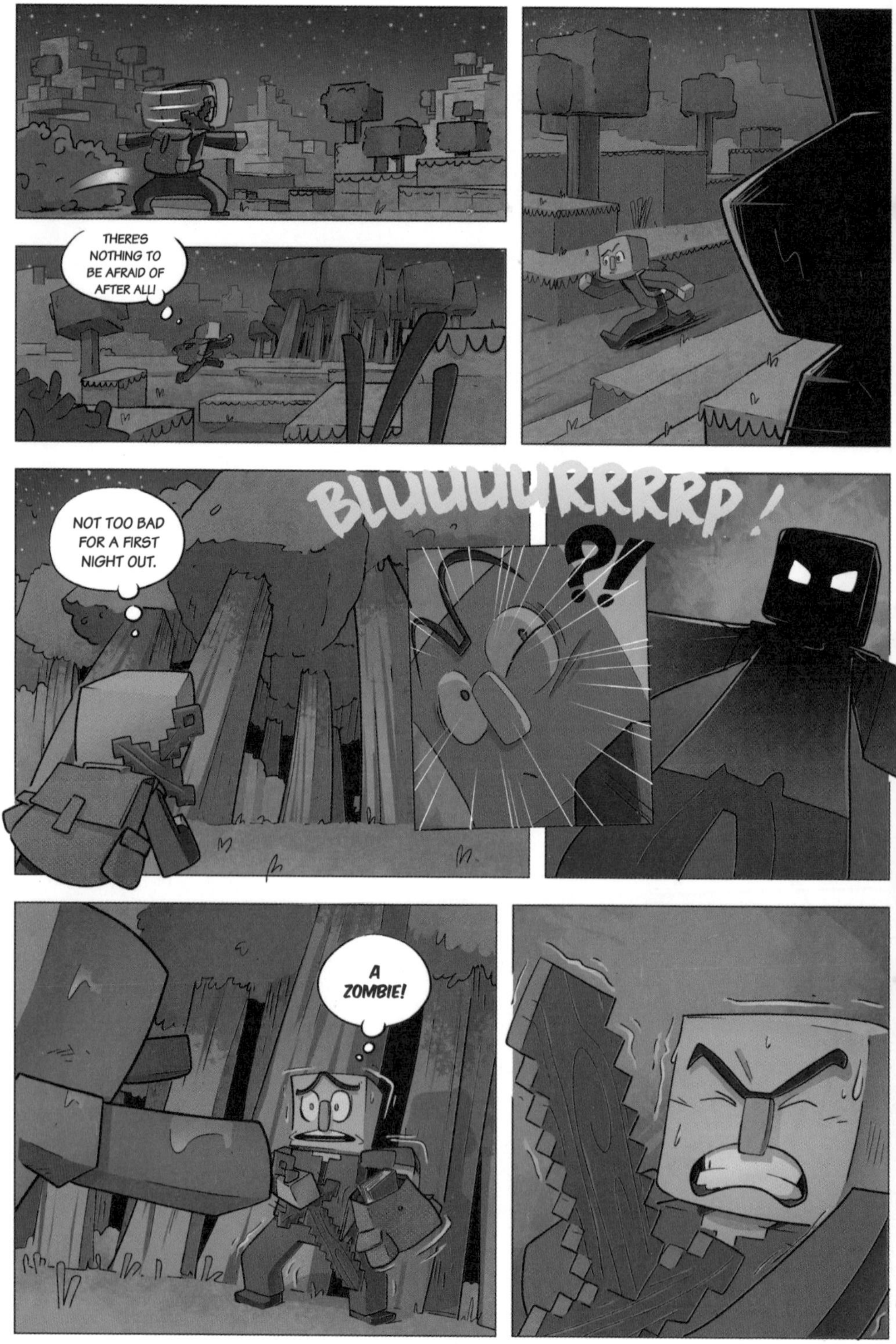
THERE'S NOTHING TO BE AFRAID OF AFTER ALL!
NOT TOO BAD FOR A FIRST NIGHT OUT.
BLUUUURRRRP!
?!
A ZOMBIE!

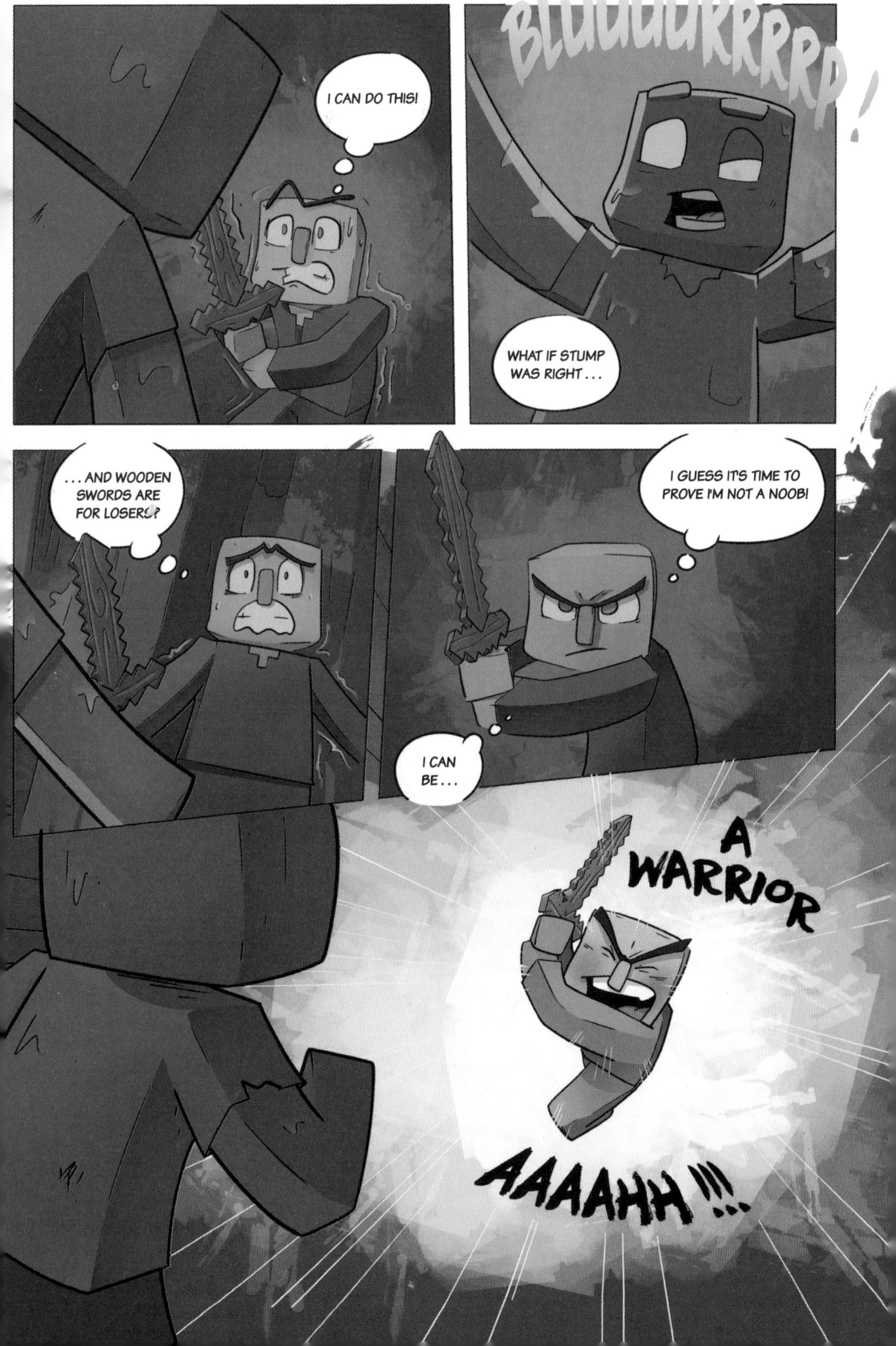
I CAN DO THIS!
BLUUUURRRRP!
WHAT IF STUMP WAS RIGHT . . .
. . . AND WOODEN SWORDS ARE FOR LOSERS?
I GUESS IT'S TIME TO PROVE I'M NOT A NOOB!
I CAN BE . . .
A WARRIOR
AAAAHH!!!

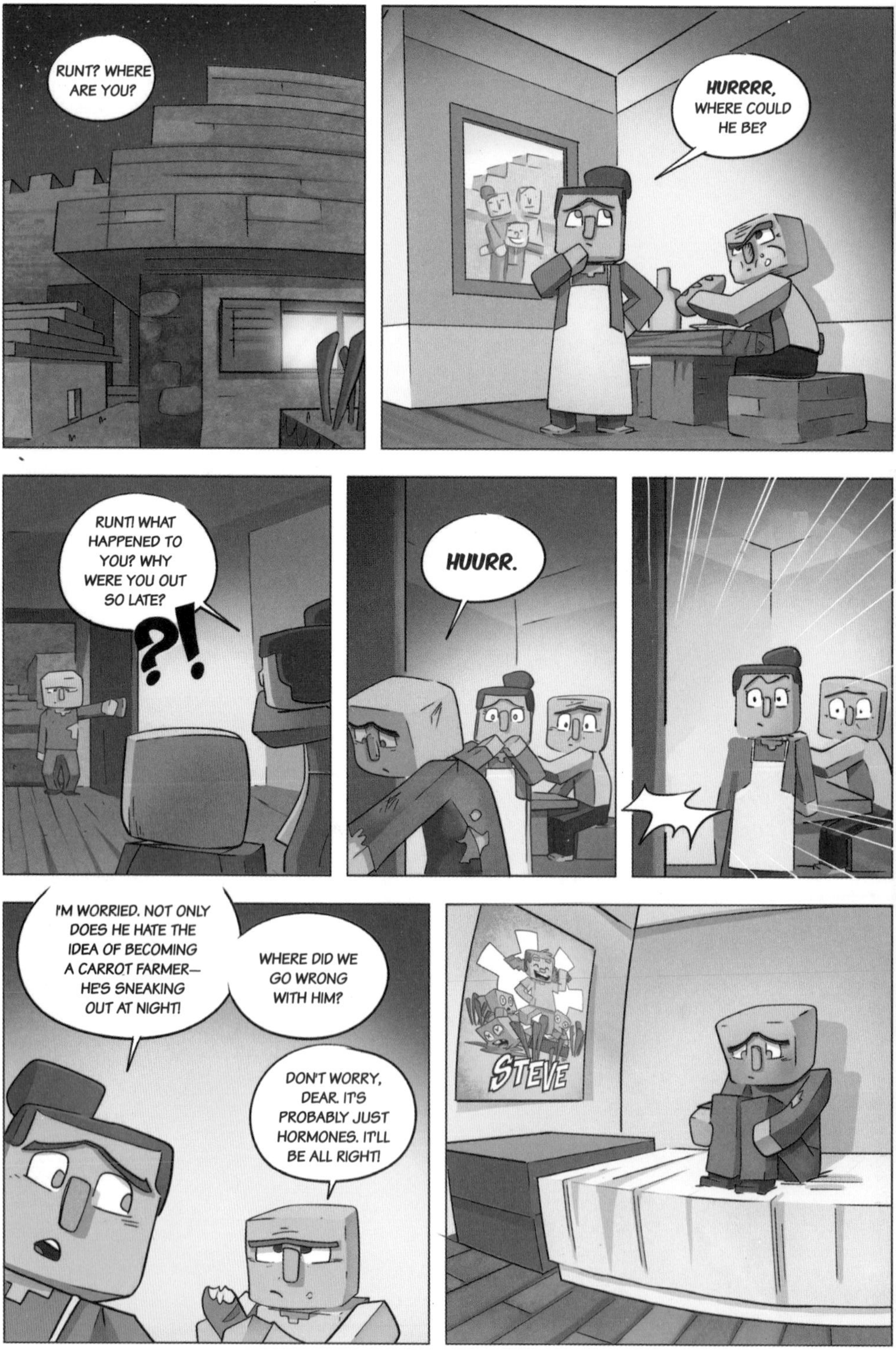
RUNT? WHERE ARE YOU?
HURRRR, WHERE COULD HE BE?
RUNT! WHAT HAPPENED TO YOU? WHY WERE YOU OUT SO LATE?
?!
HUURR.
I'M WORRIED. NOT ONLY DOES HE HATE THE IDEA OF BECOMING A CARROT FARMER— HE'S SNEAKING OUT AT NIGHT!
WHERE DID WE GO WRONG WITH HIM?
DON'T WORRY, DEAR. IT'S PROBABLY JUST HORMONES. IT'LL BE ALL RIGHT!
STEVE

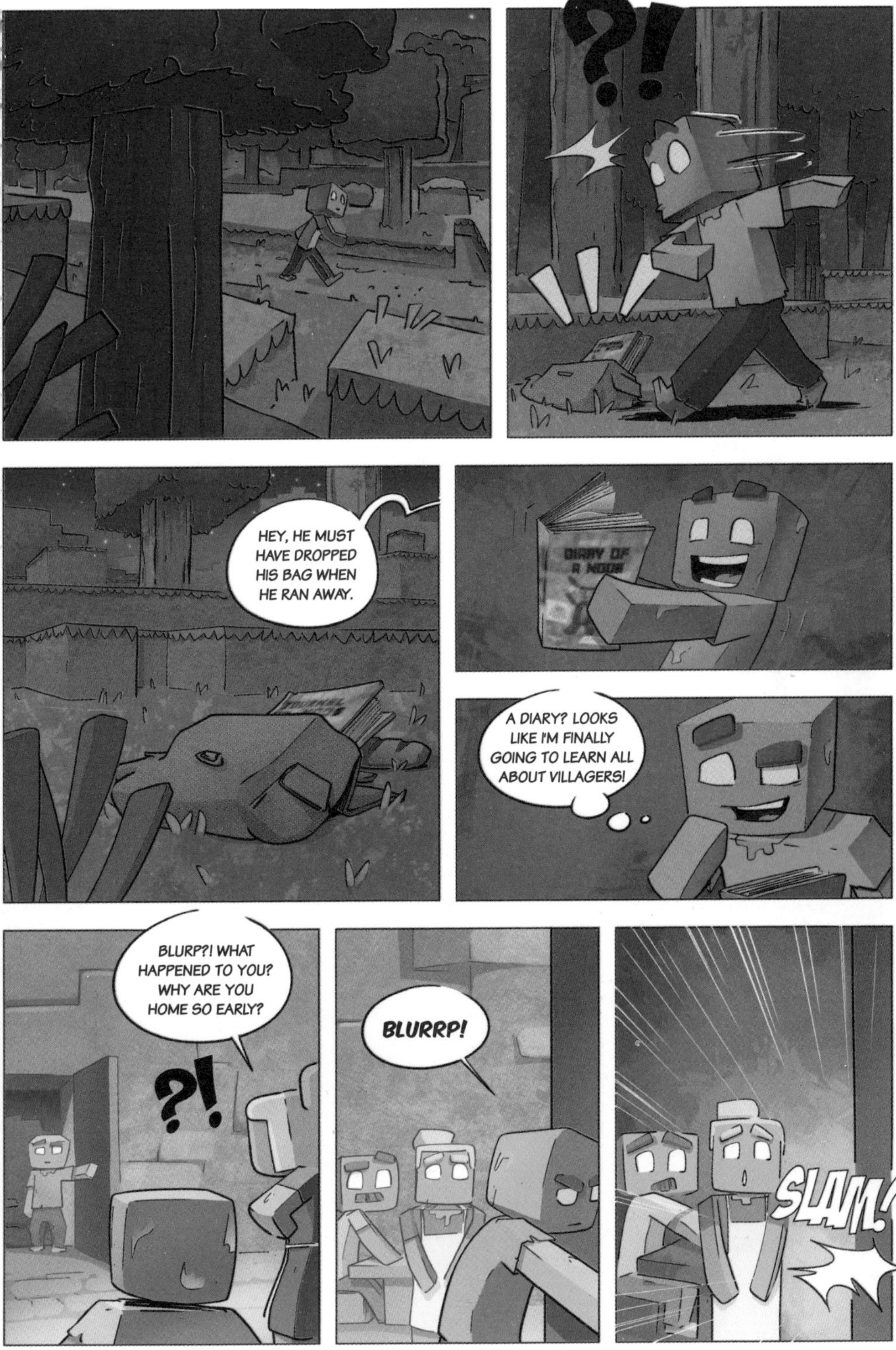
?!
HEY, HE MUST HAVE DROPPED HIS BAG WHEN HE RAN AWAY.
DIARY OF A NOOB
A DIARY? LOOKS LIKE I'M FINALLY GOING TO LEARN ALL ABOUT VILLAGERS!
BLURP?! WHAT HAPPENED TO YOU? WHY ARE YOU HOME SO EARLY?
?!
BLURRP!
SLAM!

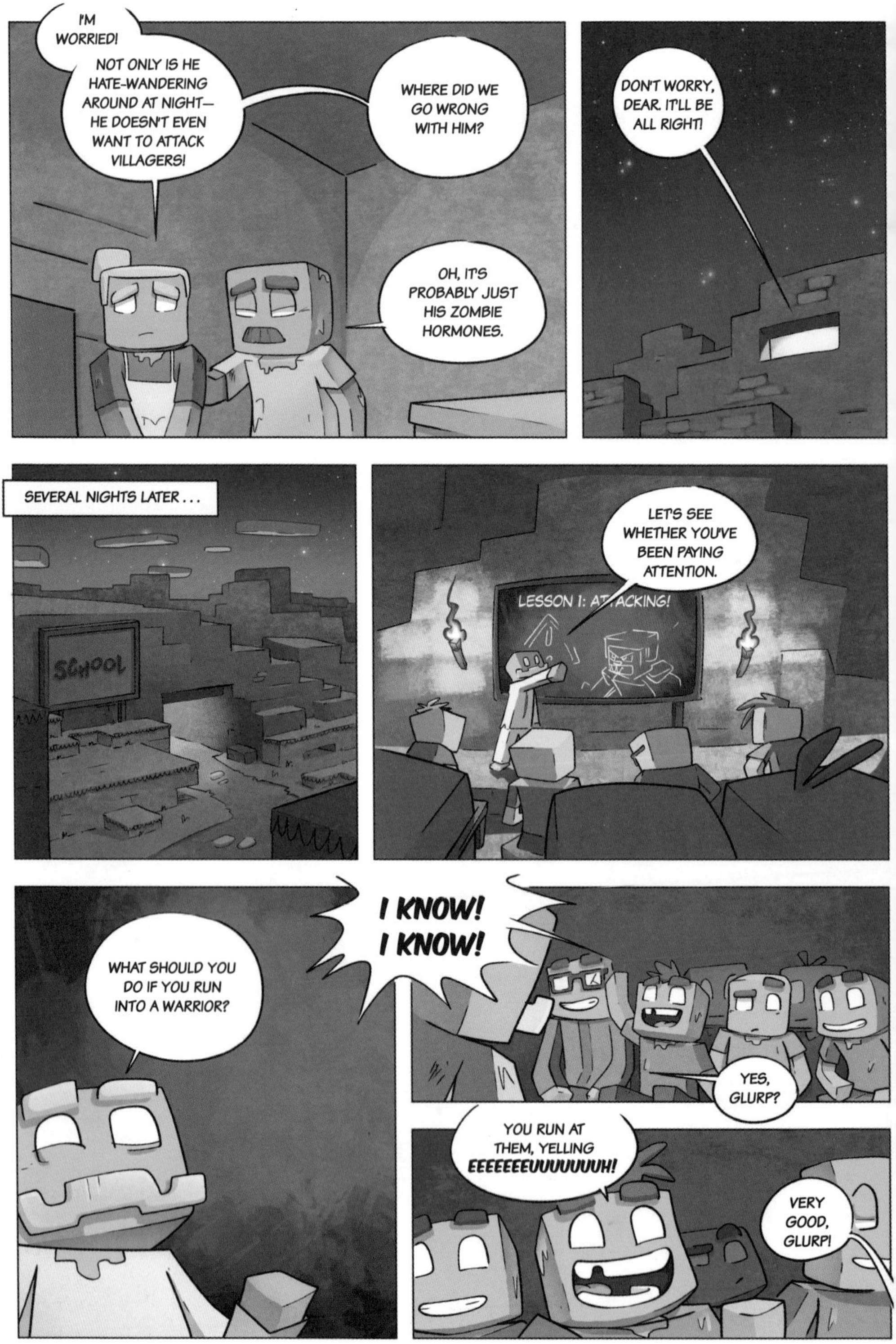
I'M WORRIED!
NOT ONLY IS HE HATE-WANDERING AROUND AT NIGHT— HE DOESN'T EVEN WANT TO ATTACK VILLAGERS!
WHERE DID WE GO WRONG WITH HIM?
OH, IT'S PROBABLY JUST HIS ZOMBIE HORMONES.
DON'T WORRY, DEAR. IT'LL BE ALL RIGHT!
SEVERAL NIGHTS LATER . . .
SCHOOL
LET'S SEE WHETHER YOU'VE BEEN PAYING ATTENTION.
WHAT SHOULD YOU DO IF YOU RUN INTO A WARRIOR?
I KNOW! I KNOW!
YES, GLURP?
YOU RUN AT THEM, YELLING EEEEEEEUUUUUUUH!
VERY GOOD, GLURP!

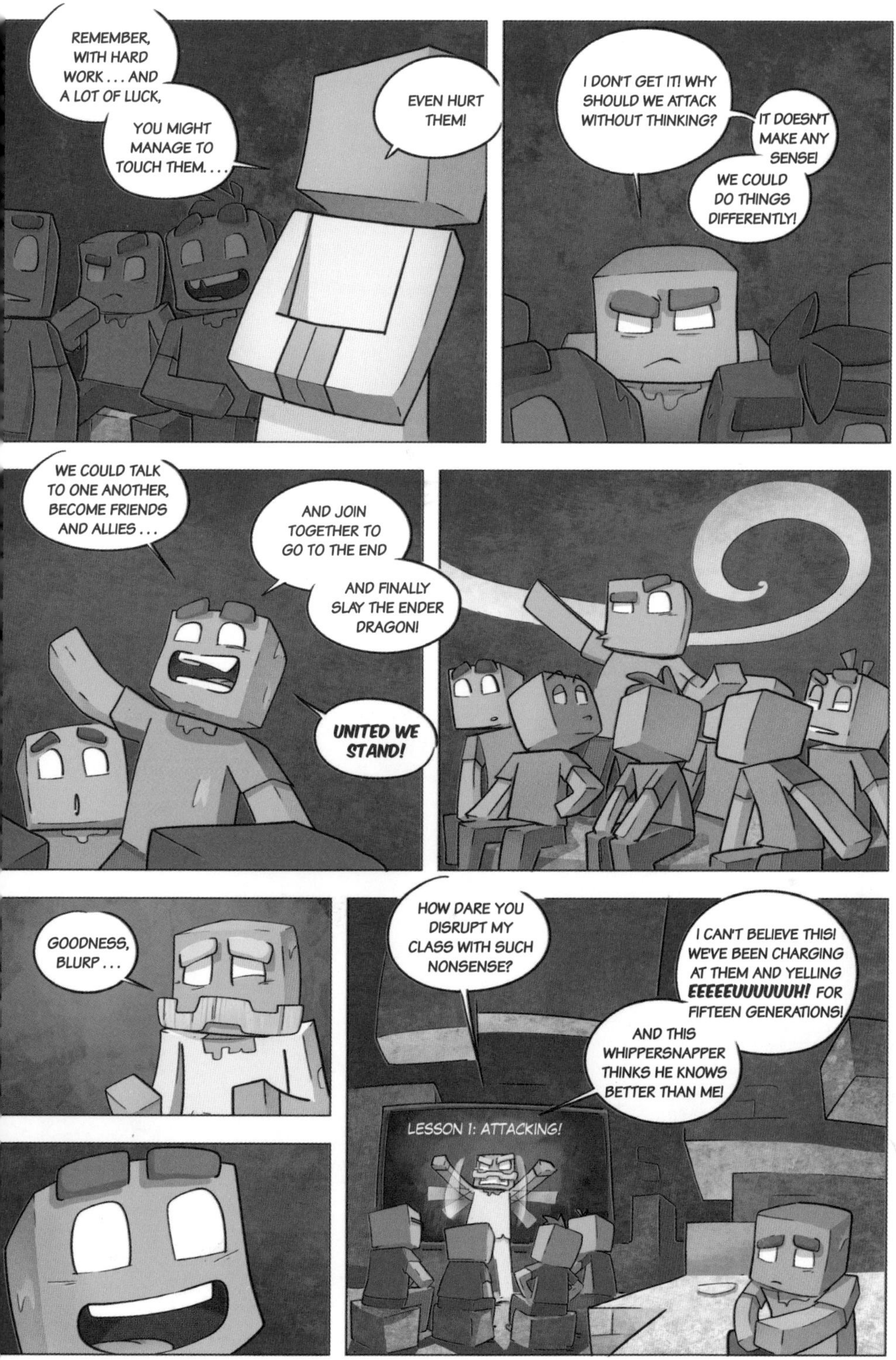
REMEMBER, WITH HARD WORK . . . AND A LOT OF LUCK,
YOU MIGHT MANAGE TO TOUCH THEM. . . .
EVEN HURT THEM!
I DON'T GET IT! WHY SHOULD WE ATTACK WITHOUT THINKING?
IT DOESN'T MAKE ANY SENSE!
WE COULD DO THINGS DIFFERENTLY!
WE COULD TALK TO ONE ANOTHER, BECOME FRIENDS AND ALLIES . . .
AND JOIN TOGETHER TO GO TO THE END
AND FINALLY SLAY THE ENDER DRAGON!
UNITED WE STAND!
GOODNESS, BLURP . . .
HOW DARE YOU DISRUPT MY CLASS WITH SUCH NONSENSE?
I CAN'T BELIEVE THIS! WE'VE BEEN CHARGING AT THEM AND YELLING EEEEEUUUUUUH! FOR FIFTEEN GENERATIONS!
AND THIS WHIPPERSNAPPER THINKS HE KNOWS BETTER THAN ME!
LESSON 1: ATTACKING!

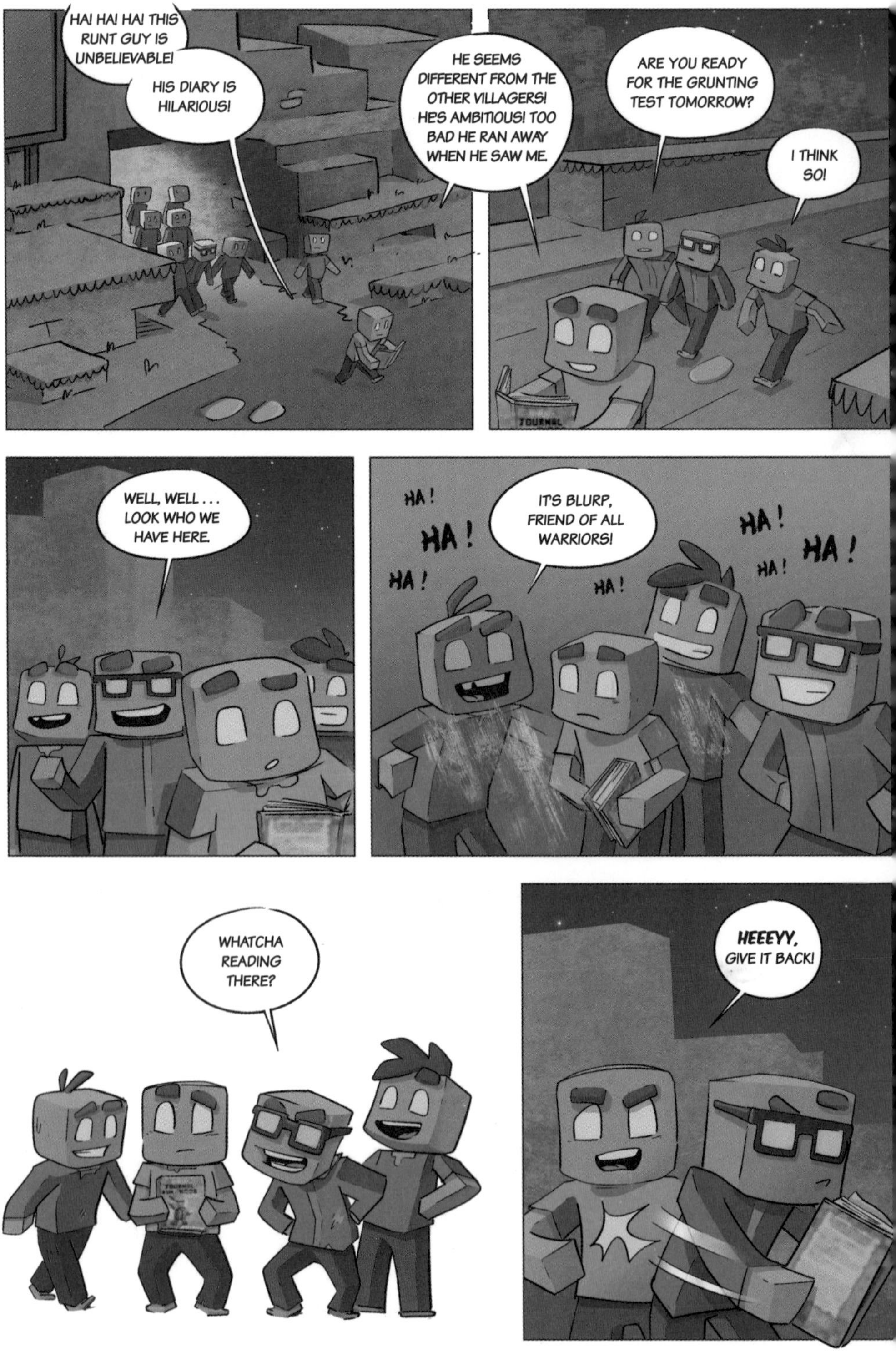

HA! HA! HA! THIS RUNT GUY IS UNBELIEVABLE!
HIS DIARY IS HILARIOUS!
HE SEEMS DIFFERENT FROM THE OTHER VILLAGERS! HE'S AMBITIOUS! TOO BAD HE RAN AWAY WHEN HE SAW ME.
ARE YOU READY FOR THE GRUNTING TEST TOMORROW?
I THINK SO!
WELL, WELL . . . LOOK WHO WE HAVE HERE.
HA! HA! HA!
IT'S BLURP, FRIEND OF ALL WARRIORS!
HA! HA! HA! HA! HA!
WHATCHA READING THERE?
HEEEYY, GIVE IT BACK!

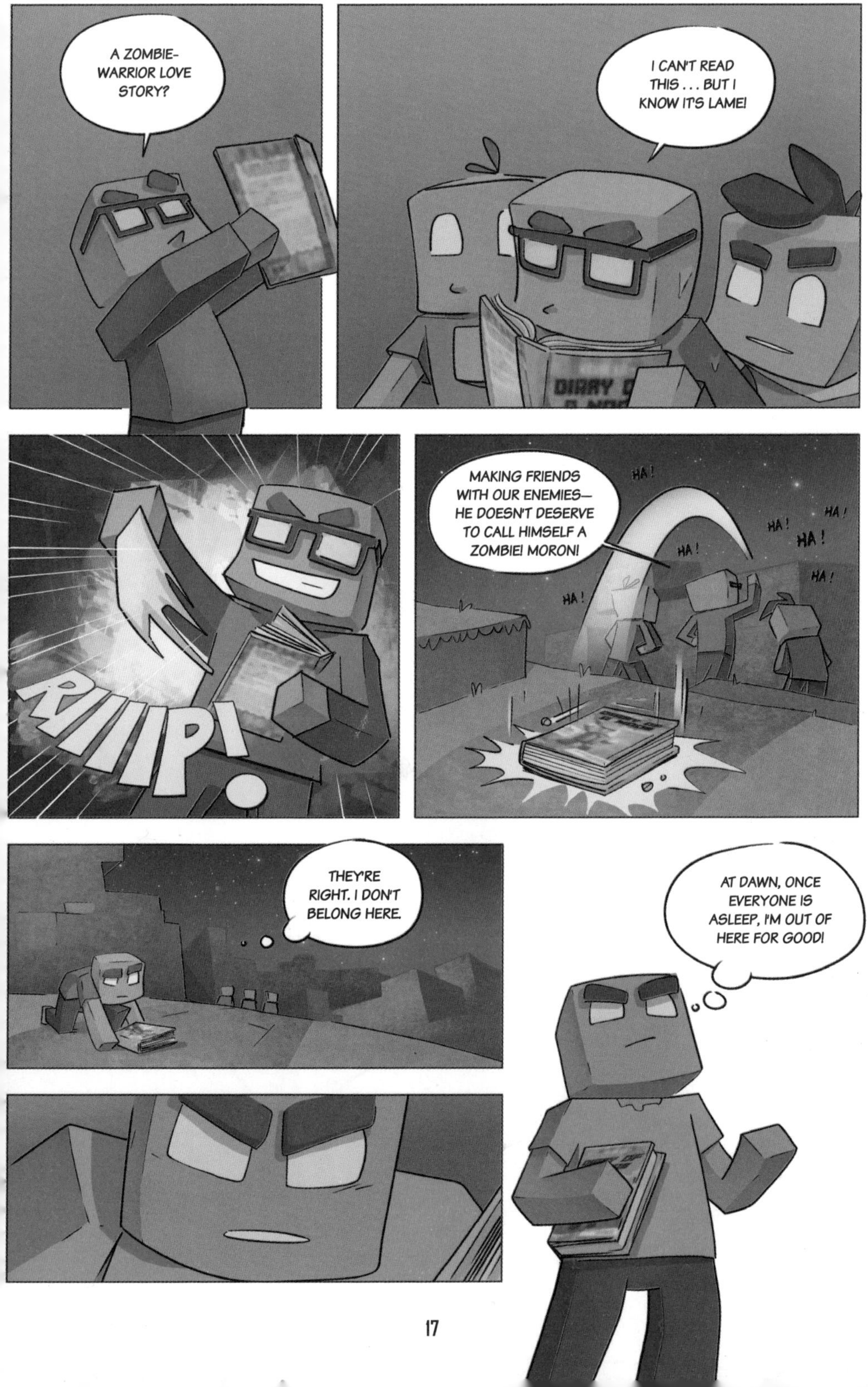
A ZOMBIE-WARRIOR LOVE STORY?
I CAN'T READ THIS . . . BUT I KNOW IT'S LAME!
RIIIP!
MAKING FRIENDS WITH OUR ENEMIES—HE DOESN'T DESERVE TO CALL HIMSELF A ZOMBIE! MORON!
HA!
HA!
HA!
HA!
HA!
HA!
THEY'RE RIGHT. I DON'T BELONG HERE.
AT DAWN, ONCE EVERYONE IS ASLEEP, I'M OUT OF HERE FOR GOOD!

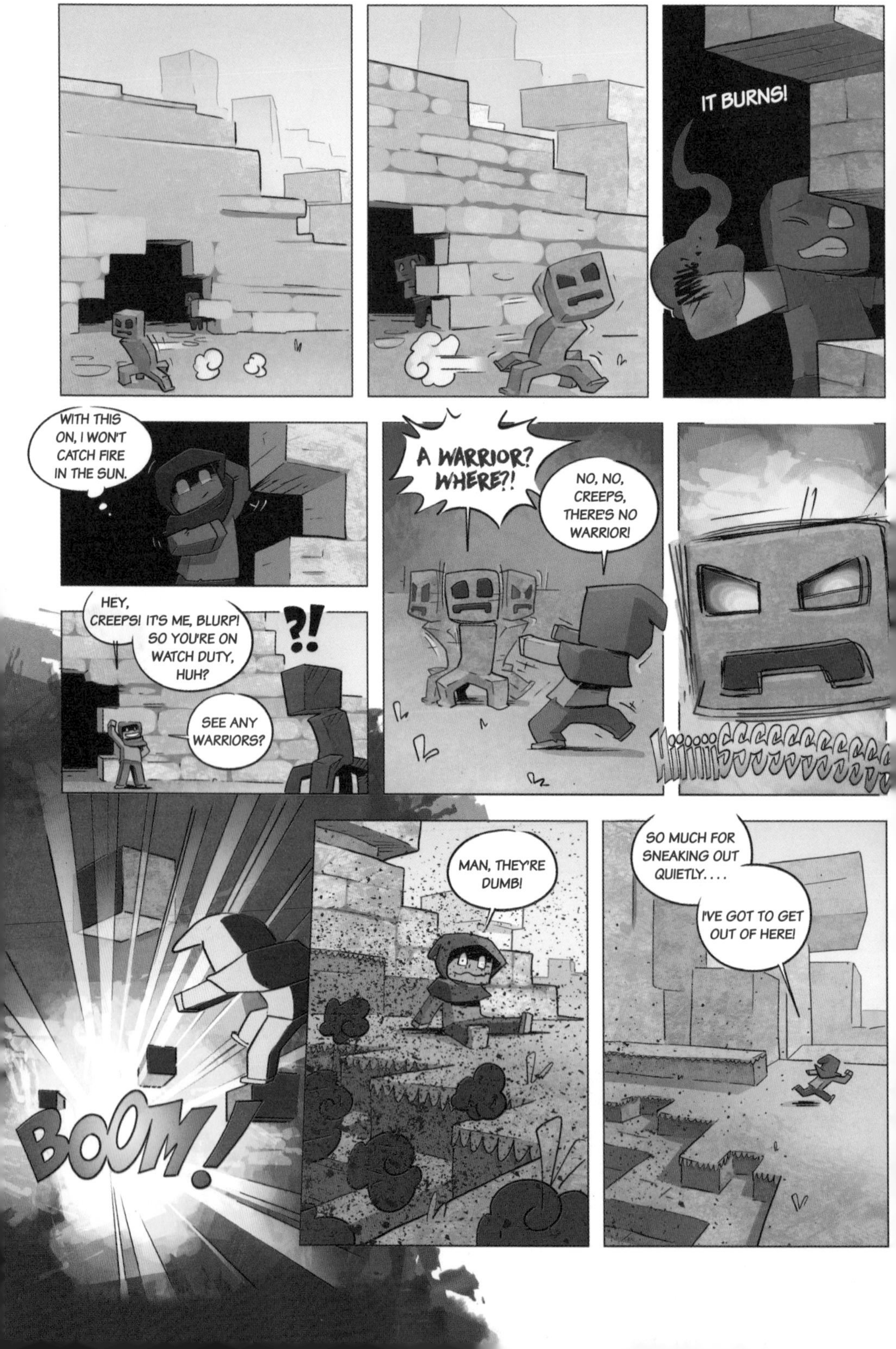
IT BURNS!
WITH THIS ON, I WON'T CATCH FIRE IN THE SUN.
HEY, CREEPS! IT'S ME, BLURP! SO YOU'RE ON WATCH DUTY, HUH?
SEE ANY WARRIORS?
?!
A WARRIOR? WHERE?!
NO, NO, CREEPS, THERE'S NO WARRIOR!
HiiiiiiSSSSSSSSSS
BOOM!
MAN, THEY'RE DUMB!
SO MUCH FOR SNEAKING OUT QUIETLY. . . .
I'VE GOT TO GET OUT OF HERE!

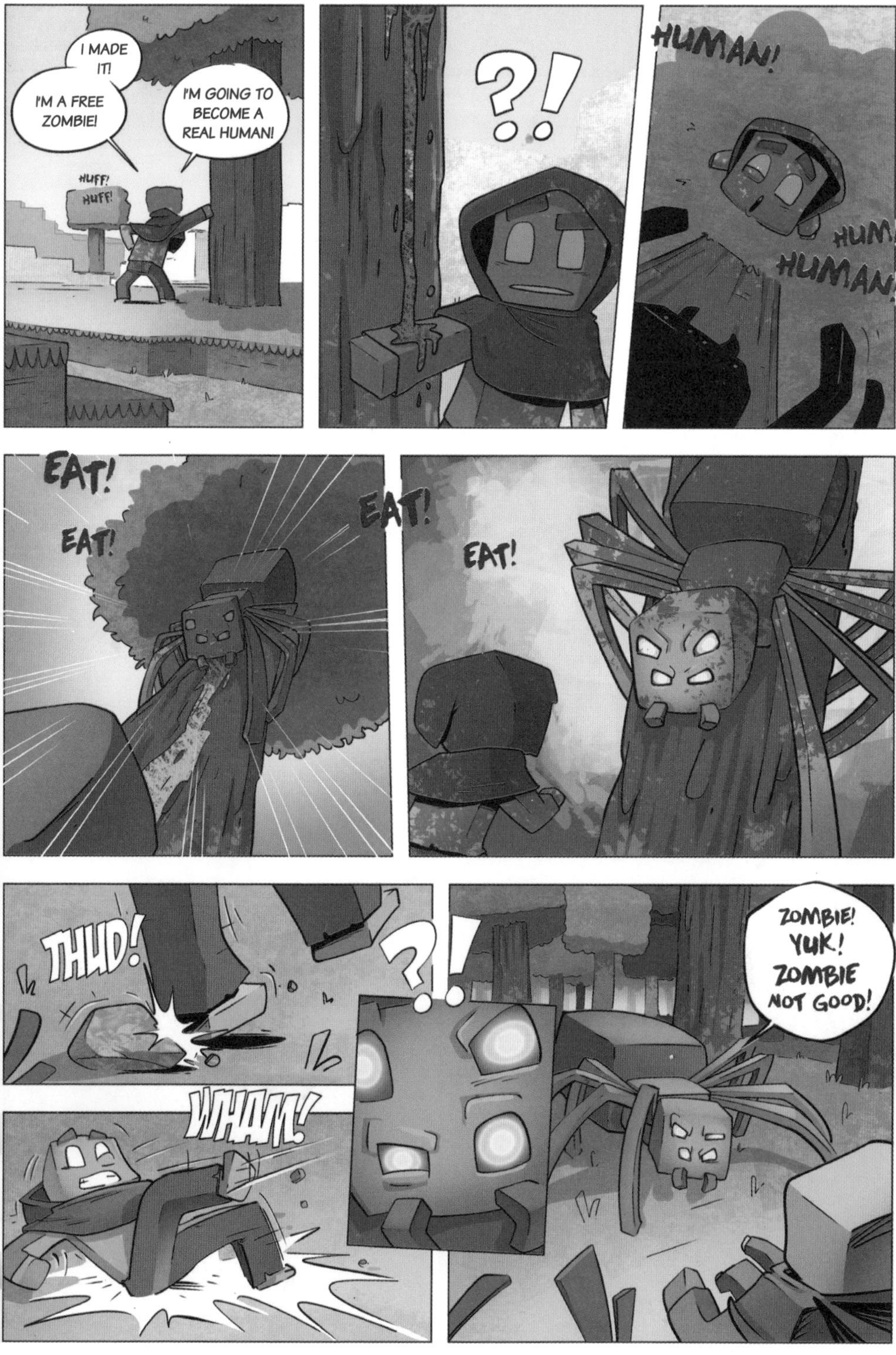
I MADE IT!
I'M A FREE ZOMBIE!
I'M GOING TO BECOME A REAL HUMAN!
HUFF! HUFF!
?!
HUMAN!
HUMAN!
HUMAN!
EAT!
EAT!
EAT!
EAT!
THUD!
WHAM!
?!
ZOMBIE! YUK! ZOMBIE NOT GOOD!

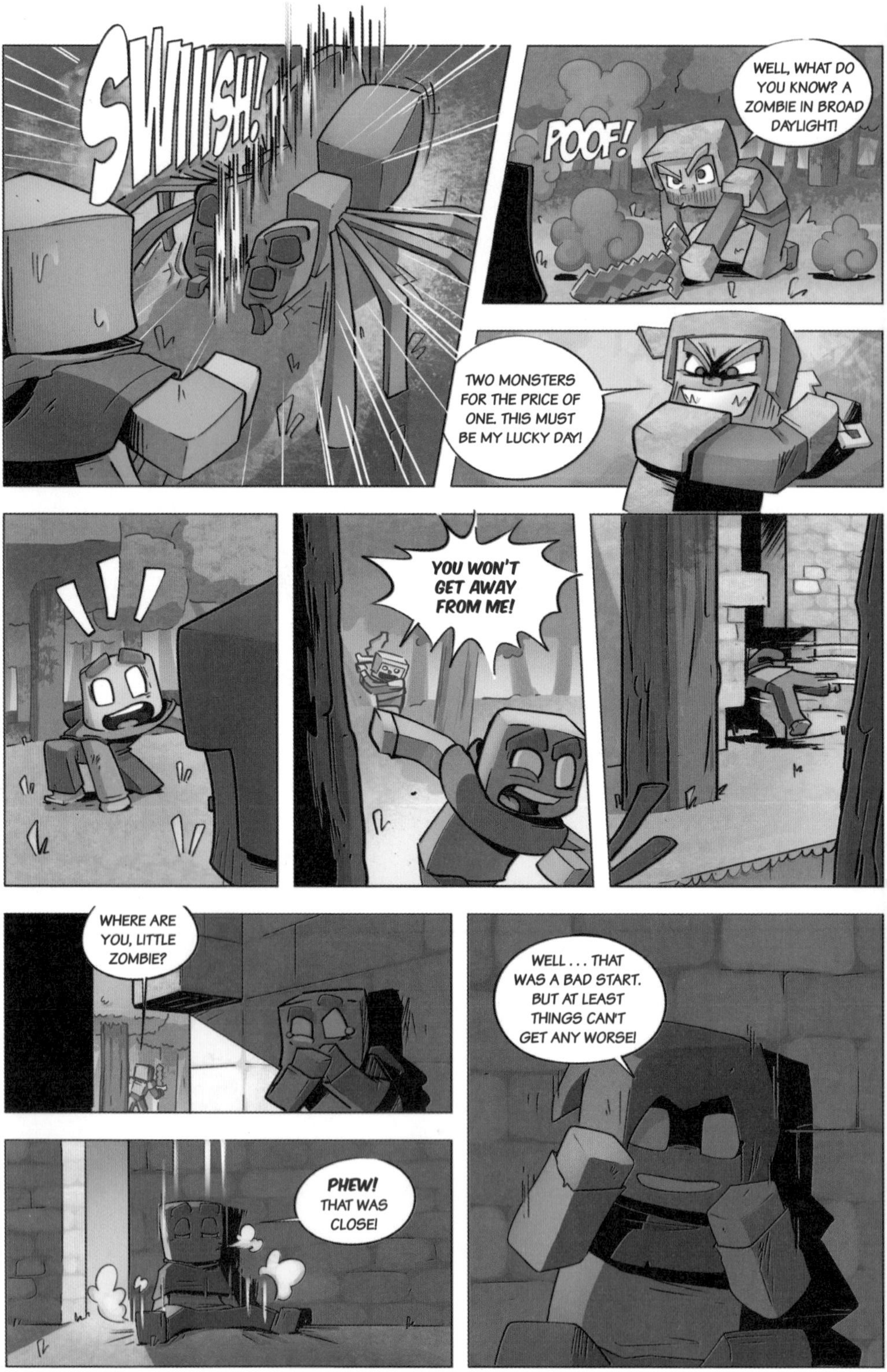
SWIIISH!
POOF!
WELL, WHAT DO YOU KNOW? A ZOMBIE IN BROAD DAYLIGHT!
TWO MONSTERS FOR THE PRICE OF ONE. THIS MUST BE MY LUCKY DAY!
YOU WON'T GET AWAY FROM ME!
WHERE ARE YOU, LITTLE ZOMBIE?
PHEW! THAT WAS CLOSE!
WELL . . . THAT WAS A BAD START. BUT AT LEAST THINGS CAN'T GET ANY WORSE!

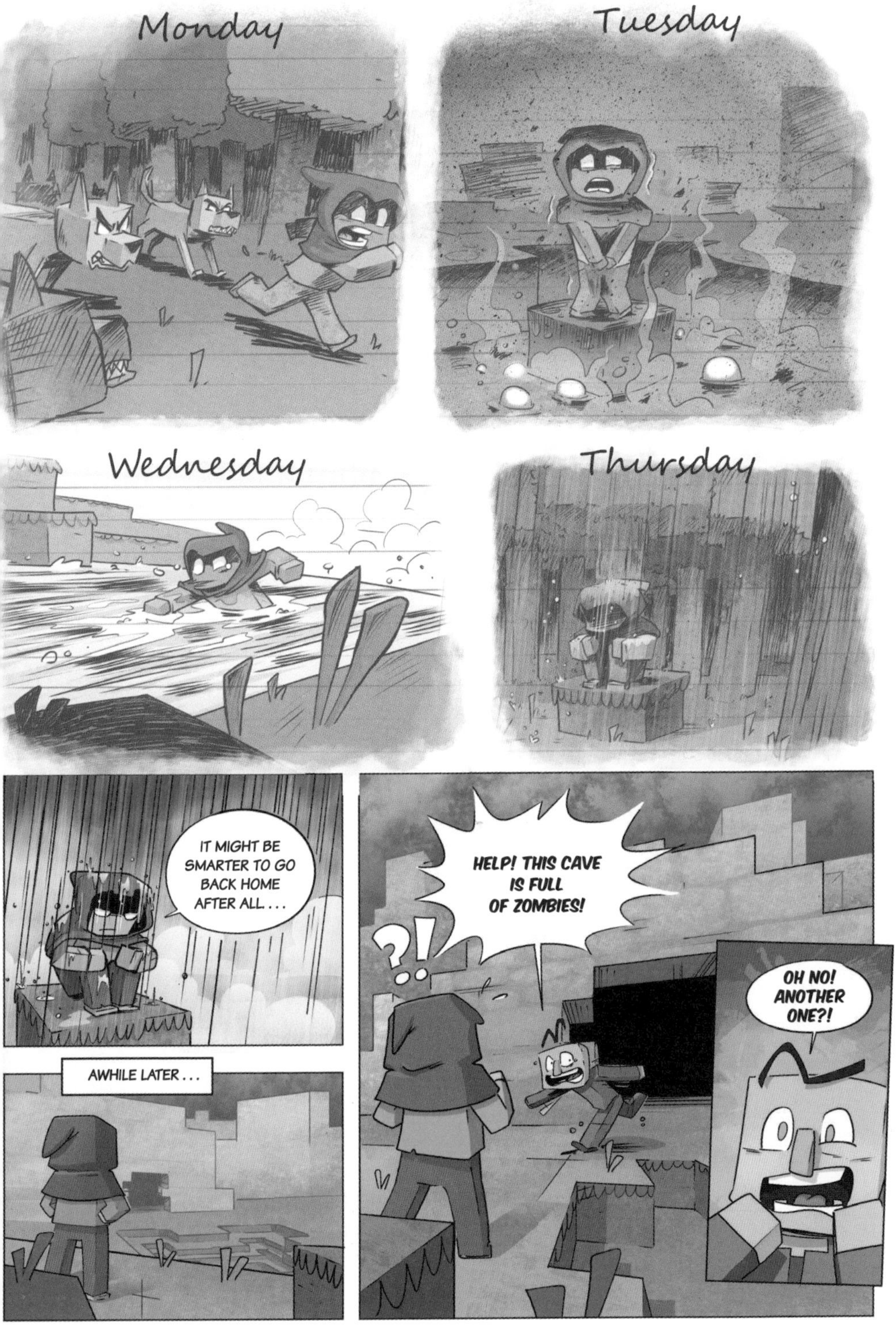
Monday
Tuesday
Wednesday
Thursday
IT MIGHT BE SMARTER TO GO BACK HOME AFTER ALL . . .
AWHILE LATER . . .
HELP! THIS CAVE IS FULL OF ZOMBIES!
?!
OH NO! ANOTHER ONE?!

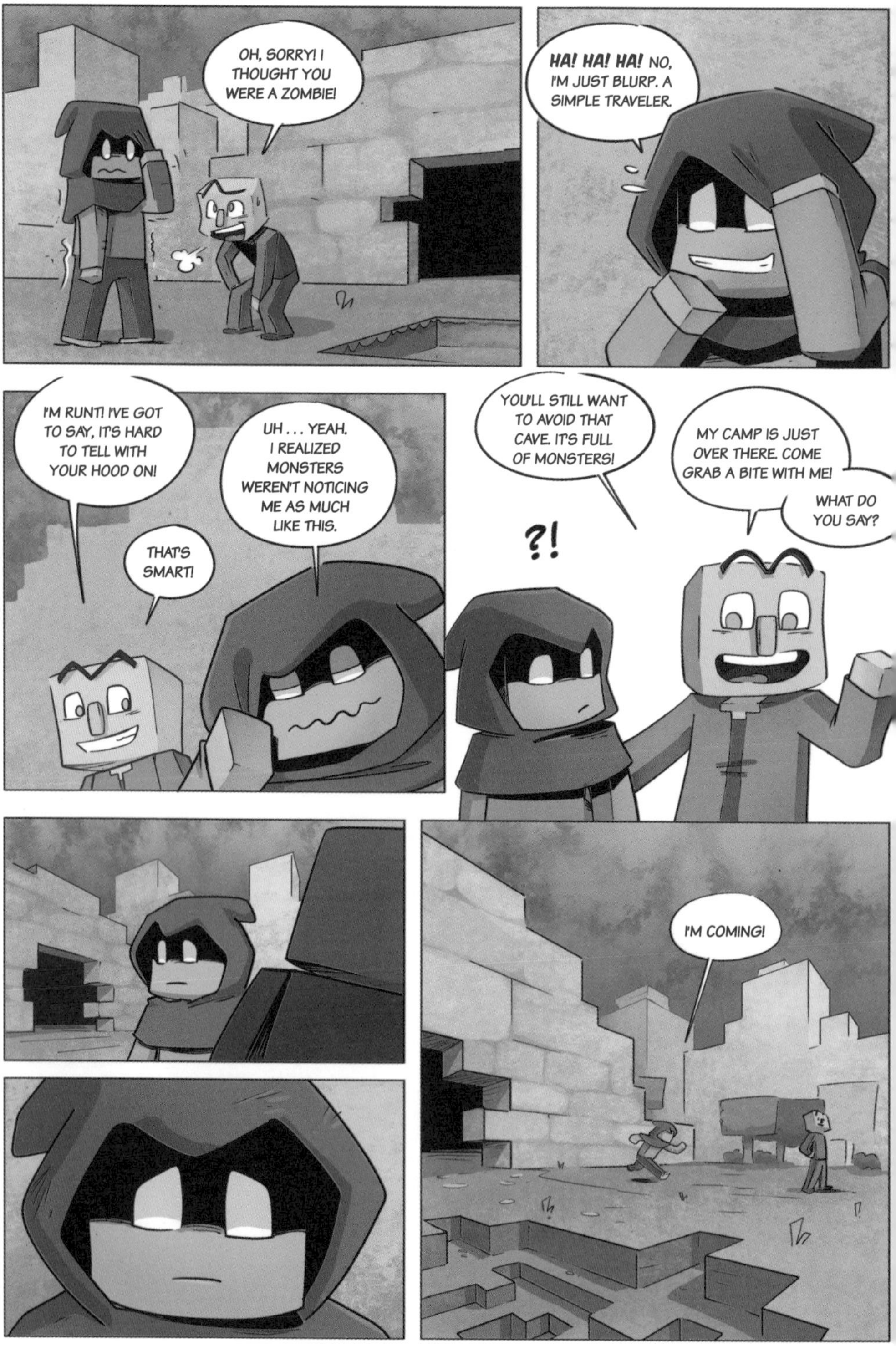
OH, SORRY! I THOUGHT YOU WERE A ZOMBIE!
HA! HA! HA! NO, I'M JUST BLURP. A SIMPLE TRAVELER.
I'M RUNT! I'VE GOT TO SAY, IT'S HARD TO TELL WITH YOUR HOOD ON!
THAT'S SMART!
UH . . . YEAH. I REALIZED MONSTERS WEREN'T NOTICING ME AS MUCH LIKE THIS.
YOU'LL STILL WANT TO AVOID THAT CAVE. IT'S FULL OF MONSTERS!
?!
MY CAMP IS JUST OVER THERE. COME GRAB A BITE WITH ME!
WHAT DO YOU SAY?
I'M COMING!

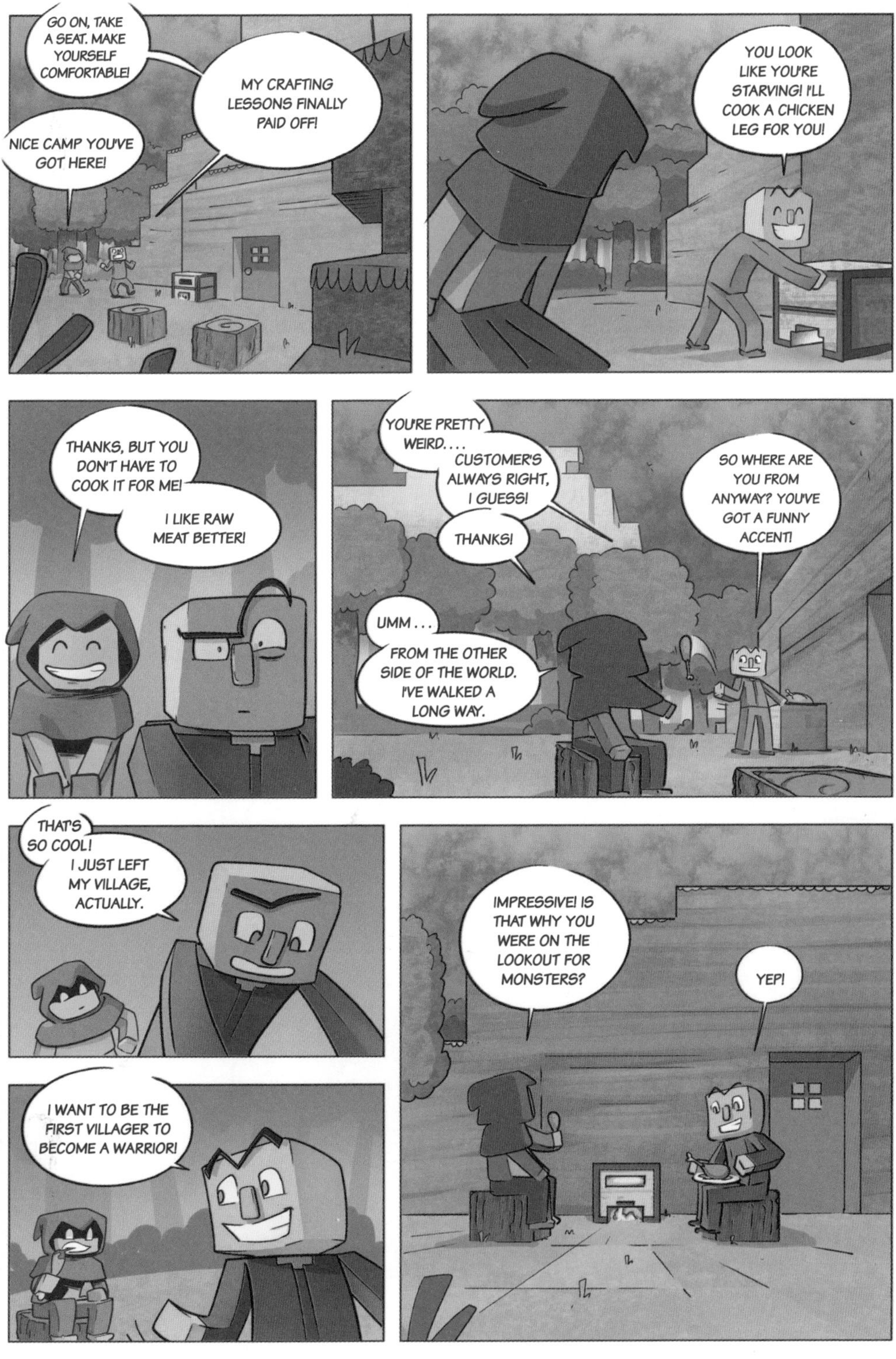
GO ON, TAKE A SEAT. MAKE YOURSELF COMFORTABLE!
NICE CAMP YOU'VE GOT HERE!
MY CRAFTING LESSONS FINALLY PAID OFF!
YOU LOOK LIKE YOU'RE STARVING! I'LL COOK A CHICKEN LEG FOR YOU!
THANKS, BUT YOU DON'T HAVE TO COOK IT FOR ME!
I LIKE RAW MEAT BETTER!
YOU'RE PRETTY WEIRD. . . .
CUSTOMER'S ALWAYS RIGHT, I GUESS!
THANKS!
SO WHERE ARE YOU FROM ANYWAY? YOU'VE GOT A FUNNY ACCENT!
UMM . . .
FROM THE OTHER SIDE OF THE WORLD. I'VE WALKED A LONG WAY.
THAT'S SO COOL!
I JUST LEFT MY VILLAGE, ACTUALLY.
I WANT TO BE THE FIRST VILLAGER TO BECOME A WARRIOR!
IMPRESSIVE! IS THAT WHY YOU WERE ON THE LOOKOUT FOR MONSTERS?
YEP!

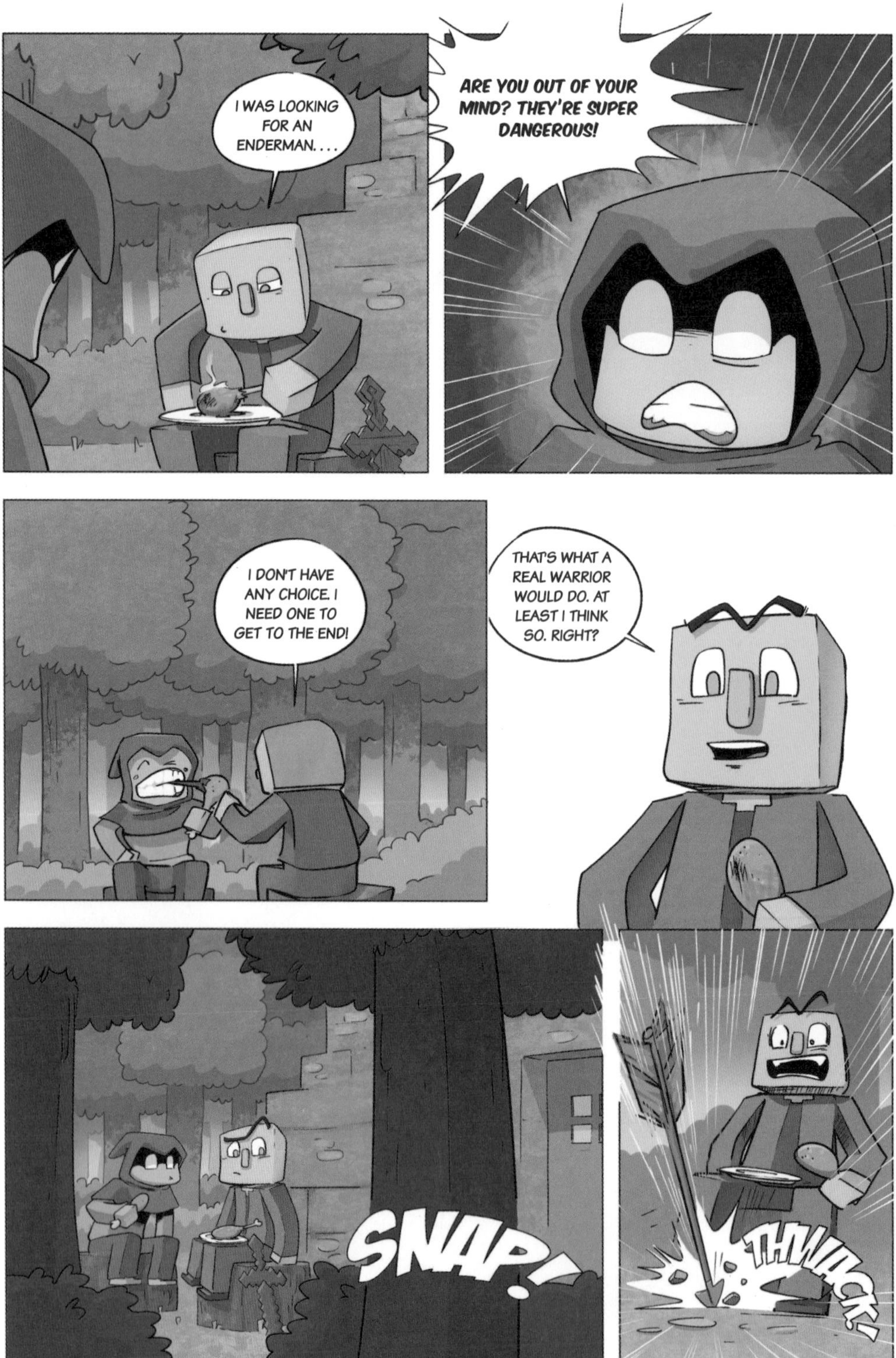
I WAS LOOKING FOR AN ENDERMAN. . . .
ARE YOU OUT OF YOUR MIND? THEY'RE SUPER DANGEROUS!
I DON'T HAVE ANY CHOICE. I NEED ONE TO GET TO THE END!
THAT'S WHAT A REAL WARRIOR WOULD DO. AT LEAST I THINK SO. RIGHT?
SNAP!
THWACK!

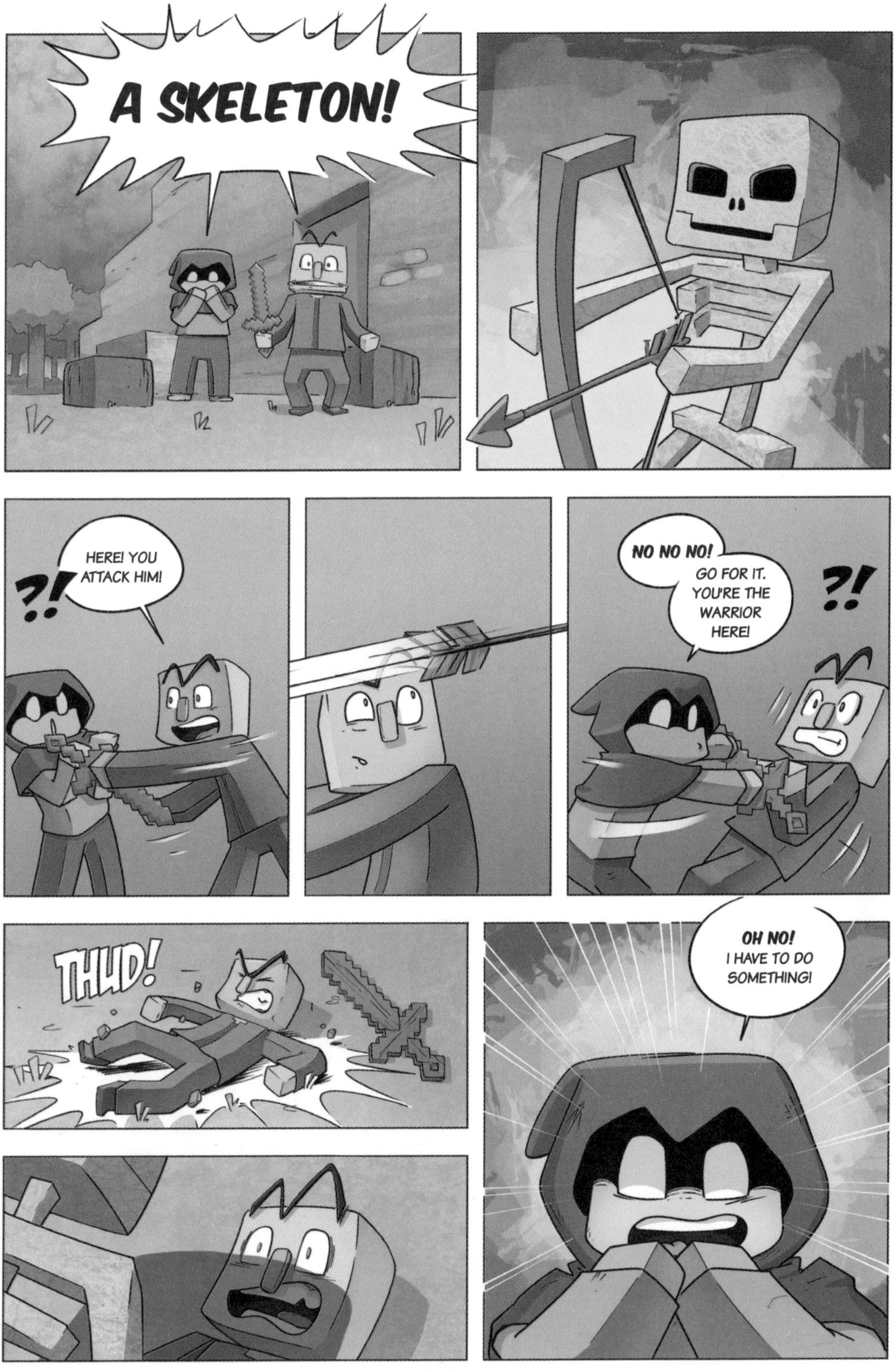

A SKELETON!
HERE! YOU ATTACK HIM!
?!
NO NO NO!
GO FOR IT. YOU'RE THE WARRIOR HERE!
?!
THUD!
OH NO!
I HAVE TO DO SOMETHING!

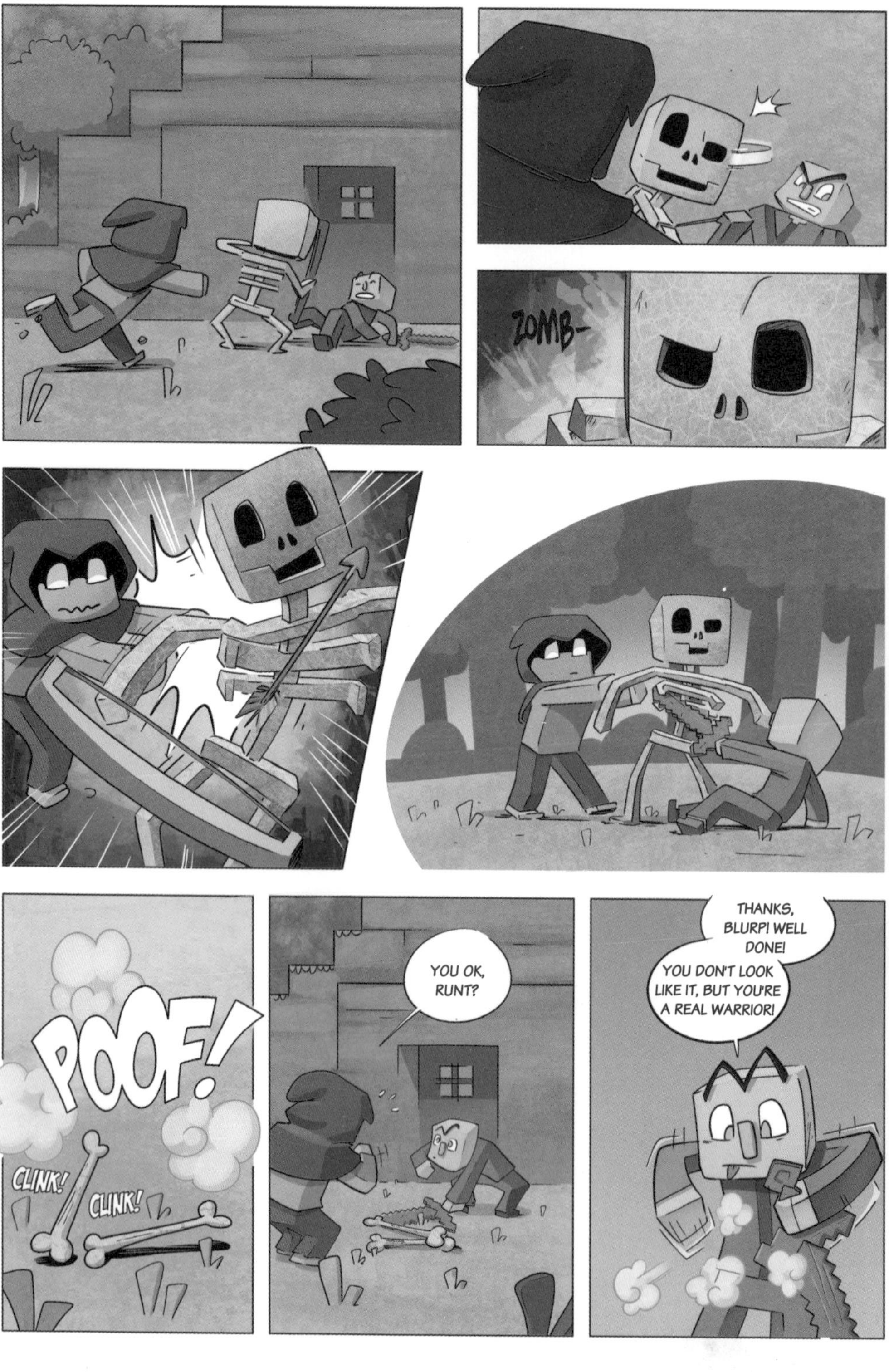
ZOMB-
POOF!
CLINK!
CLINK!
YOU OK, RUNT?
THANKS, BLURP! WELL DONE!
YOU DON'T LOOK LIKE IT, BUT YOU'RE A REAL WARRIOR!

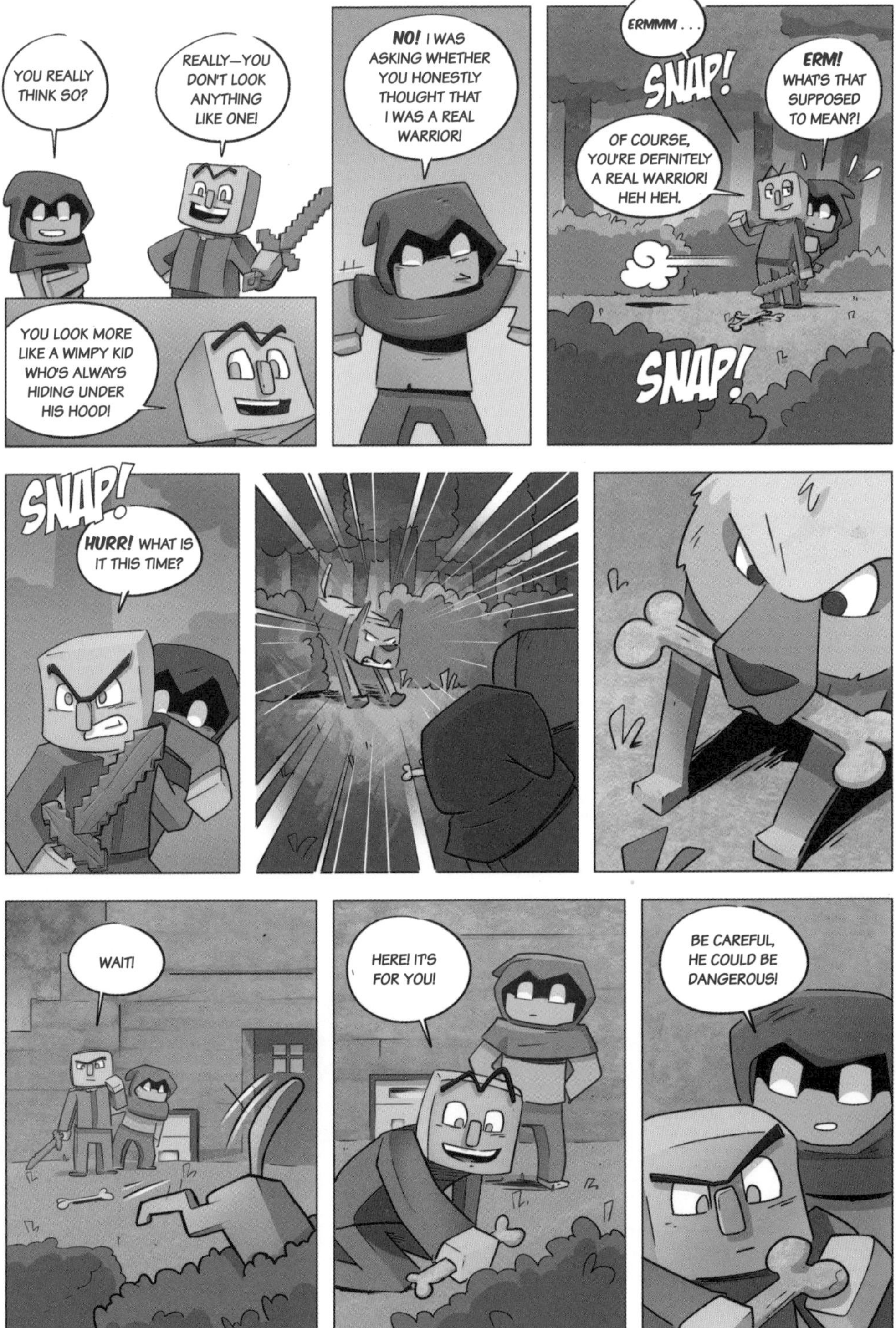
YOU REALLY THINK SO?
REALLY—YOU DON'T LOOK ANYTHING LIKE ONE!
YOU LOOK MORE LIKE A WIMPY KID WHO'S ALWAYS HIDING UNDER HIS HOOD!
NO! I WAS ASKING WHETHER YOU HONESTLY THOUGHT THAT I WAS A REAL WARRIOR!
ERMMM . . .
OF COURSE, YOU'RE DEFINITELY A REAL WARRIOR! HEH HEH.
SNAP!
ERM! WHAT'S THAT SUPPOSED TO MEAN?!
SNAP!
SNAP!
HURR! WHAT IS IT THIS TIME?
WAIT!
HERE! IT'S FOR YOU!
BE CAREFUL, HE COULD BE DANGEROUS!

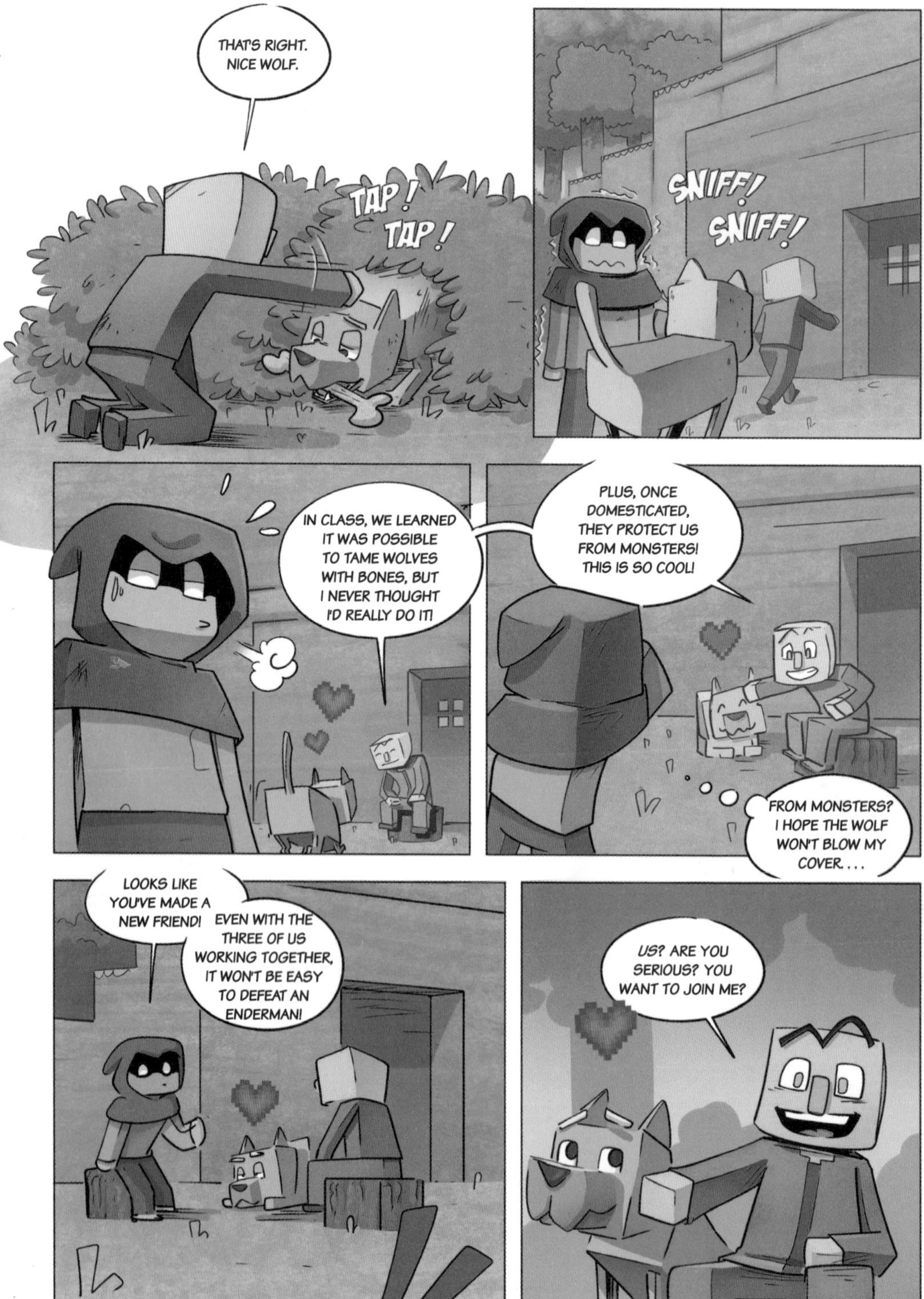

THAT'S RIGHT. NICE WOLF.
TAP! TAP!
SNIFF! SNIFF!
IN CLASS, WE LEARNED IT WAS POSSIBLE TO TAME WOLVES WITH BONES, BUT I NEVER THOUGHT I'D REALLY DO IT!
PLUS, ONCE DOMESTICATED, THEY PROTECT US FROM MONSTERS! THIS IS SO COOL!
FROM MONSTERS? I HOPE THE WOLF WON'T BLOW MY COVER . . .
LOOKS LIKE YOU'VE MADE A NEW FRIEND!
EVEN WITH THE THREE OF US WORKING TOGETHER, IT WON'T BE EASY TO DEFEAT AN ENDERMAN!
US? ARE YOU SERIOUS? YOU WANT TO JOIN ME?

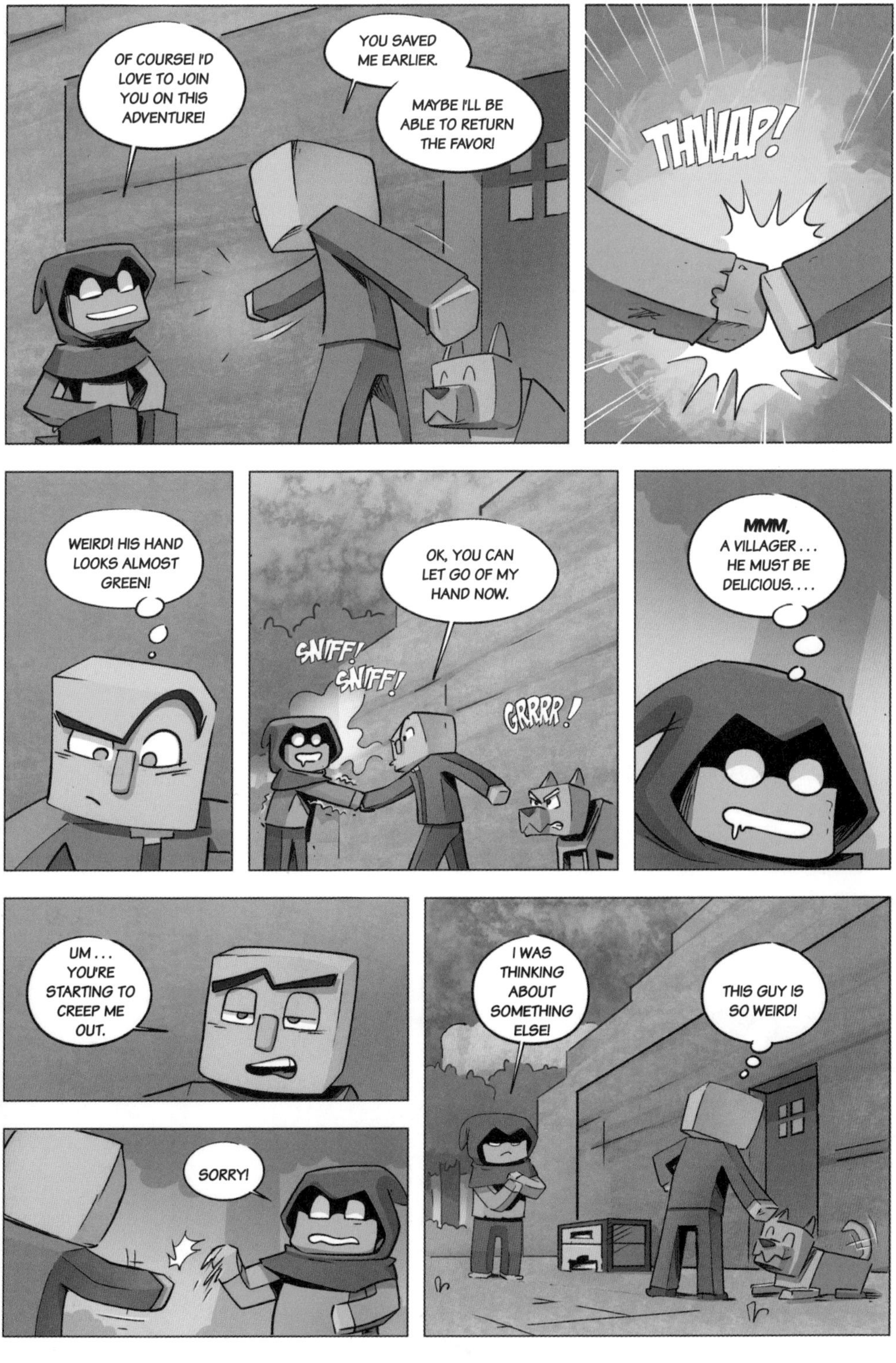
OF COURSE! I'D LOVE TO JOIN YOU ON THIS ADVENTURE!
YOU SAVED ME EARLIER.
MAYBE I'LL BE ABLE TO RETURN THE FAVOR!
THWAP!
WEIRD! HIS HAND LOOKS ALMOST GREEN!
OK, YOU CAN LET GO OF MY HAND NOW.
SNIFF!
SNIFF!
GRRRR!
MMM, A VILLAGER . . . HE MUST BE DELICIOUS. . . .
UM . . . YOU'RE STARTING TO CREEP ME OUT.
SORRY!
I WAS THINKING ABOUT SOMETHING ELSE!
THIS GUY IS SO WEIRD!

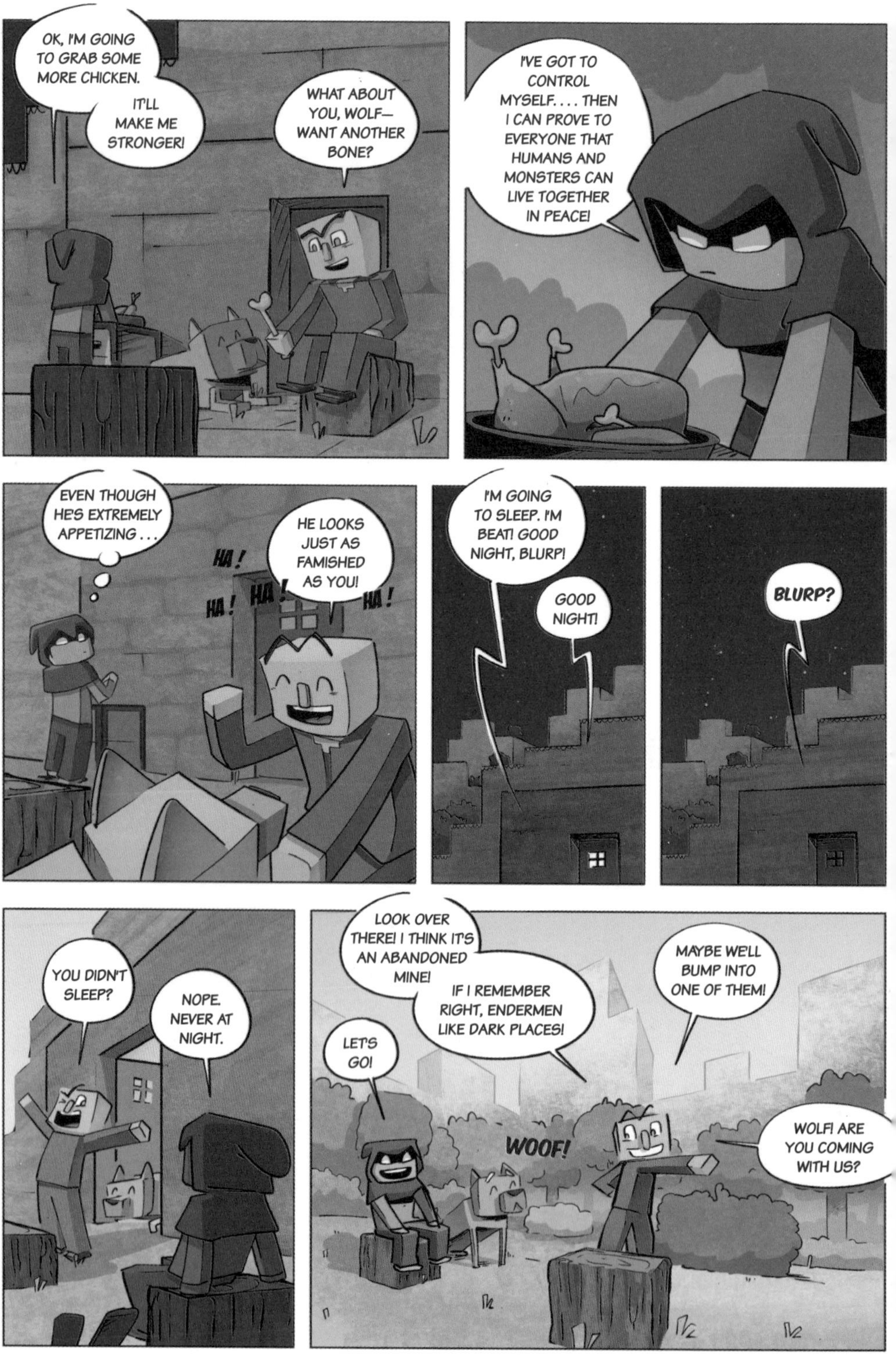
OK, I'M GOING TO GRAB SOME MORE CHICKEN.
IT'LL MAKE ME STRONGER!
WHAT ABOUT YOU, WOLF— WANT ANOTHER BONE?
I'VE GOT TO CONTROL MYSELF. . . . THEN I CAN PROVE TO EVERYONE THAT HUMANS AND MONSTERS CAN LIVE TOGETHER IN PEACE!
EVEN THOUGH HE'S EXTREMELY APPETIZING . . .
HE LOOKS JUST AS FAMISHED AS YOU!
HA! HA! HA! HA!
I'M GOING TO SLEEP. I'M BEAT! GOOD NIGHT, BLURP!
GOOD NIGHT!
BLURP?
YOU DIDN'T SLEEP?
NOPE. NEVER AT NIGHT.
LOOK OVER THERE! I THINK IT'S AN ABANDONED MINE!
IF I REMEMBER RIGHT, ENDERMEN LIKE DARK PLACES!
LET'S GO!
MAYBE WE'LL BUMP INTO ONE OF THEM!
WOOF!
WOLF! ARE YOU COMING WITH US?

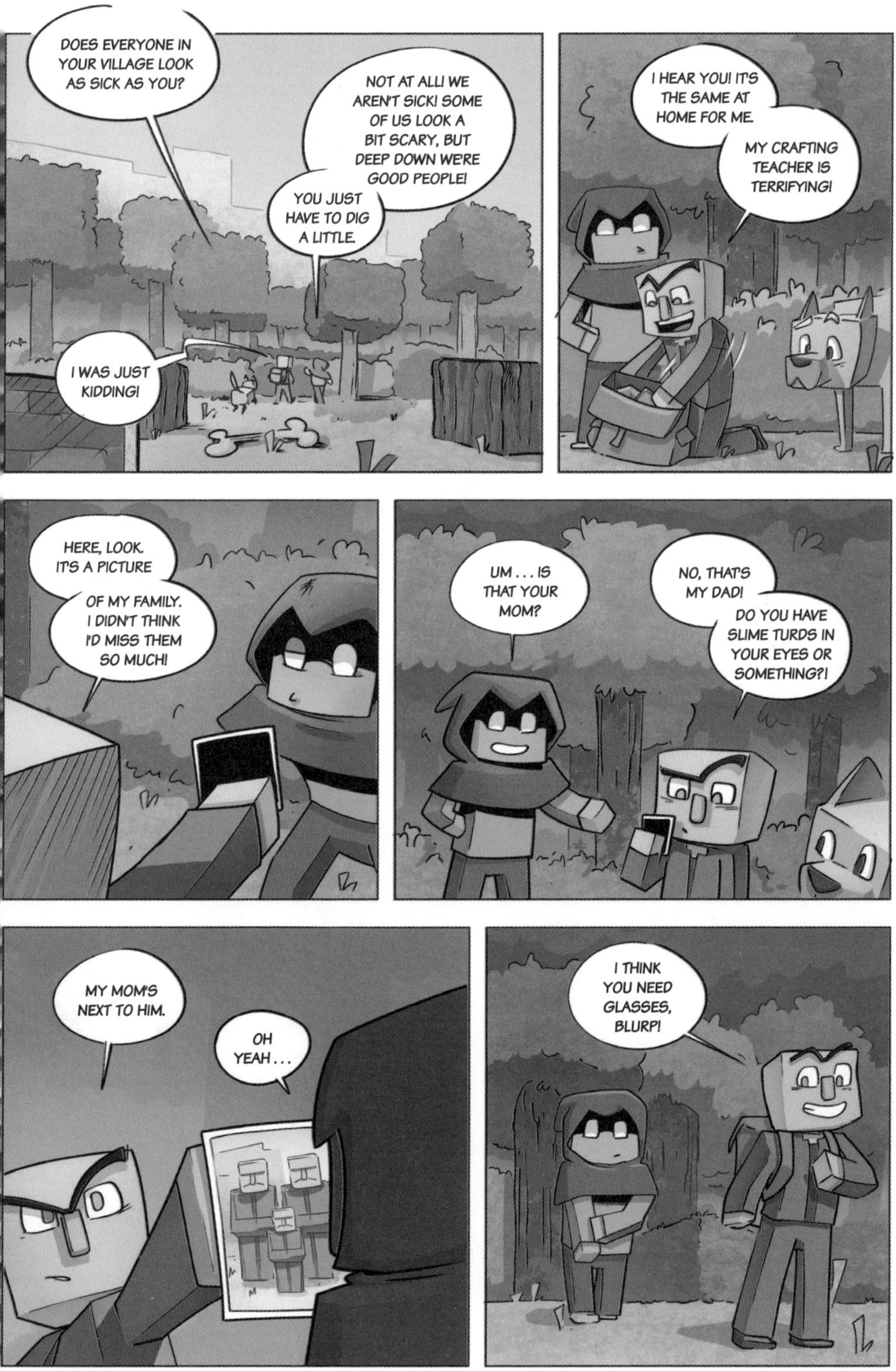

DOES EVERYONE IN YOUR VILLAGE LOOK AS SICK AS YOU?
NOT AT ALL! WE AREN'T SICK! SOME OF US LOOK A BIT SCARY, BUT DEEP DOWN WE'RE GOOD PEOPLE!
YOU JUST HAVE TO DIG A LITTLE.
I WAS JUST KIDDING!
I HEAR YOU! IT'S THE SAME AT HOME FOR ME.
MY CRAFTING TEACHER IS TERRIFYING!
HERE, LOOK. IT'S A PICTURE
OF MY FAMILY. I DIDN'T THINK I'D MISS THEM SO MUCH!
UM . . . IS THAT YOUR MOM?
NO, THAT'S MY DAD!
DO YOU HAVE SLIME TURDS IN YOUR EYES OR SOMETHING?!
MY MOM'S NEXT TO HIM.
OH YEAH . . .
I THINK YOU NEED GLASSES, BLURP!

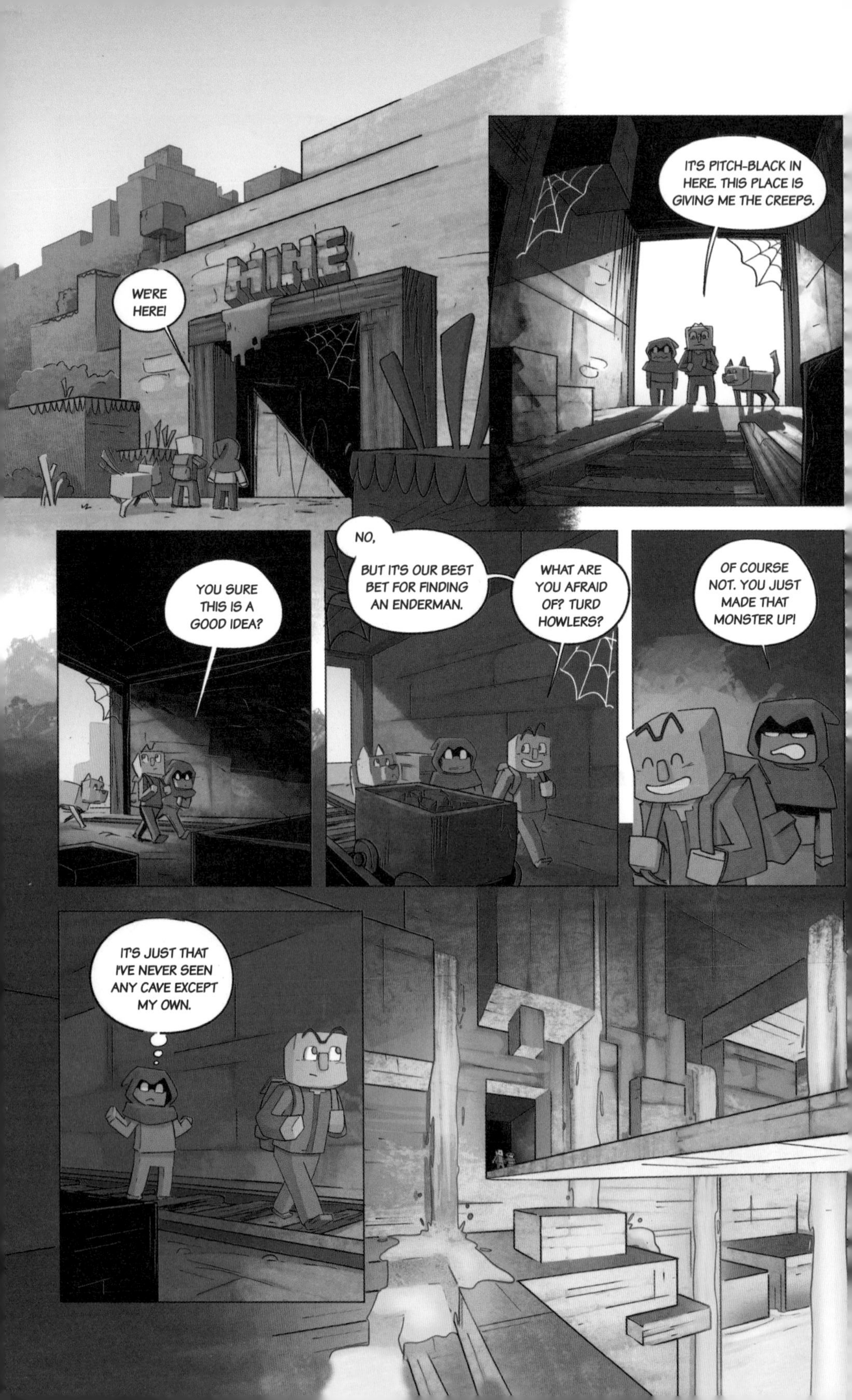
MINE
WE'RE HERE!
IT'S PITCH-BLACK IN HERE. THIS PLACE IS GIVING ME THE CREEPS.
YOU SURE THIS IS A GOOD IDEA?
NO,
BUT IT'S OUR BEST BET FOR FINDING AN ENDERMAN.
WHAT ARE YOU AFRAID OF? TURD HOWLERS?
OF COURSE NOT. YOU JUST MADE THAT MONSTER UP!
IT'S JUST THAT I'VE NEVER SEEN ANY CAVE EXCEPT MY OWN.

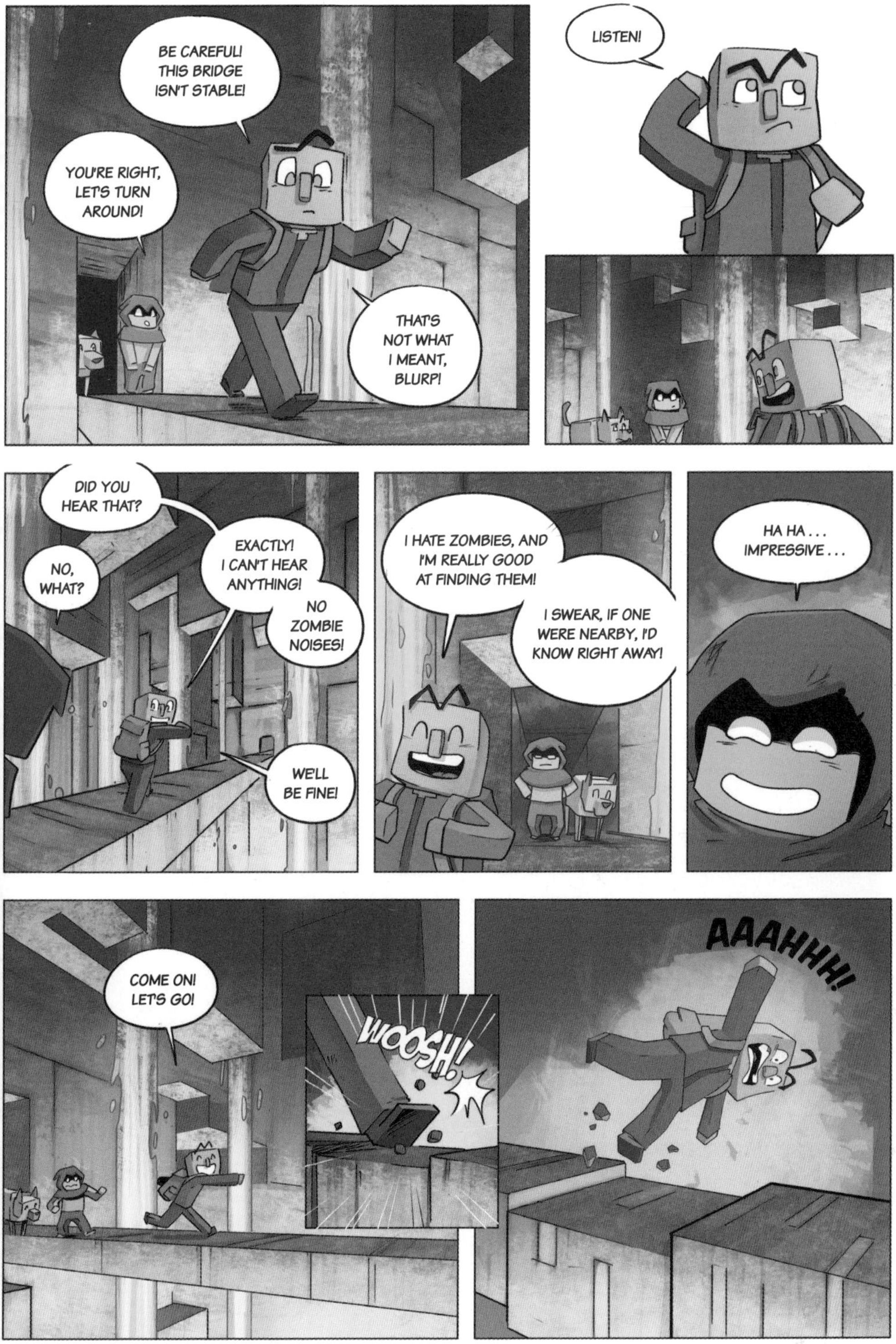
BE CAREFUL! THIS BRIDGE ISN'T STABLE!
YOU'RE RIGHT, LET'S TURN AROUND!
THAT'S NOT WHAT I MEANT, BLURP!
LISTEN!
DID YOU HEAR THAT?
NO, WHAT?
EXACTLY! I CAN'T HEAR ANYTHING!
NO ZOMBIE NOISES!
WE'LL BE FINE!
I HATE ZOMBIES, AND I'M REALLY GOOD AT FINDING THEM!
I SWEAR, IF ONE WERE NEARBY, I'D KNOW RIGHT AWAY!
HA HA . . . IMPRESSIVE . . .
COME ON! LET'S GO!
WOOSH!
AAAHHH!

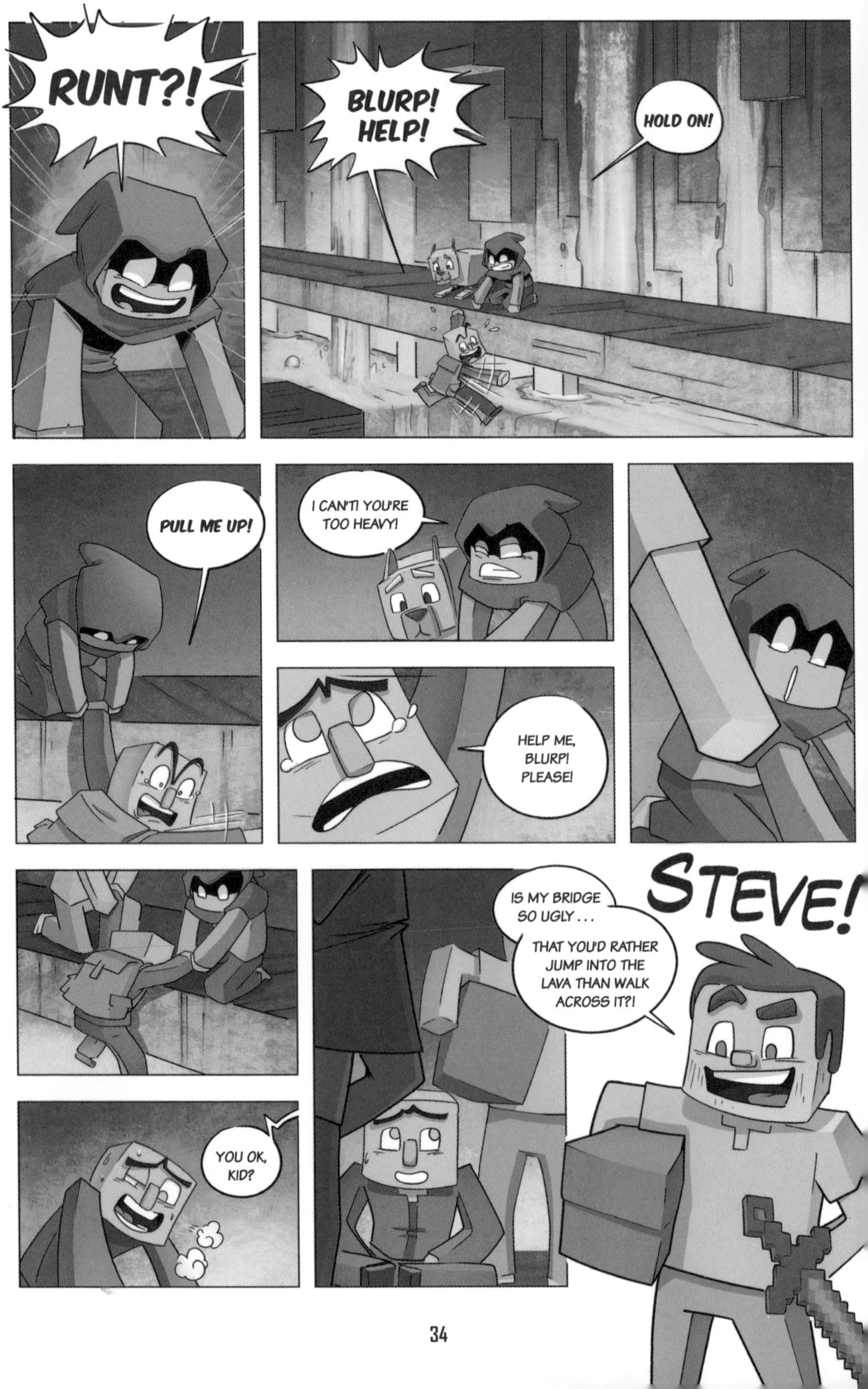
RUNT?!
BLURP! HELP!
HOLD ON!
PULL ME UP!
I CAN'T! YOU'RE TOO HEAVY!
HELP ME, BLURP! PLEASE!
YOU OK, KID?
STEVE!
IS MY BRIDGE SO UGLY . . .
THAT YOU'D RATHER JUMP INTO THE LAVA THAN WALK ACROSS IT?!

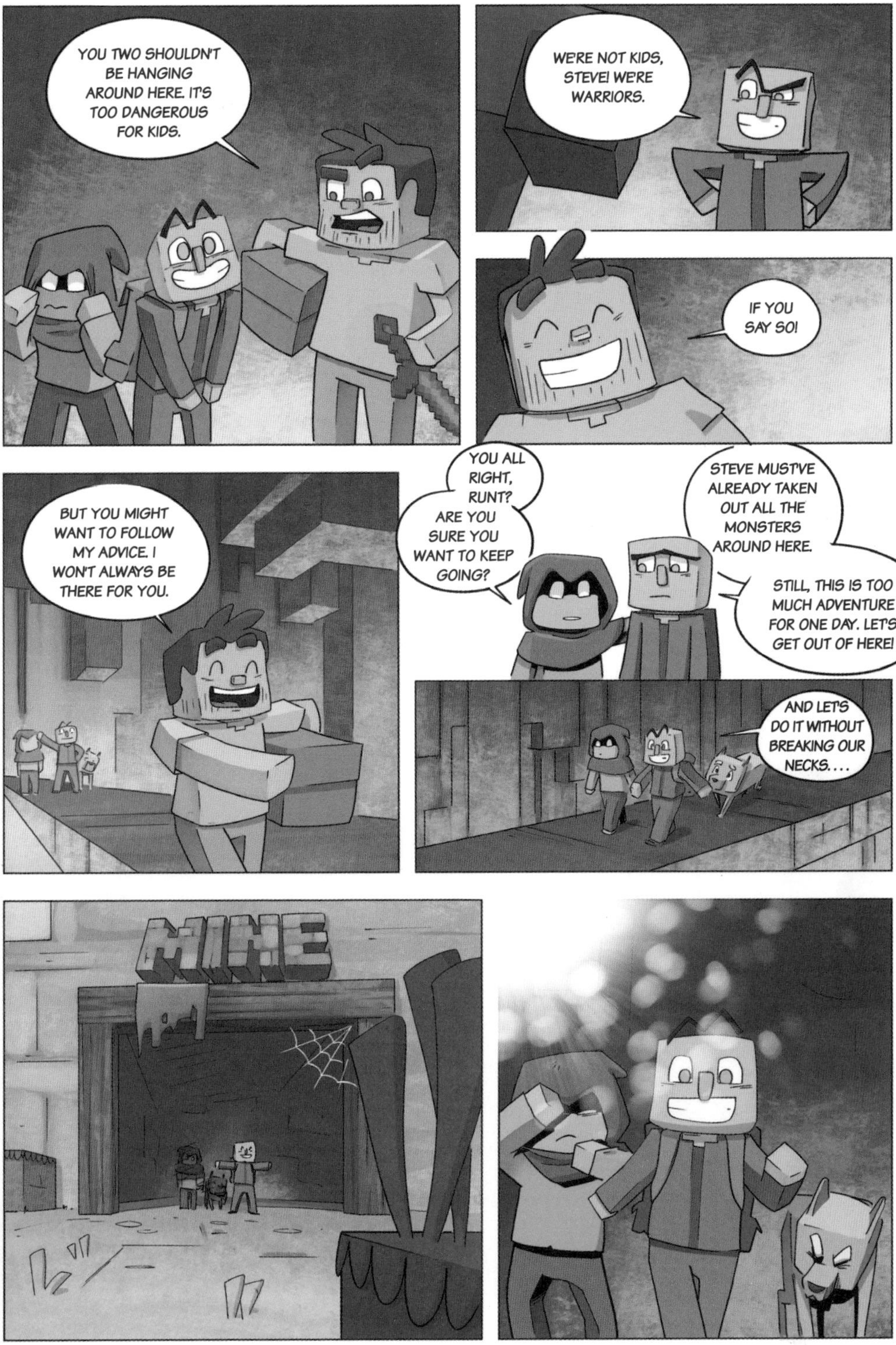
YOU TWO SHOULDN'T BE HANGING AROUND HERE. IT'S TOO DANGEROUS FOR KIDS.
WE'RE NOT KIDS, STEVE! WE'RE WARRIORS.
IF YOU SAY SO!
BUT YOU MIGHT WANT TO FOLLOW MY ADVICE. I WON'T ALWAYS BE THERE FOR YOU.
YOU ALL RIGHT, RUNT?
ARE YOU SURE YOU WANT TO KEEP GOING?
STEVE MUST'VE ALREADY TAKEN OUT ALL THE MONSTERS AROUND HERE.
STILL, THIS IS TOO MUCH ADVENTURE FOR ONE DAY. LET'S GET OUT OF HERE!
AND LET'S DO IT WITHOUT BREAKING OUR NECKS. . . .
MINE

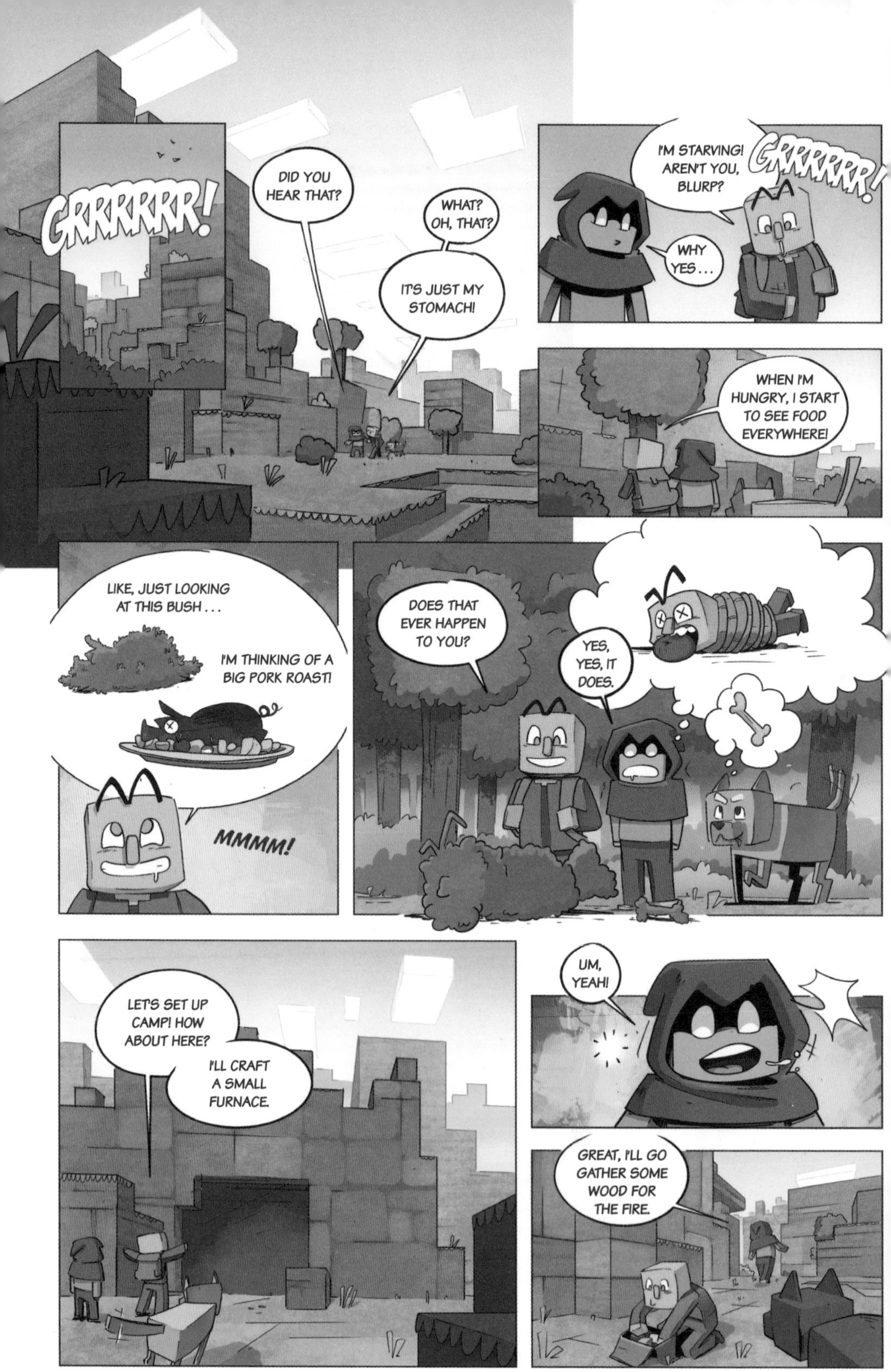
GRRRRRR!
DID YOU HEAR THAT?
WHAT? OH, THAT?
IT'S JUST MY STOMACH!
I'M STARVING! AREN'T YOU, BLURP?
GRRRRRRR!
WHY YES . . .
WHEN I'M HUNGRY, I START TO SEE FOOD EVERYWHERE!
LIKE, JUST LOOKING AT THIS BUSH . . .
I'M THINKING OF A BIG PORK ROAST!
MMMM!
DOES THAT EVER HAPPEN TO YOU?
YES, YES, IT DOES.
LET'S SET UP CAMP! HOW ABOUT HERE?
I'LL CRAFT A SMALL FURNACE.
UM, YEAH!
GREAT, I'LL GO GATHER SOME WOOD FOR THE FIRE.

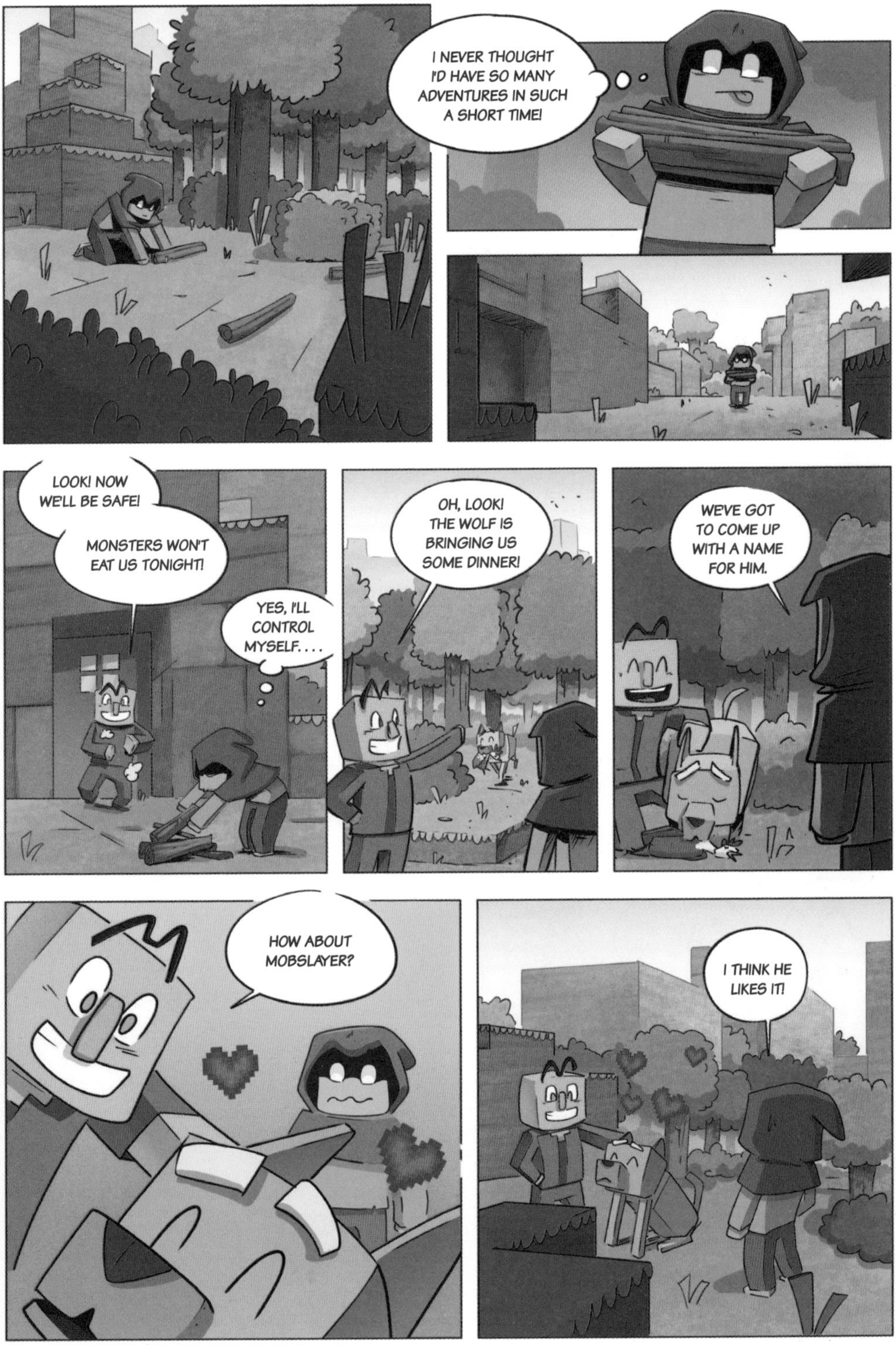
I NEVER THOUGHT I'D HAVE SO MANY ADVENTURES IN SUCH A SHORT TIME!
LOOK! NOW WE'LL BE SAFE!
MONSTERS WON'T EAT US TONIGHT!
YES, I'LL CONTROL MYSELF. . . .
OH, LOOK! THE WOLF IS BRINGING US SOME DINNER!
WE'VE GOT TO COME UP WITH A NAME FOR HIM.
HOW ABOUT MOBSLAYER?
I THINK HE LIKES IT!

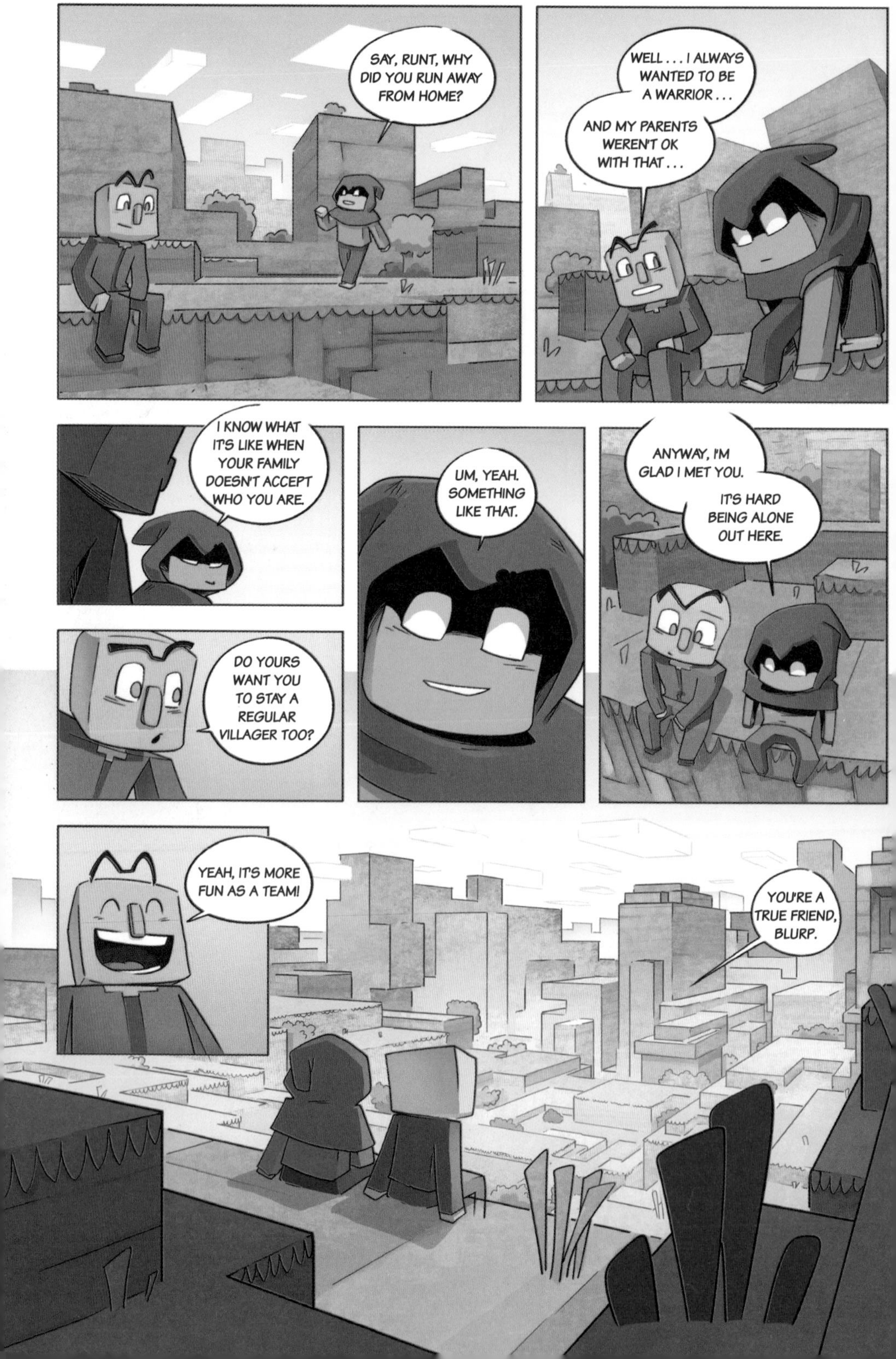
SAY, RUNT, WHY DID YOU RUN AWAY FROM HOME?
WELL . . . I ALWAYS WANTED TO BE A WARRIOR . . .
AND MY PARENTS WEREN'T OK WITH THAT . . .
I KNOW WHAT IT'S LIKE WHEN YOUR FAMILY DOESN'T ACCEPT WHO YOU ARE.
DO YOURS WANT YOU TO STAY A REGULAR VILLAGER TOO?
UM, YEAH. SOMETHING LIKE THAT.
ANYWAY, I'M GLAD I MET YOU.
IT'S HARD BEING ALONE OUT HERE.
YEAH, IT'S MORE FUN AS A TEAM!
YOU'RE A TRUE FRIEND, BLURP.

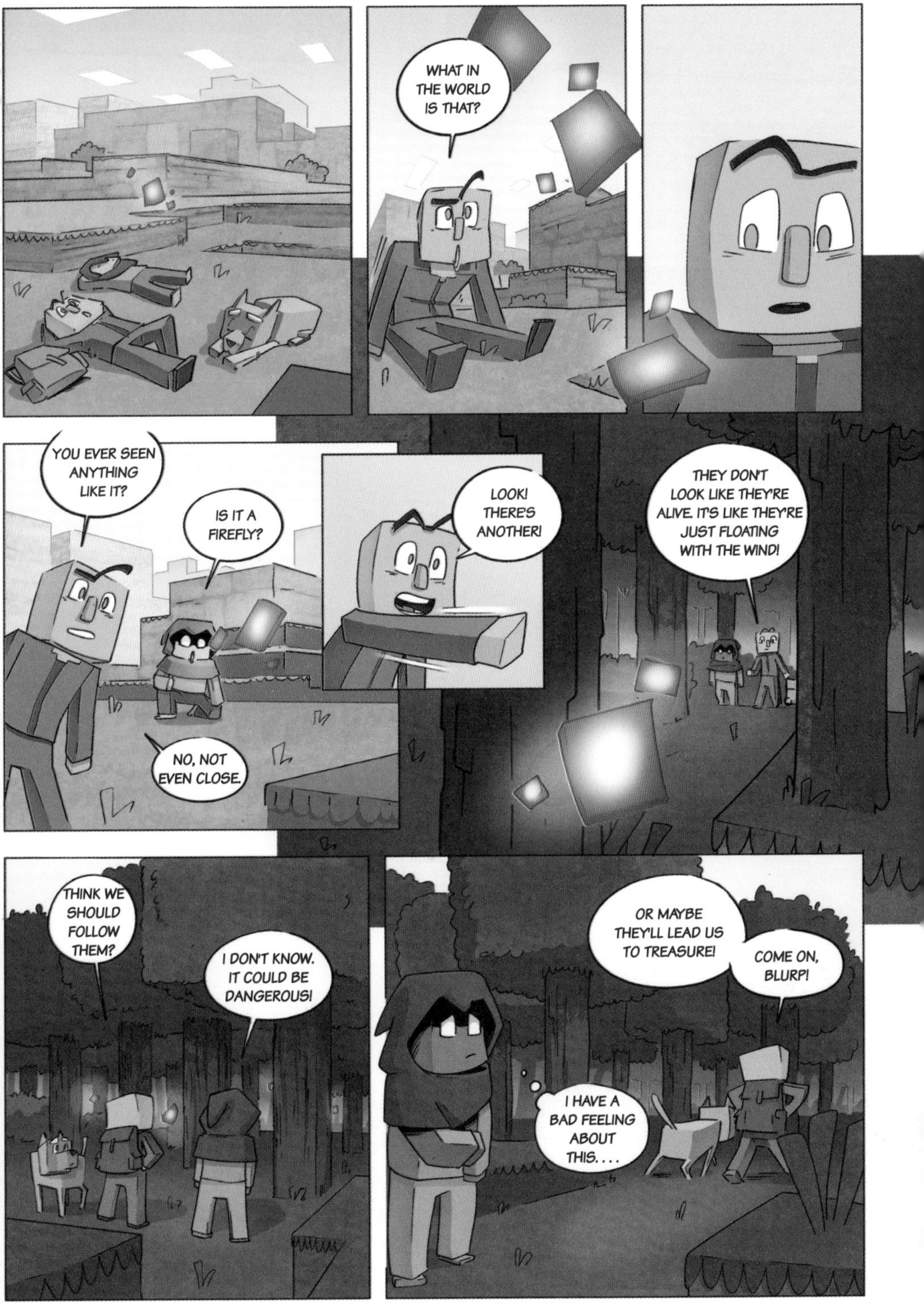
WHAT IN THE WORLD IS THAT?
YOU EVER SEEN ANYTHING LIKE IT?
IS IT A FIREFLY?
NO, NOT EVEN CLOSE.
LOOK! THERE'S ANOTHER!
THEY DON'T LOOK LIKE THEY'RE ALIVE. IT'S LIKE THEY'RE JUST FLOATING WITH THE WIND!
THINK WE SHOULD FOLLOW THEM?
I DON'T KNOW. IT COULD BE DANGEROUS!
OR MAYBE THEY'LL LEAD US TO TREASURE!
COME ON, BLURP!
I HAVE A BAD FEELING ABOUT THIS. . . .

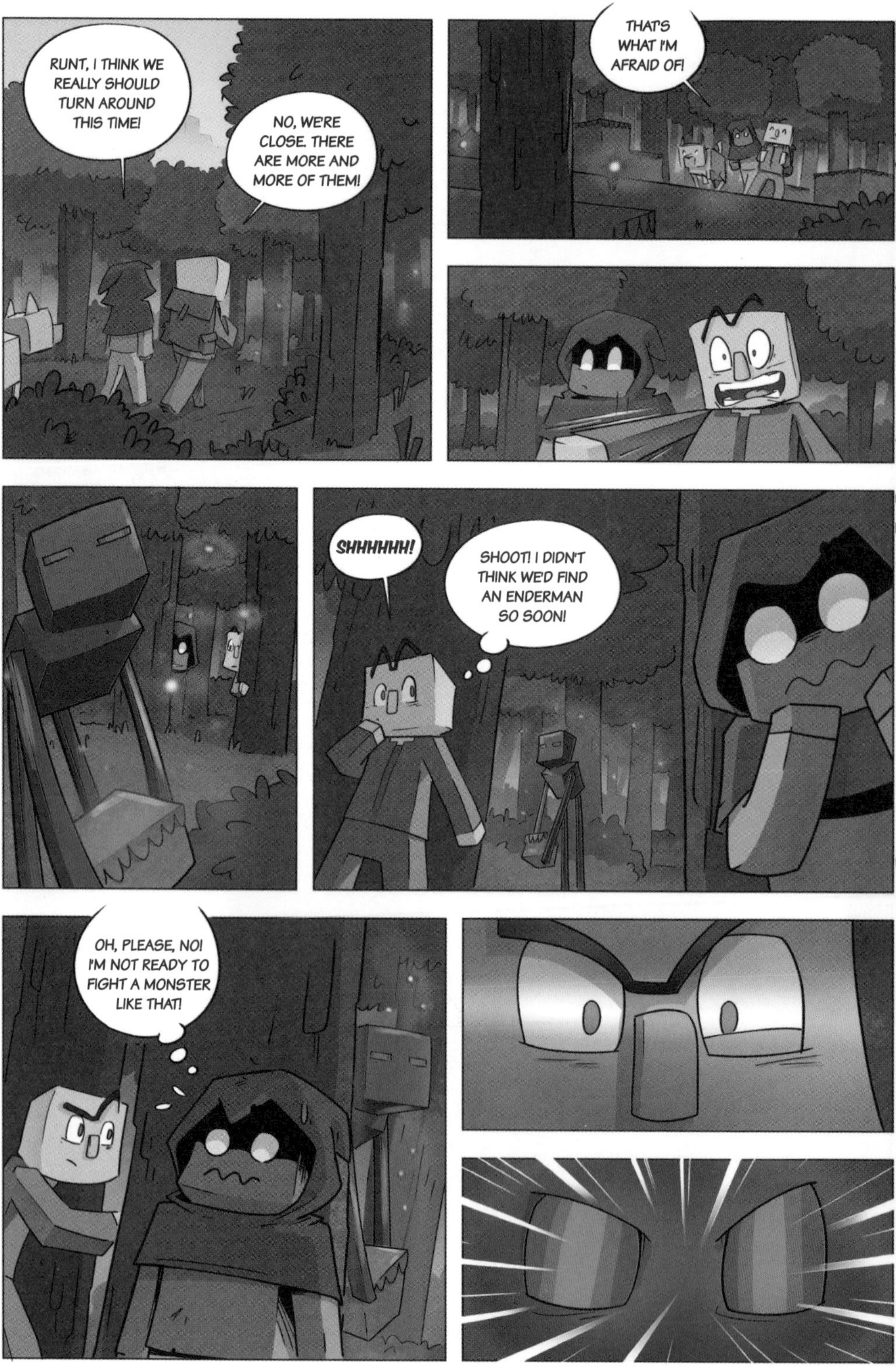
RUNT, I THINK WE REALLY SHOULD TURN AROUND THIS TIME!
NO, WE'RE CLOSE. THERE ARE MORE AND MORE OF THEM!
THAT'S WHAT I'M AFRAID OF!
SHHHHHH!
SHOOT! I DIDN'T THINK WE'D FIND AN ENDERMAN SO SOON!
OH, PLEASE, NO! I'M NOT READY TO FIGHT A MONSTER LIKE THAT!

EEEEEERRRRRRREEEEEEEE!!

OH NO, I LOOKED HIM IN THE EYE! WE'RE DEAD!!

I CAN'T MESS THIS UP!

HE . . .

TELEPORTED.

RUN!!!

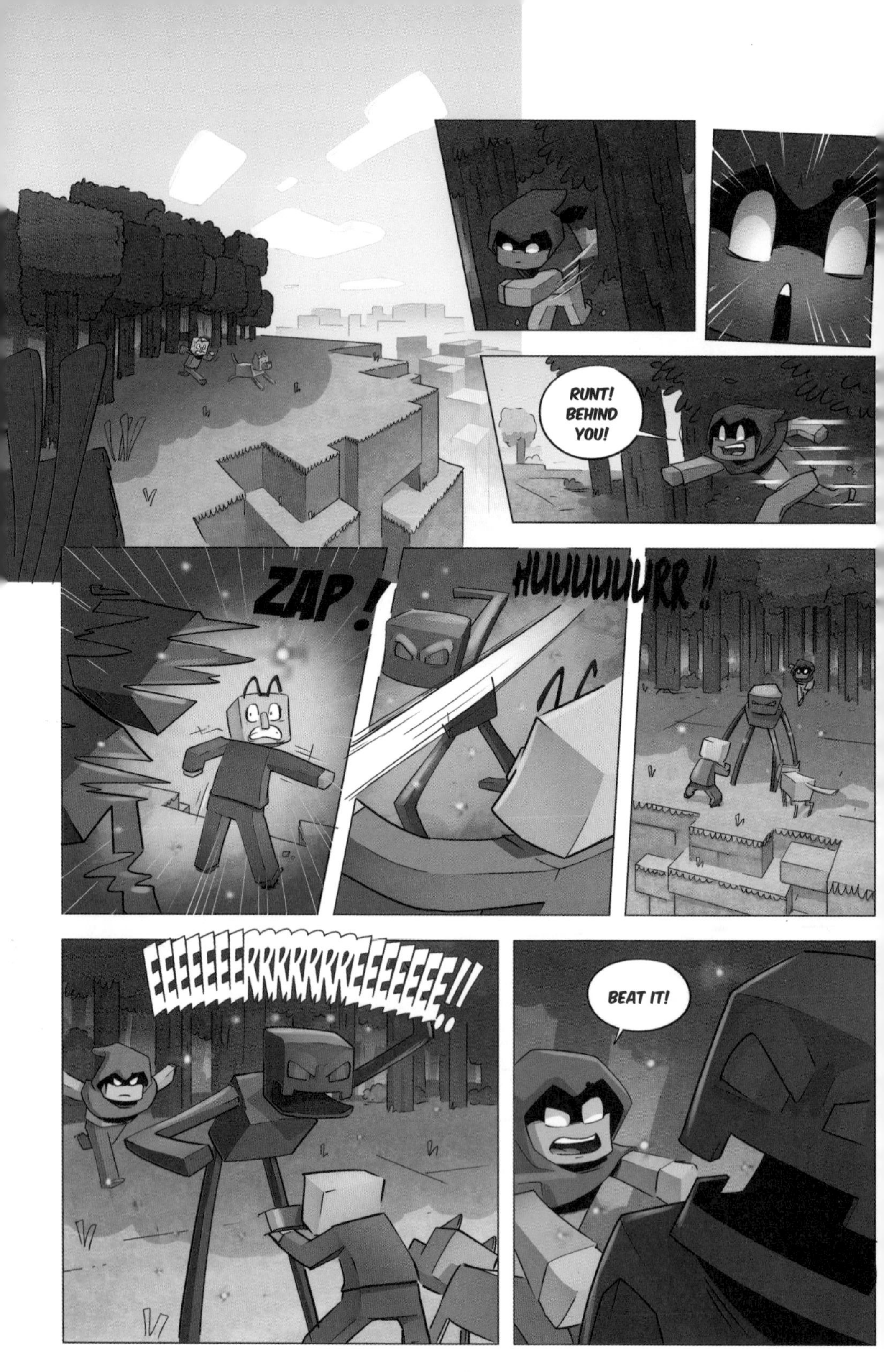

RUNT! BEHIND YOU!
ZAP!
HUUUUUURR!!
EEEEEEERRRRRREEEEEEE!!
BEAT IT!

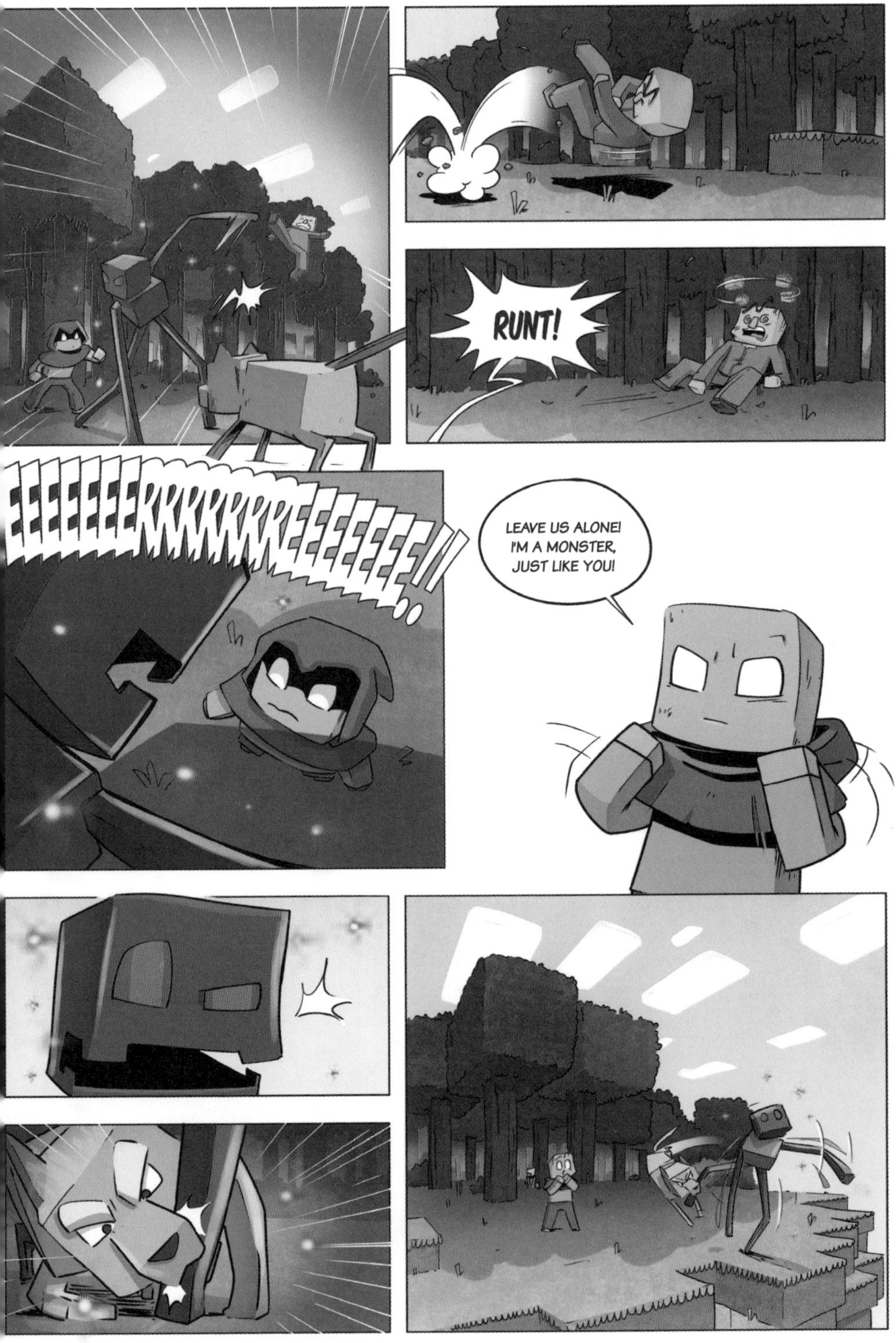
RUNT!
EEEEEEEERRRRRRREEEEEEE!!
LEAVE US ALONE!
I'M A MONSTER,
JUST LIKE YOU!

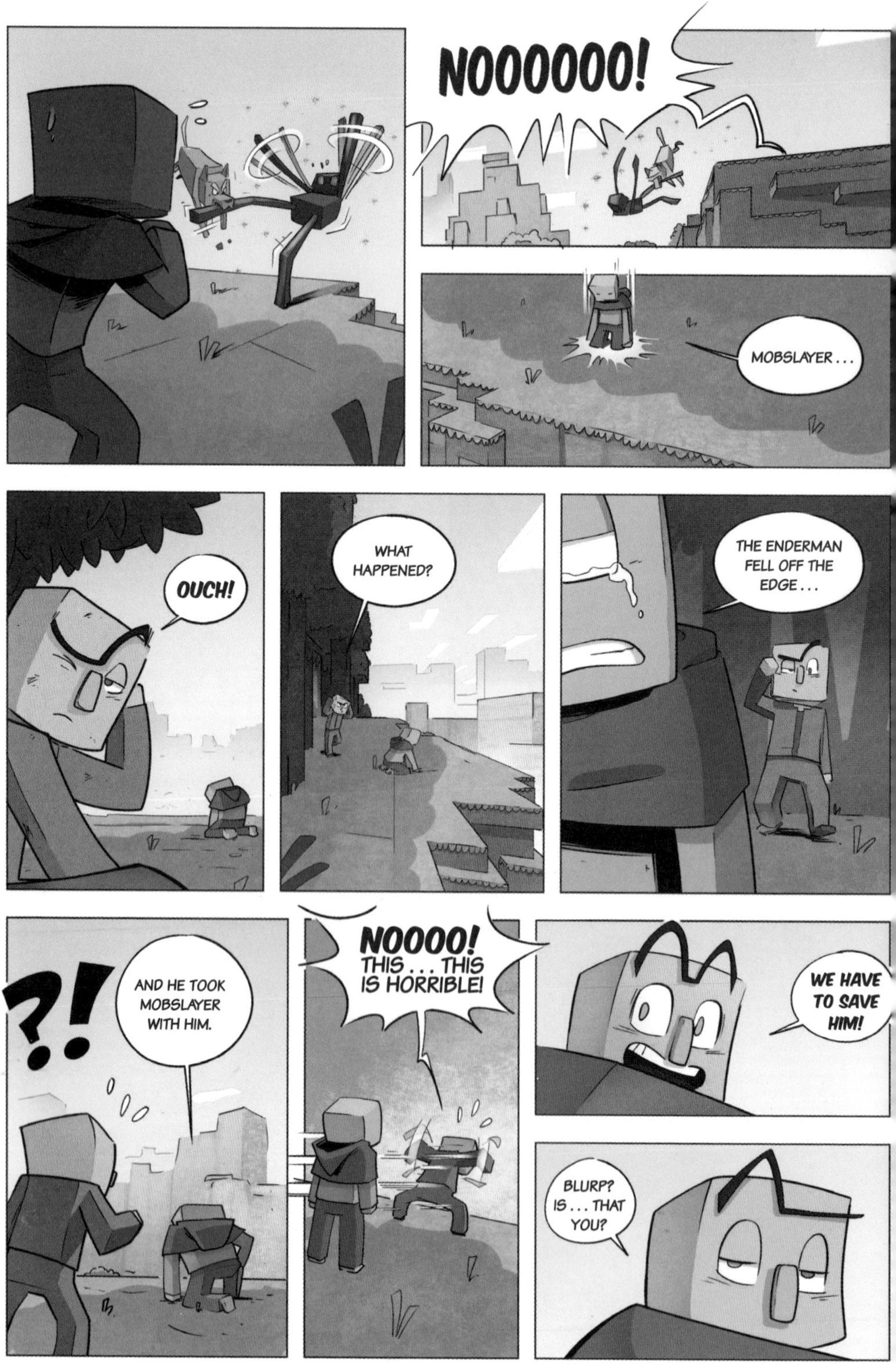
NOOOOOO!
MOBSLAYER . . .
OUCH!
WHAT HAPPENED?
THE ENDERMAN FELL OFF THE EDGE . . .
?!
AND HE TOOK MOBSLAYER WITH HIM.
NOOOO! THIS . . . THIS IS HORRIBLE!
WE HAVE TO SAVE HIM!
BLURP? IS . . . THAT YOU?

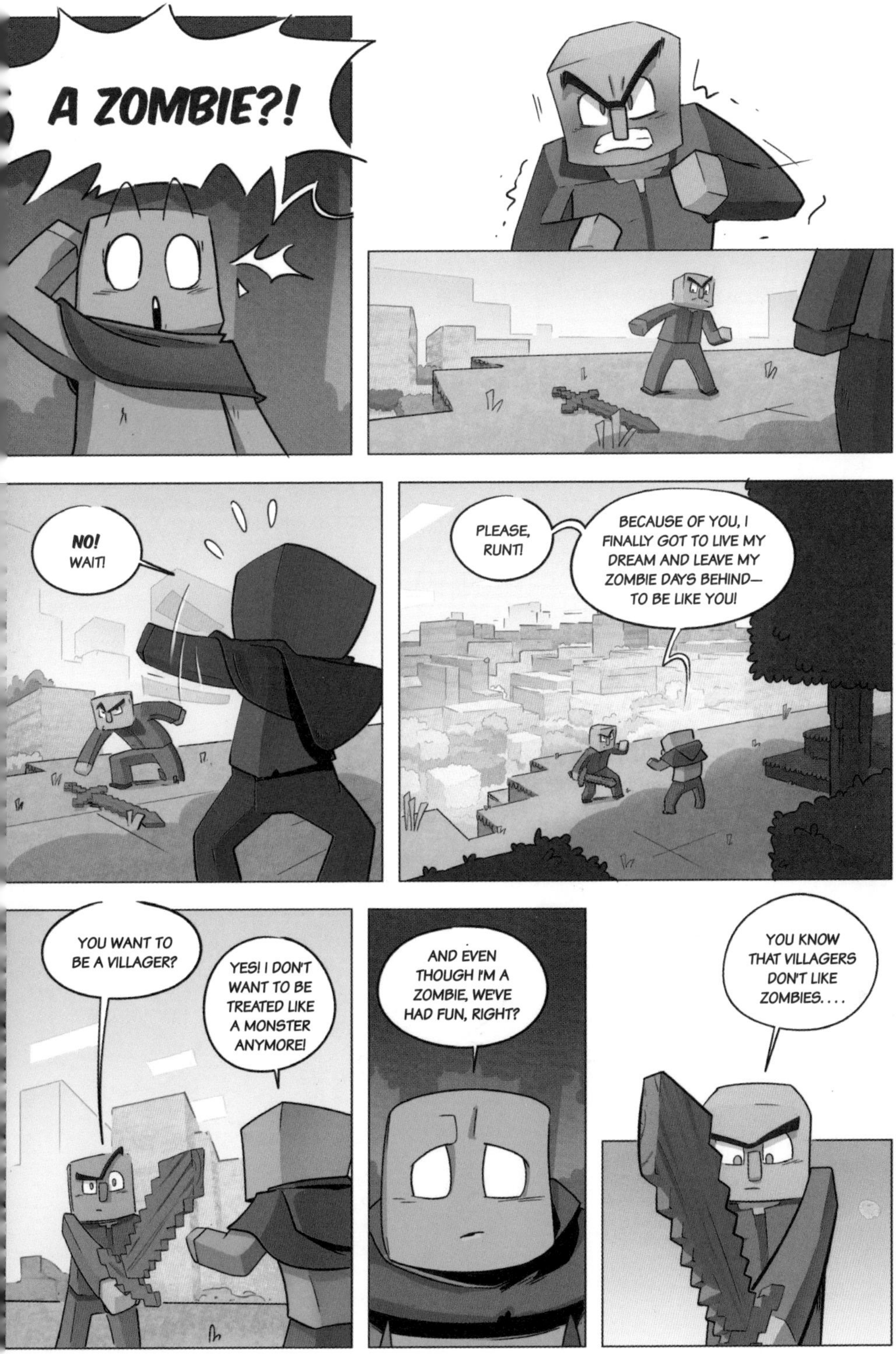
A ZOMBIE?!
NO! WAIT!
PLEASE, RUNT!
BECAUSE OF YOU, I FINALLY GOT TO LIVE MY DREAM AND LEAVE MY ZOMBIE DAYS BEHIND—TO BE LIKE YOU!
YOU WANT TO BE A VILLAGER?
YES! I DON'T WANT TO BE TREATED LIKE A MONSTER ANYMORE!
AND EVEN THOUGH I'M A ZOMBIE, WE'VE HAD FUN, RIGHT?
YOU KNOW THAT VILLAGERS DON'T LIKE ZOMBIES. . . .

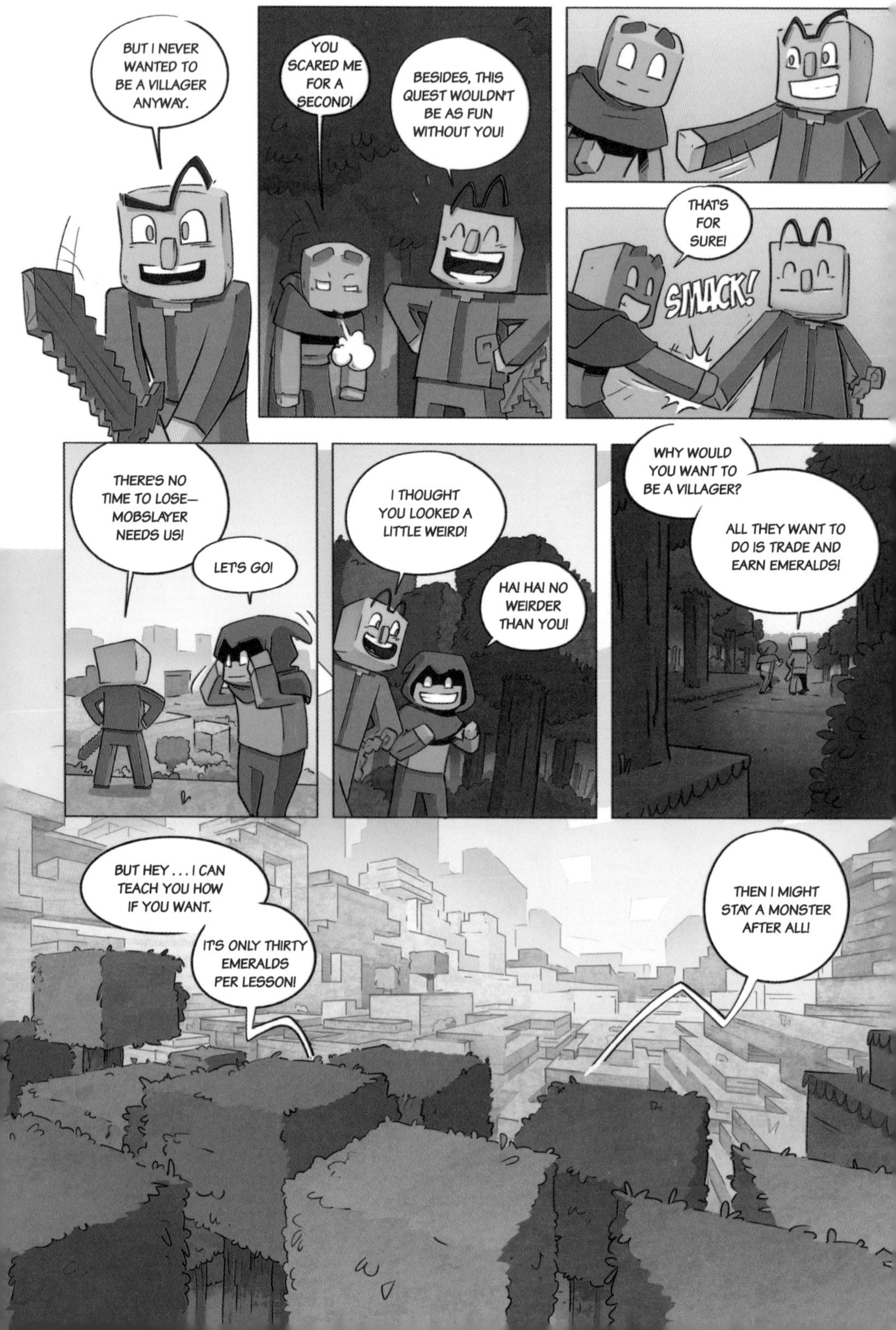
BUT I NEVER WANTED TO BE A VILLAGER ANYWAY.
YOU SCARED ME FOR A SECOND!
BESIDES, THIS QUEST WOULDN'T BE AS FUN WITHOUT YOU!
THAT'S FOR SURE!
SMACK!
THERE'S NO TIME TO LOSE— MOBSLAYER NEEDS US!
LET'S GO!
I THOUGHT YOU LOOKED A LITTLE WEIRD!
HA! HA! NO WEIRDER THAN YOU!
WHY WOULD YOU WANT TO BE A VILLAGER?
ALL THEY WANT TO DO IS TRADE AND EARN EMERALDS!
BUT HEY . . . I CAN TEACH YOU HOW IF YOU WANT.
IT'S ONLY THIRTY EMERALDS PER LESSON!
THEN I MIGHT STAY A MONSTER AFTER ALL!

PART TWO

A STROLL THROUGH THE NETHER

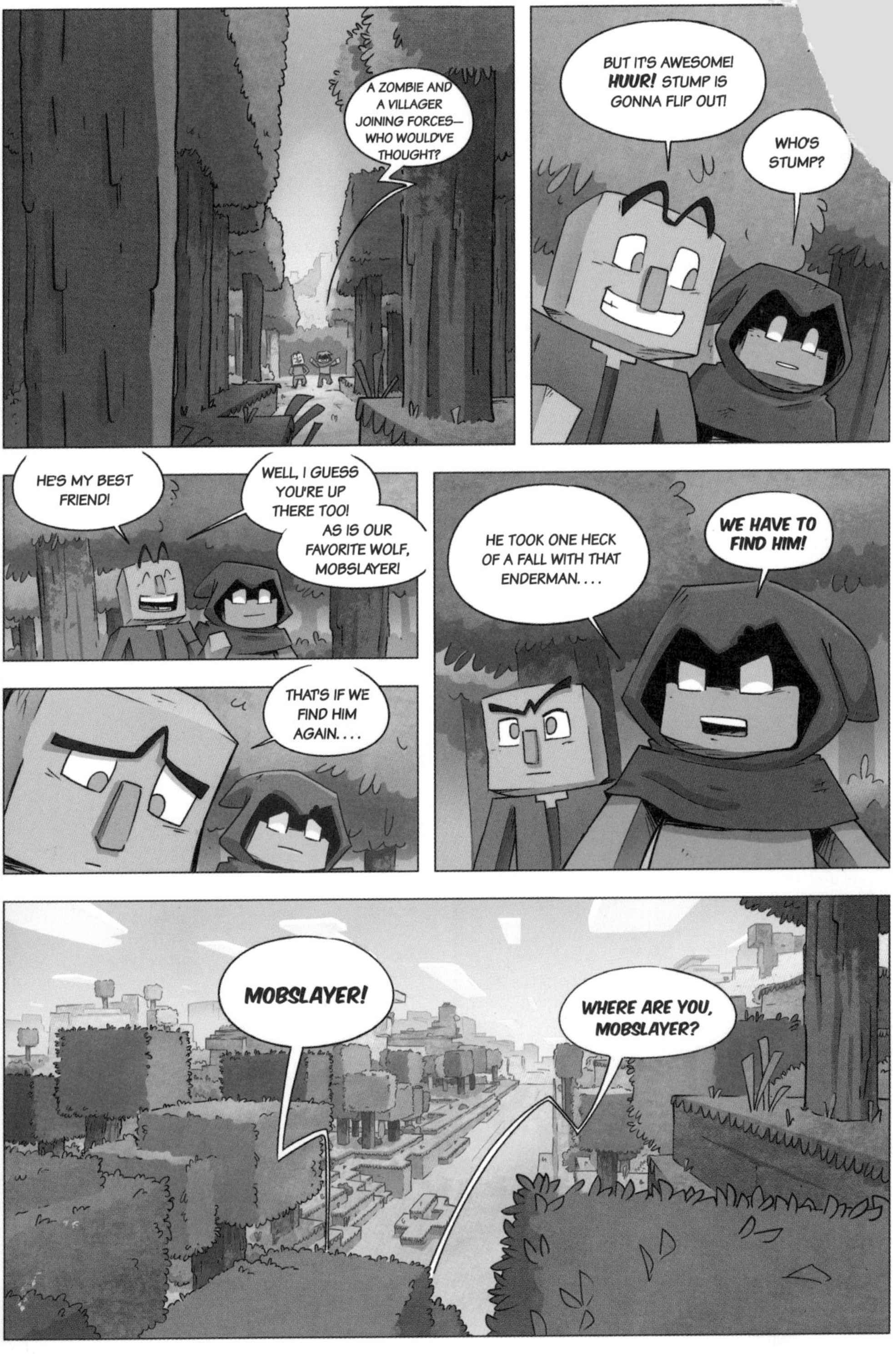
A ZOMBIE AND A VILLAGER JOINING FORCES— WHO WOULD'VE THOUGHT?
BUT IT'S AWESOME! **HUUR!** STUMP IS GONNA FLIP OUT!
WHO'S STUMP?
HE'S MY BEST FRIEND!
WELL, I GUESS YOU'RE UP THERE TOO!
AS IS OUR FAVORITE WOLF, MOBSLAYER!
THAT'S IF WE FIND HIM AGAIN. . . .
HE TOOK ONE HECK OF A FALL WITH THAT ENDERMAN. . . .
WE HAVE TO FIND HIM!
MOBSLAYER!
WHERE ARE YOU, MOBSLAYER?

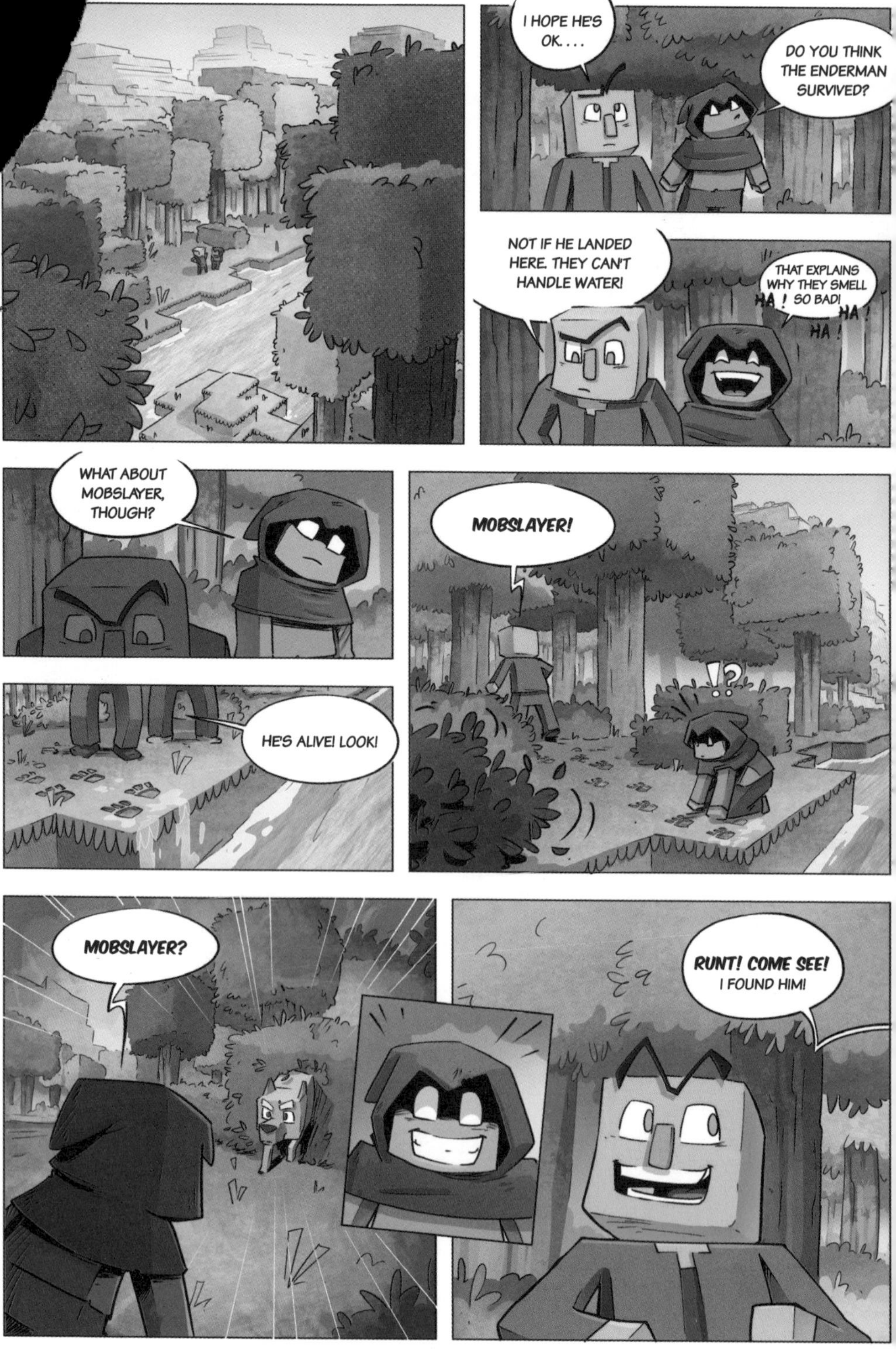
I HOPE HE'S OK. . . .
DO YOU THINK THE ENDERMAN SURVIVED?
NOT IF HE LANDED HERE. THEY CAN'T HANDLE WATER!
THAT EXPLAINS WHY THEY SMELL SO BAD!
HA! HA! HA!
WHAT ABOUT MOBSLAYER, THOUGH?
HE'S ALIVE! LOOK!
MOBSLAYER!
!?
MOBSLAYER?
RUNT! COME SEE! I FOUND HIM!

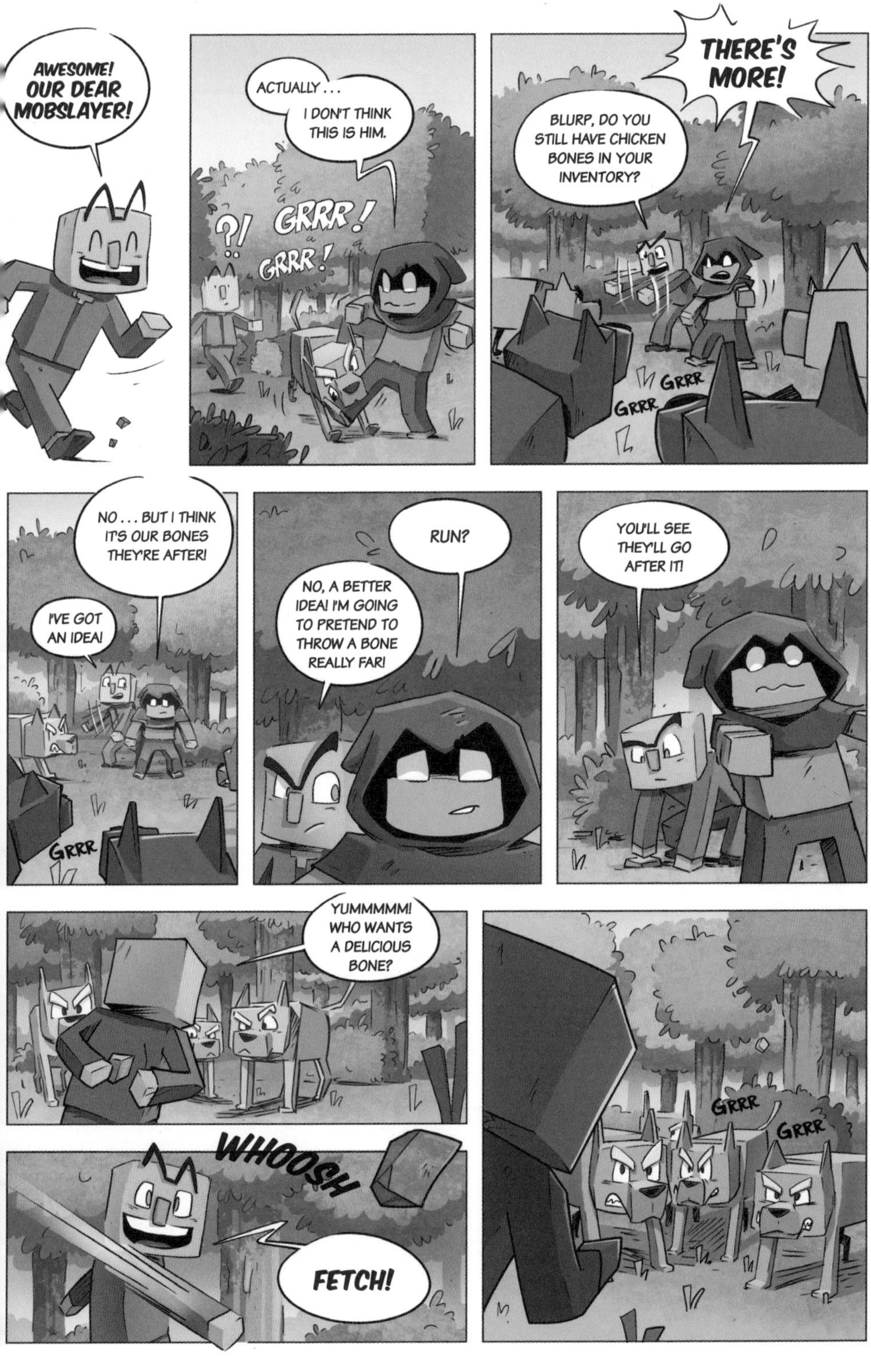
AWESOME! OUR DEAR MOBSLAYER!
ACTUALLY . . .
I DON'T THINK THIS IS HIM.
?!
GRRR!
GRRR!
THERE'S MORE!
BLURP, DO YOU STILL HAVE CHICKEN BONES IN YOUR INVENTORY?
GRRR
GRRR
NO . . . BUT I THINK IT'S OUR BONES THEY'RE AFTER!
I'VE GOT AN IDEA!
GRRR
RUN?
NO, A BETTER IDEA! I'M GOING TO PRETEND TO THROW A BONE REALLY FAR!
YOU'LL SEE. THEY'LL GO AFTER IT!
YUMMMMM! WHO WANTS A DELICIOUS BONE?
WHOOSH
FETCH!
GRRR
GRRR

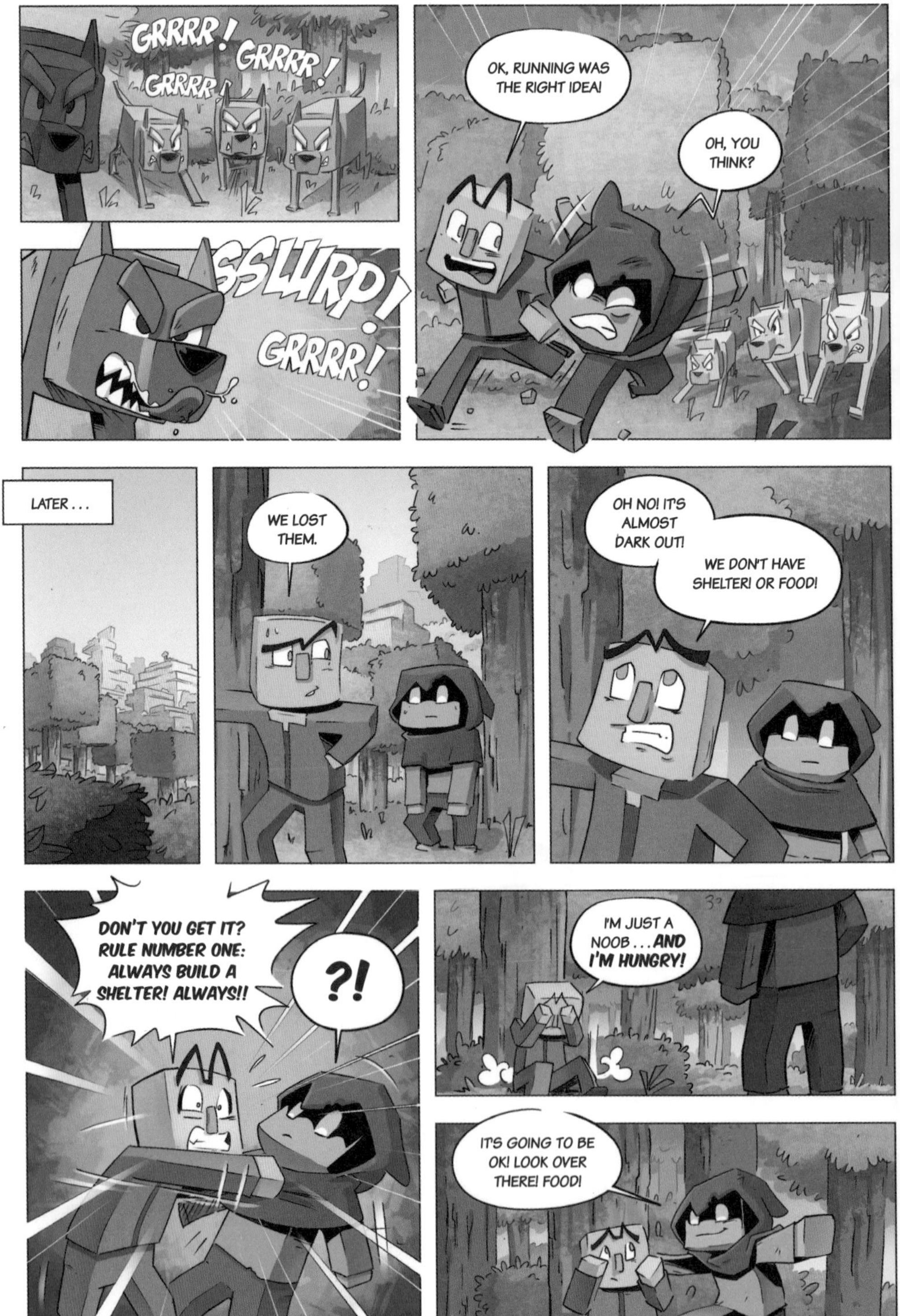
GRRRR! GRRRR! GRRRR!
OK, RUNNING WAS THE RIGHT IDEA!
OH, YOU THINK?
SSLURP!
GRRRR!
LATER . . .
WE LOST THEM.
OH NO! IT'S ALMOST DARK OUT!
WE DON'T HAVE SHELTER! OR FOOD!
DON'T YOU GET IT? RULE NUMBER ONE: ALWAYS BUILD A SHELTER! ALWAYS!!
?!
I'M JUST A NOOB . . . AND I'M HUNGRY!
IT'S GOING TO BE OK! LOOK OVER THERE! FOOD!

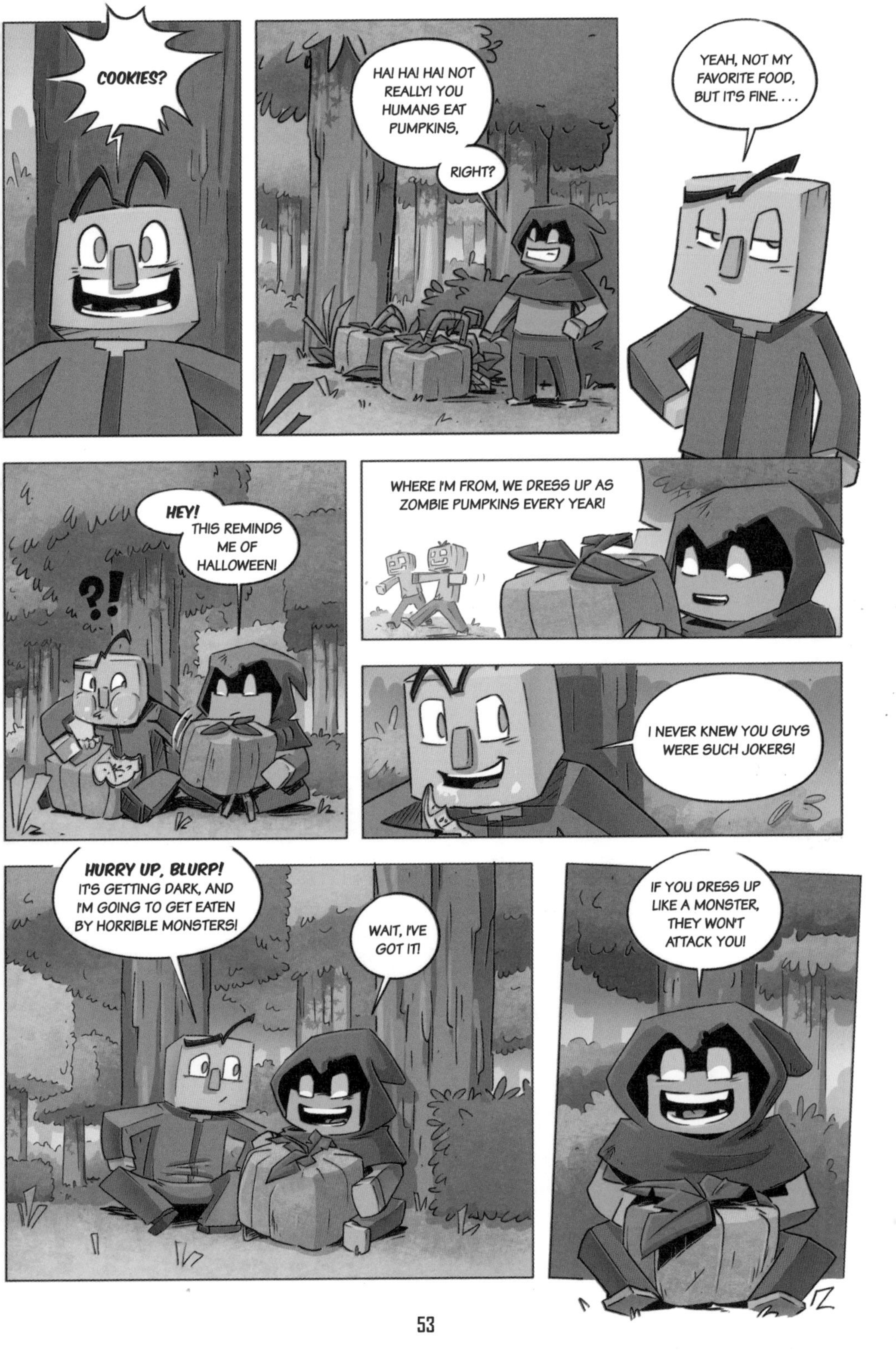
COOKIES?
HA! HA! HA! NOT REALLY! YOU HUMANS EAT PUMPKINS,
RIGHT?
YEAH, NOT MY FAVORITE FOOD, BUT IT'S FINE. . . .
HEY! THIS REMINDS ME OF HALLOWEEN!
?!
WHERE I'M FROM, WE DRESS UP AS ZOMBIE PUMPKINS EVERY YEAR!
I NEVER KNEW YOU GUYS WERE SUCH JOKERS!
HURRY UP, BLURP! IT'S GETTING DARK, AND I'M GOING TO GET EATEN BY HORRIBLE MONSTERS!
WAIT, I'VE GOT IT!
IF YOU DRESS UP LIKE A MONSTER, THEY WON'T ATTACK YOU!

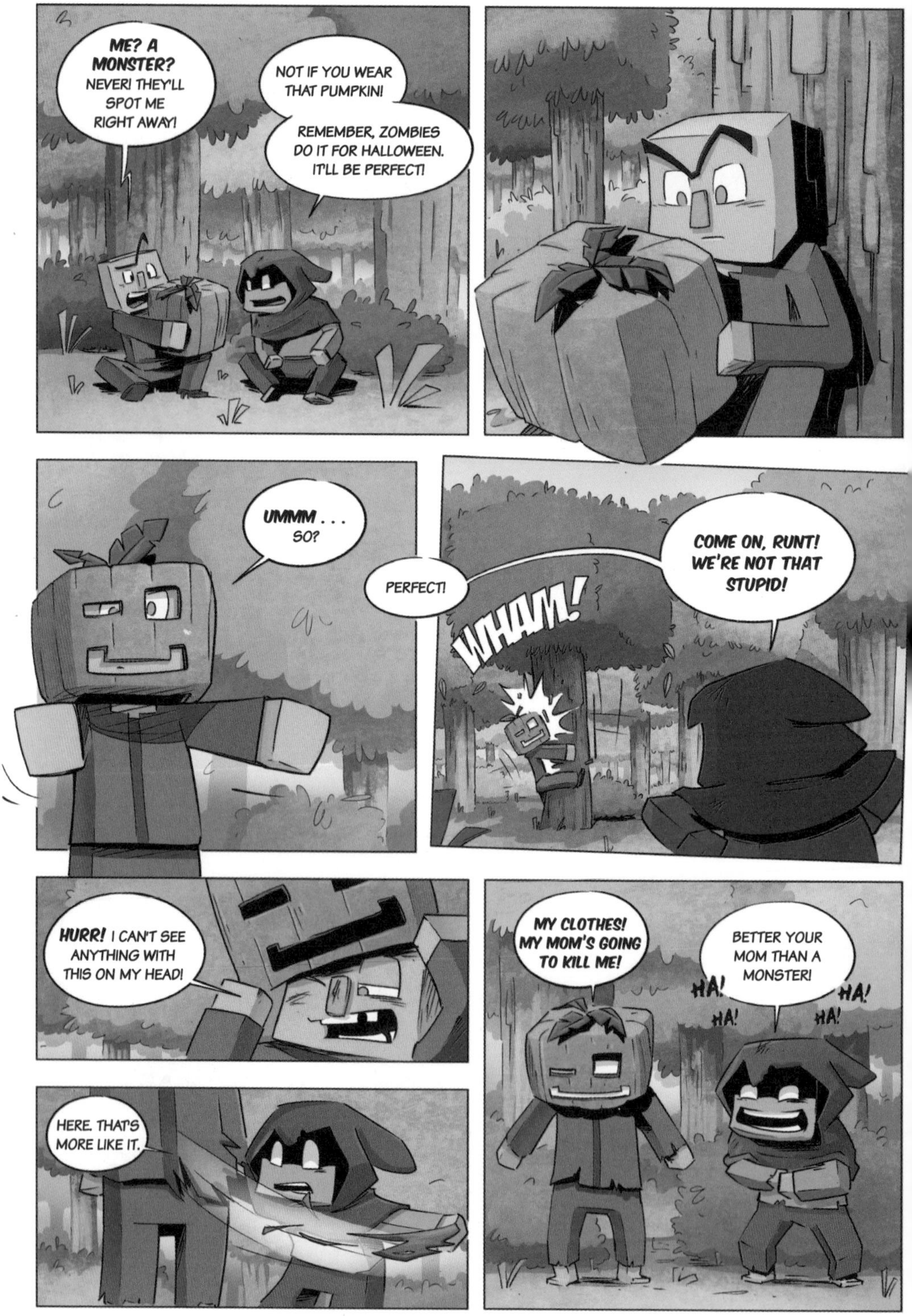
ME? A MONSTER? NEVER! THEY'LL SPOT ME RIGHT AWAY!
NOT IF YOU WEAR THAT PUMPKIN!
REMEMBER, ZOMBIES DO IT FOR HALLOWEEN. IT'LL BE PERFECT!
UMMM . . . SO?
PERFECT!
COME ON, RUNT! WE'RE NOT THAT STUPID!
WHAM!
HURR! I CAN'T SEE ANYTHING WITH THIS ON MY HEAD!
HERE. THAT'S MORE LIKE IT.
MY CLOTHES! MY MOM'S GOING TO KILL ME!
BETTER YOUR MOM THAN A MONSTER!
HA! HA! HA! HA!

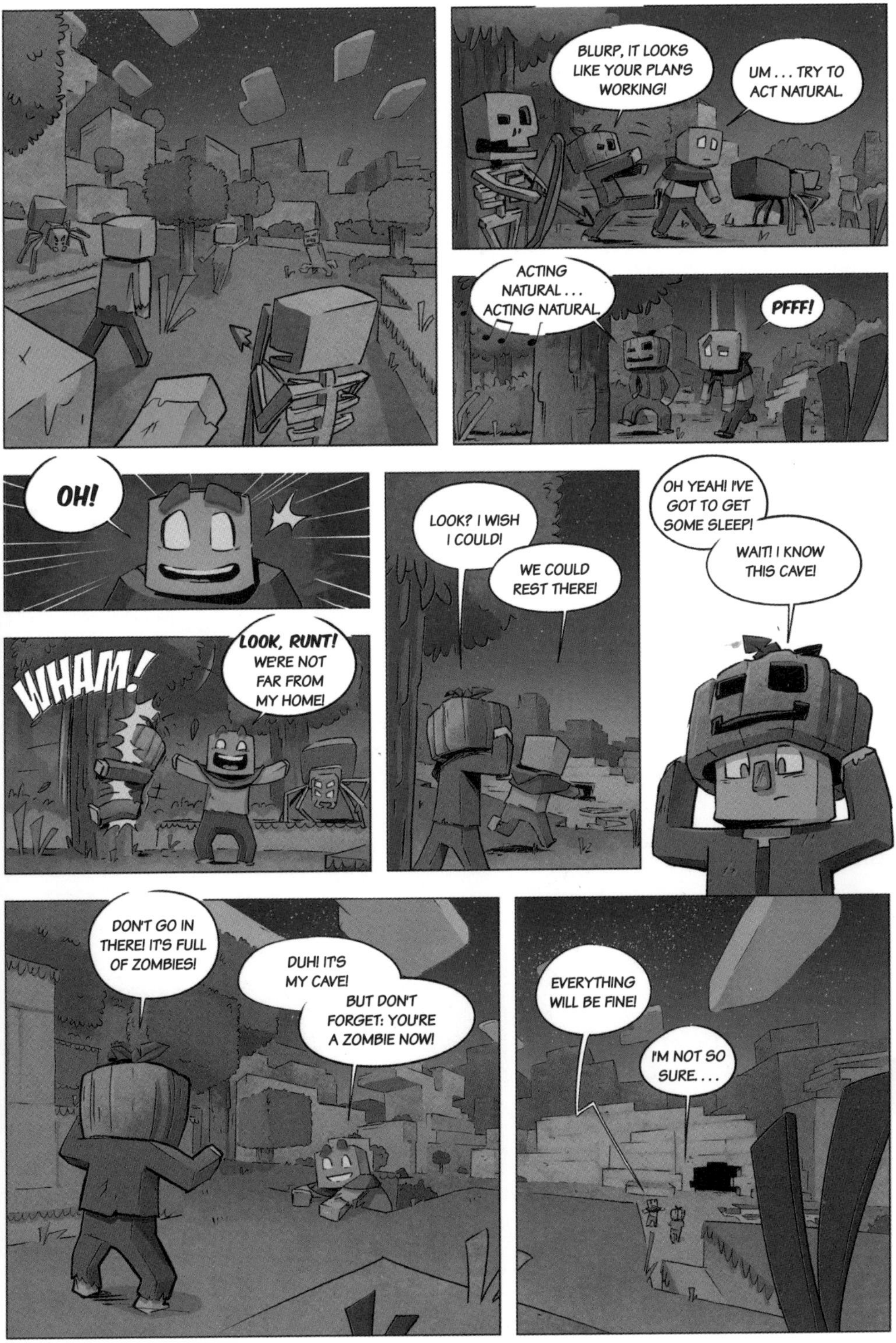
BLURP, IT LOOKS LIKE YOUR PLAN'S WORKING!
UM . . . TRY TO ACT NATURAL.
ACTING NATURAL . . . ACTING NATURAL.
PFFF!
OH!
WHAM!
LOOK, RUNT! WE'RE NOT FAR FROM MY HOME!
LOOK? I WISH I COULD!
WE COULD REST THERE!
OH YEAH! I'VE GOT TO GET SOME SLEEP!
WAIT! I KNOW THIS CAVE!
DON'T GO IN THERE! IT'S FULL OF ZOMBIES!
DUH! IT'S MY CAVE!
BUT DON'T FORGET: YOU'RE A ZOMBIE NOW!
EVERYTHING WILL BE FINE!
I'M NOT SO SURE. . .

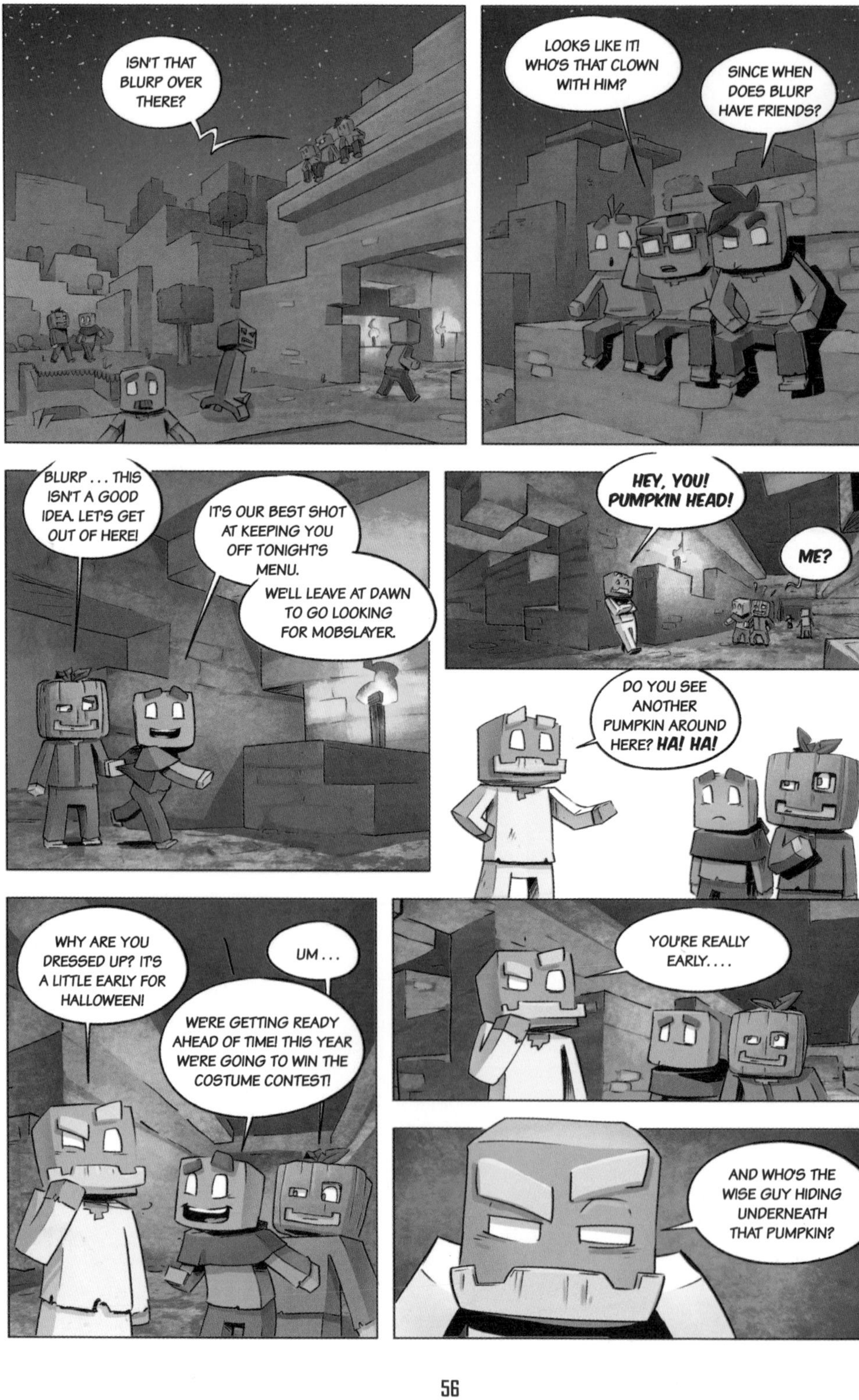
ISN'T THAT BLURP OVER THERE?
LOOKS LIKE IT! WHO'S THAT CLOWN WITH HIM?
SINCE WHEN DOES BLURP HAVE FRIENDS?
BLURP . . . THIS ISN'T A GOOD IDEA. LET'S GET OUT OF HERE!
IT'S OUR BEST SHOT AT KEEPING YOU OFF TONIGHT'S MENU.
WE'LL LEAVE AT DAWN TO GO LOOKING FOR MOBSLAYER.
HEY, YOU! PUMPKIN HEAD!
ME?
DO YOU SEE ANOTHER PUMPKIN AROUND HERE? HA! HA!
WHY ARE YOU DRESSED UP? IT'S A LITTLE EARLY FOR HALLOWEEN!
UM . . .
WE'RE GETTING READY AHEAD OF TIME! THIS YEAR WE'RE GOING TO WIN THE COSTUME CONTEST!
YOU'RE REALLY EARLY. . . .
AND WHO'S THE WISE GUY HIDING UNDERNEATH THAT PUMPKIN?

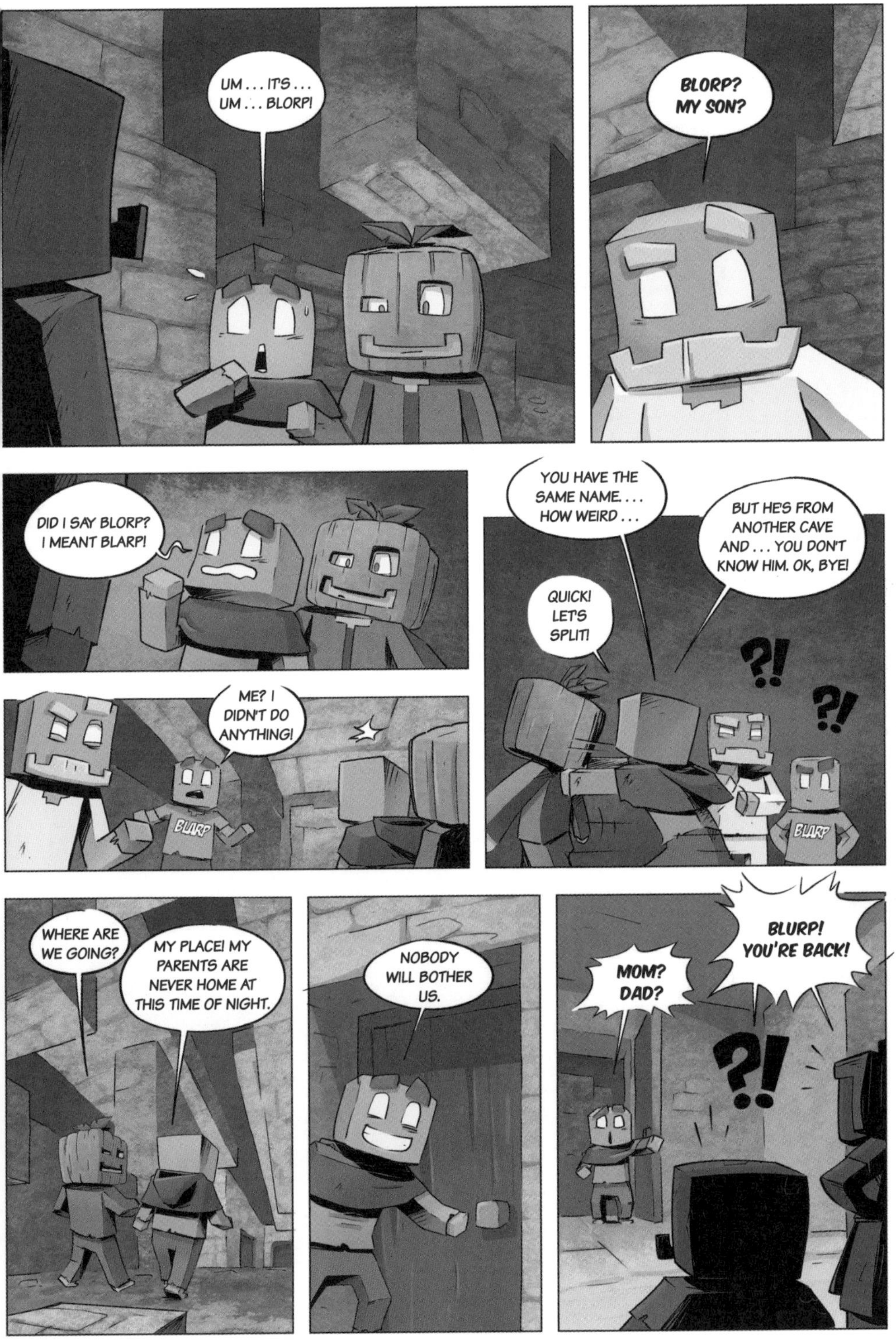
UM . . . IT'S . . . UM . . . BLORP!
BLORP? MY SON?
DID I SAY BLORP? I MEANT BLARP!
ME? I DIDN'T DO ANYTHING!
BLARP
YOU HAVE THE SAME NAME. . . . HOW WEIRD . . .
BUT HE'S FROM ANOTHER CAVE AND . . . YOU DON'T KNOW HIM. OK, BYE!
QUICK! LET'S SPLIT!
?!
?!
BLARP
WHERE ARE WE GOING?
MY PLACE! MY PARENTS ARE NEVER HOME AT THIS TIME OF NIGHT.
NOBODY WILL BOTHER US.
BLURP! YOU'RE BACK!
MOM? DAD?
?!

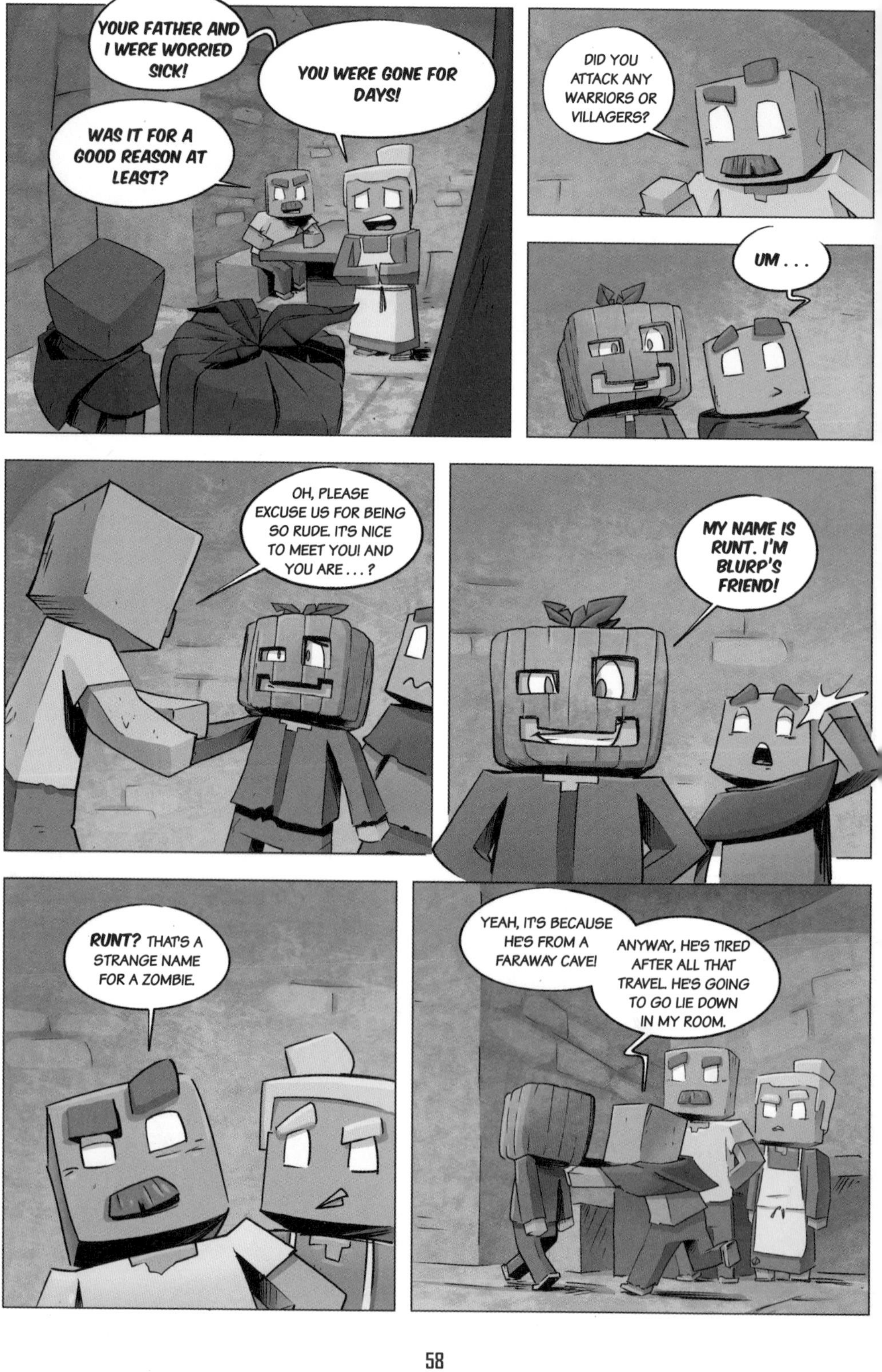
YOUR FATHER AND I WERE WORRIED SICK!
YOU WERE GONE FOR DAYS!
WAS IT FOR A GOOD REASON AT LEAST?
DID YOU ATTACK ANY WARRIORS OR VILLAGERS?
UM . . .
OH, PLEASE EXCUSE US FOR BEING SO RUDE. IT'S NICE TO MEET YOU! AND YOU ARE . . . ?
MY NAME IS RUNT. I'M BLURP'S FRIEND!
RUNT? THAT'S A STRANGE NAME FOR A ZOMBIE.
YEAH, IT'S BECAUSE HE'S FROM A FARAWAY CAVE!
ANYWAY, HE'S TIRED AFTER ALL THAT TRAVEL. HE'S GOING TO GO LIE DOWN IN MY ROOM.

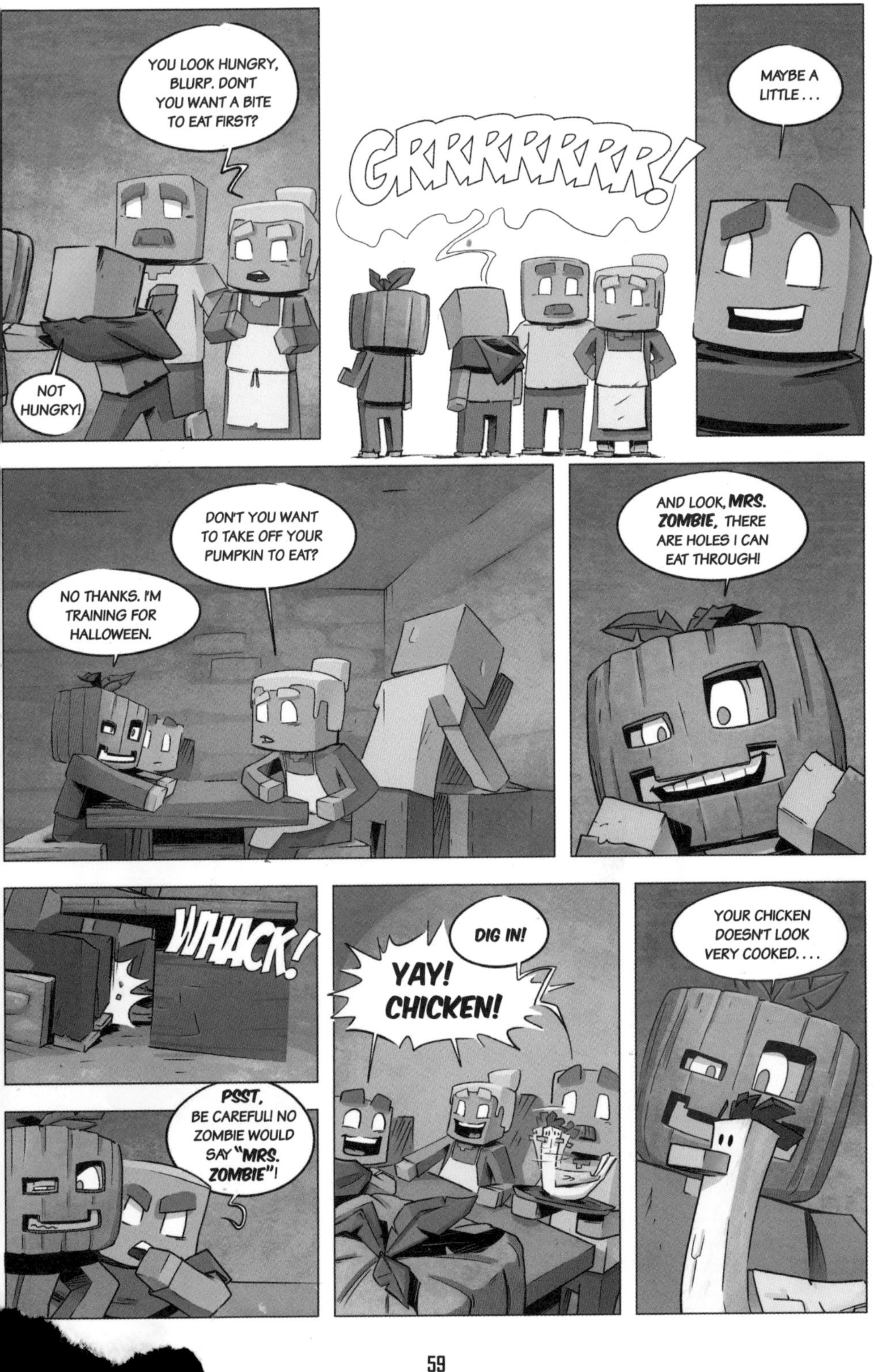
YOU LOOK HUNGRY, BLURP. DON'T YOU WANT A BITE TO EAT FIRST?
NOT HUNGRY!
GRRRRRRRRR!
MAYBE A LITTLE . . .
DON'T YOU WANT TO TAKE OFF YOUR PUMPKIN TO EAT?
NO THANKS. I'M TRAINING FOR HALLOWEEN.
AND LOOK, MRS. ZOMBIE, THERE ARE HOLES I CAN EAT THROUGH!
WHACK!
PSST, BE CAREFUL! NO ZOMBIE WOULD SAY "MRS. ZOMBIE"!
DIG IN!
YAY! CHICKEN!
YOUR CHICKEN DOESN'T LOOK VERY COOKED. . . .

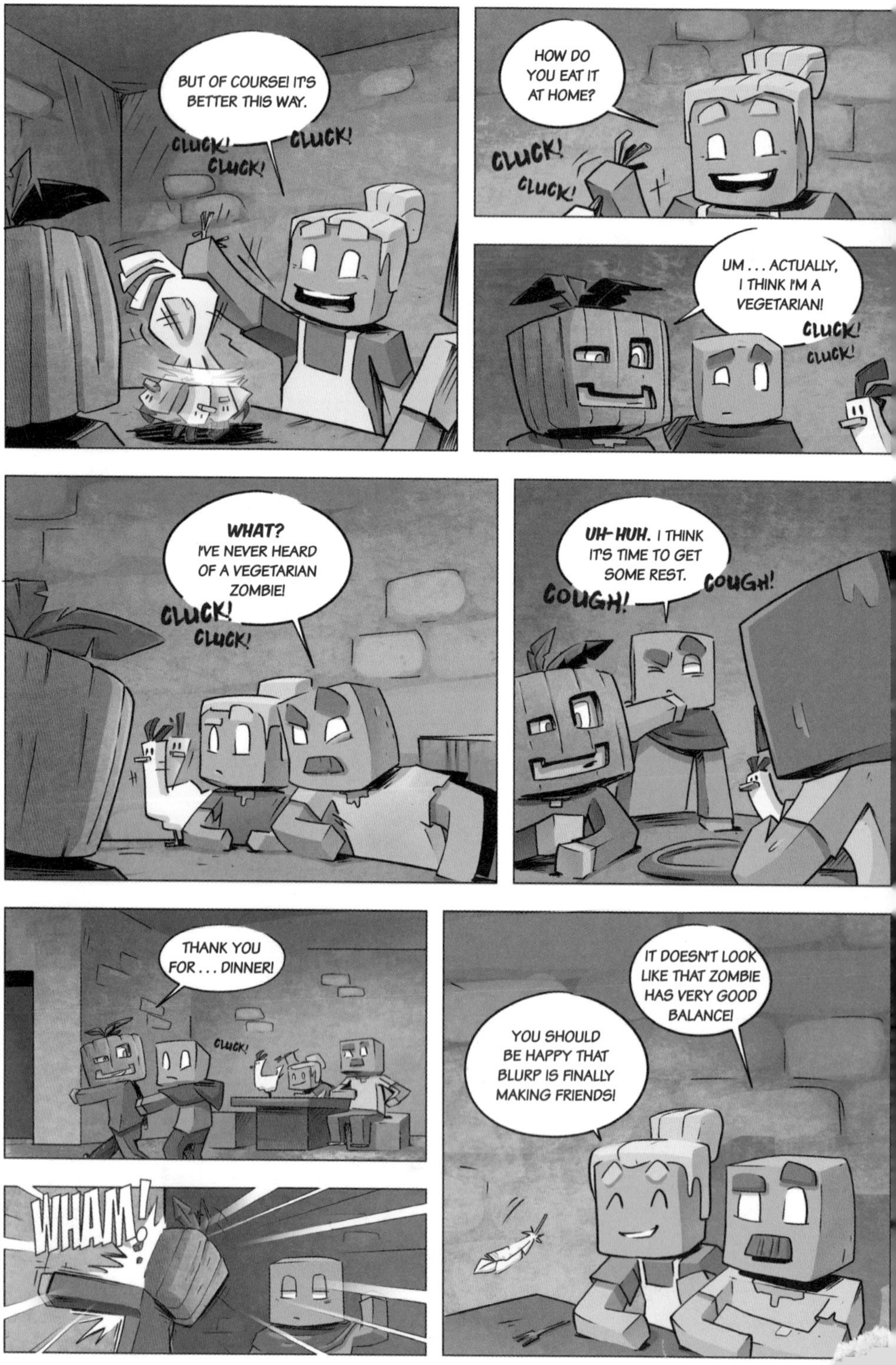
BUT OF COURSE! IT'S BETTER THIS WAY.
CLUCK!
CLUCK!
CLUCK!
HOW DO YOU EAT IT AT HOME?
CLUCK!
CLUCK!
UM . . . ACTUALLY, I THINK I'M A VEGETARIAN!
CLUCK!
CLUCK!
WHAT? I'VE NEVER HEARD OF A VEGETARIAN ZOMBIE!
CLUCK!
CLUCK!
UH-HUH. I THINK IT'S TIME TO GET SOME REST.
COUGH!
COUGH!
THANK YOU FOR . . . DINNER!
CLUCK!
WHAM!
IT DOESN'T LOOK LIKE THAT ZOMBIE HAS VERY GOOD BALANCE!
YOU SHOULD BE HAPPY THAT BLURP IS FINALLY MAKING FRIENDS!

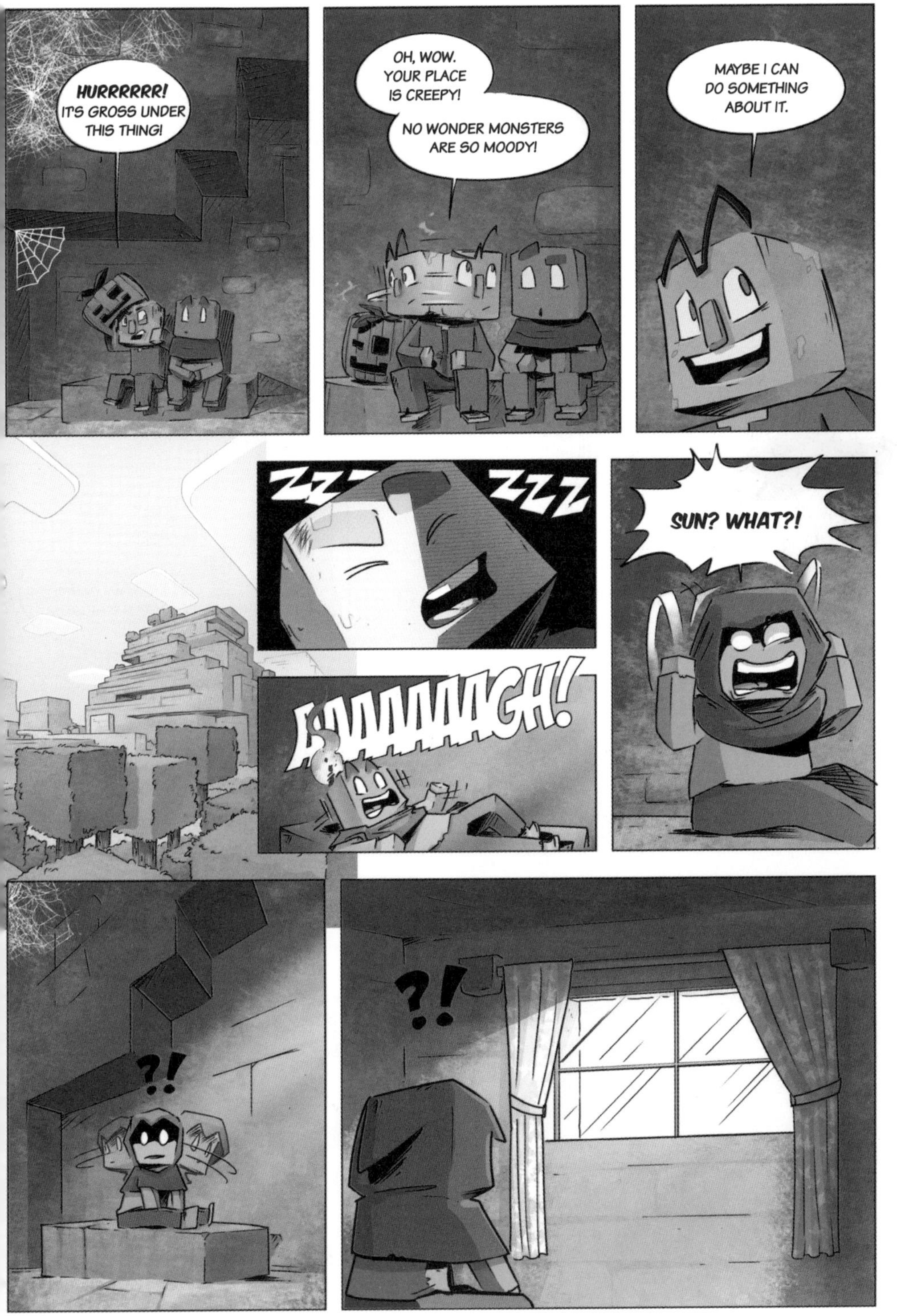
HURRRRRR!
IT'S GROSS UNDER THIS THING!
OH, WOW. YOUR PLACE IS CREEPY!
NO WONDER MONSTERS ARE SO MOODY!
MAYBE I CAN DO SOMETHING ABOUT IT.
ZZZ
ZZZ
AAAAAAAGH!
SUN? WHAT?!
?!
?!

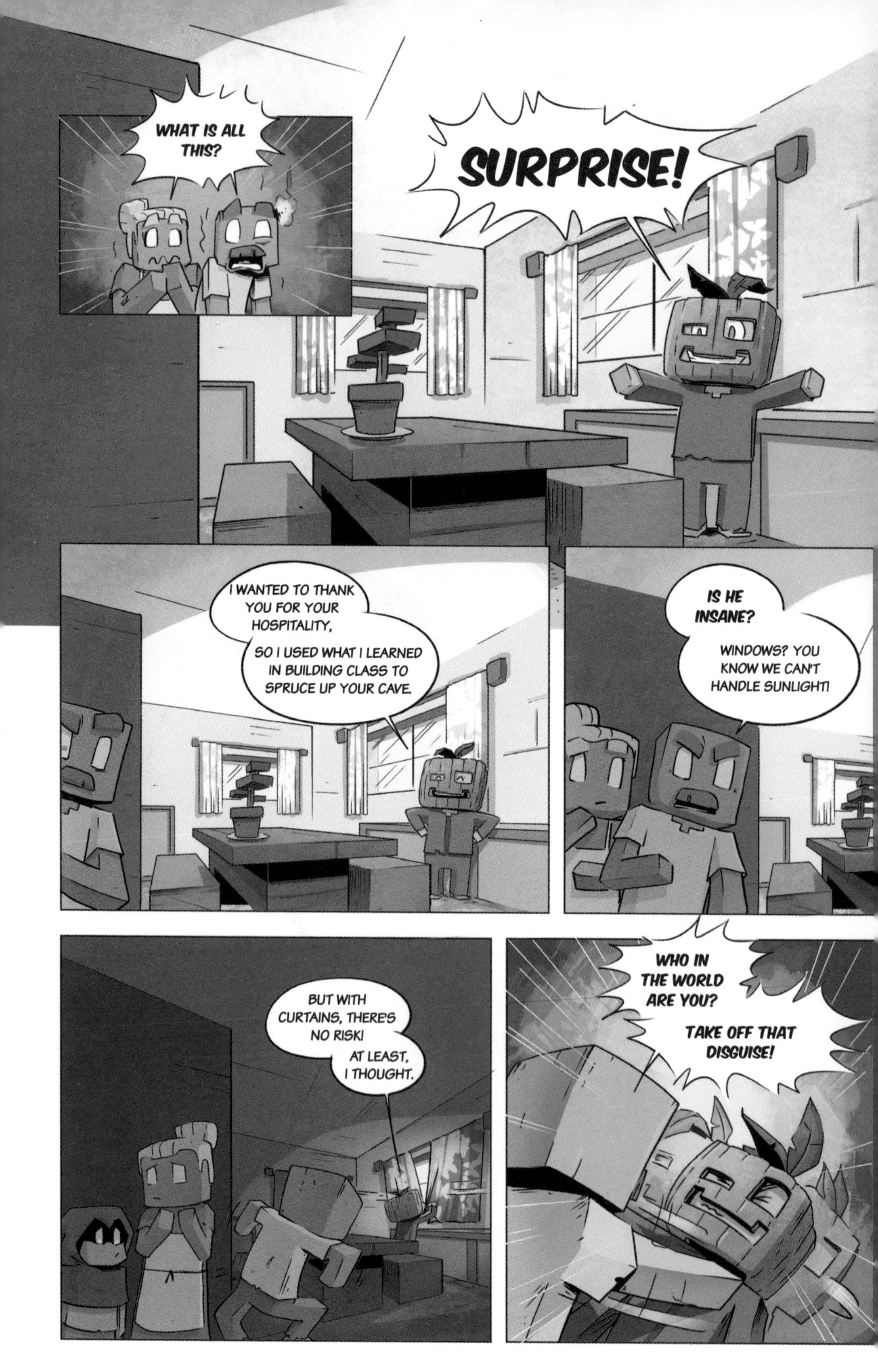
WHAT IS ALL THIS?
SURPRISE!
I WANTED TO THANK YOU FOR YOUR HOSPITALITY,
SO I USED WHAT I LEARNED IN BUILDING CLASS TO SPRUCE UP YOUR CAVE.
IS HE INSANE?
WINDOWS? YOU KNOW WE CAN'T HANDLE SUNLIGHT!
BUT WITH CURTAINS, THERE'S NO RISK!
AT LEAST, I THOUGHT.
WHO IN THE WORLD ARE YOU?
TAKE OFF THAT DISGUISE!

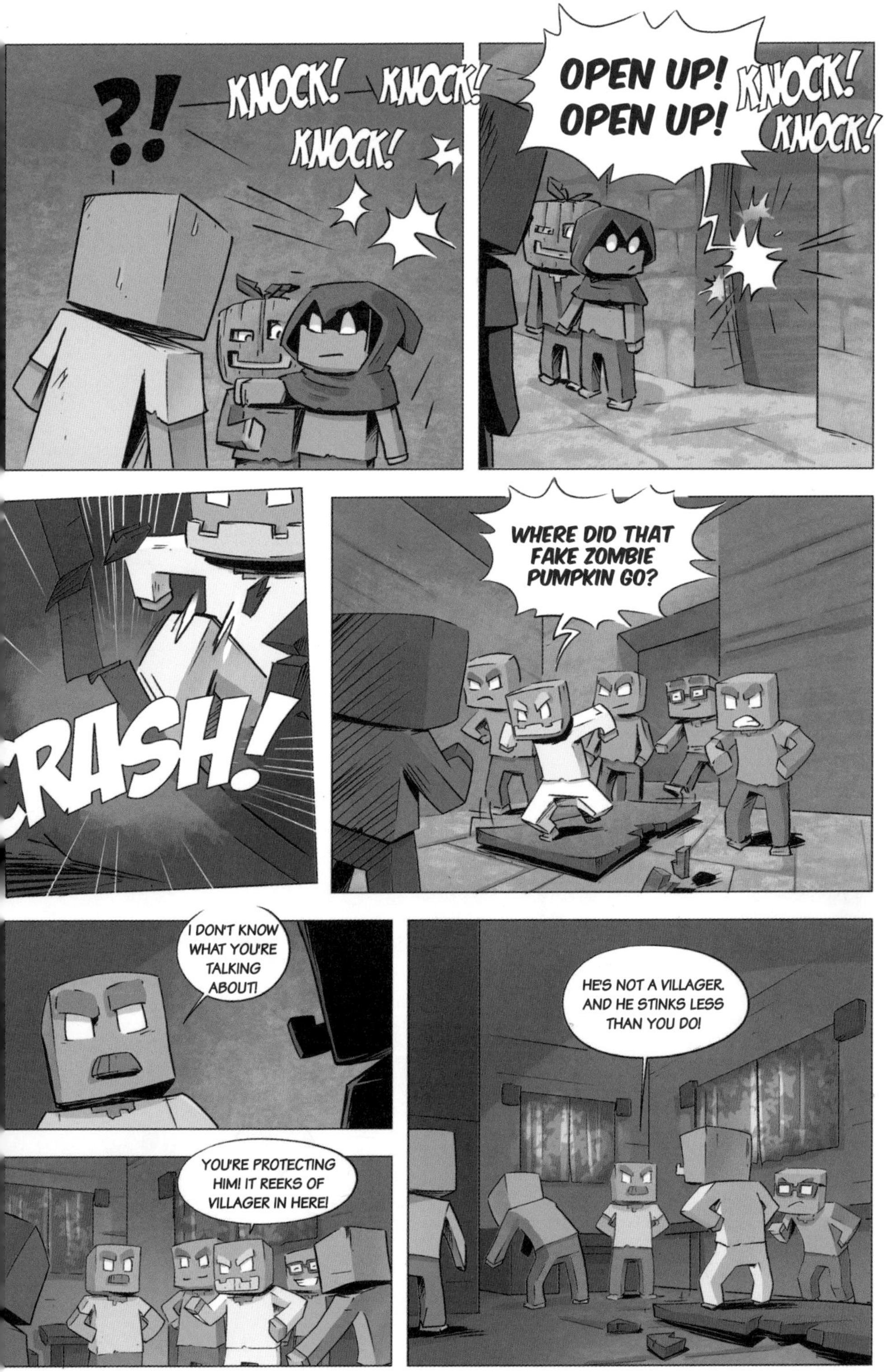

?!
KNOCK! KNOCK!
KNOCK!
OPEN UP! OPEN UP!
KNOCK!
KNOCK!
CRASH!
WHERE DID THAT FAKE ZOMBIE PUMPKIN GO?
I DON'T KNOW WHAT YOU'RE TALKING ABOUT!
YOU'RE PROTECTING HIM! IT REEKS OF VILLAGER IN HERE!
HE'S NOT A VILLAGER. AND HE STINKS LESS THAN YOU DO!

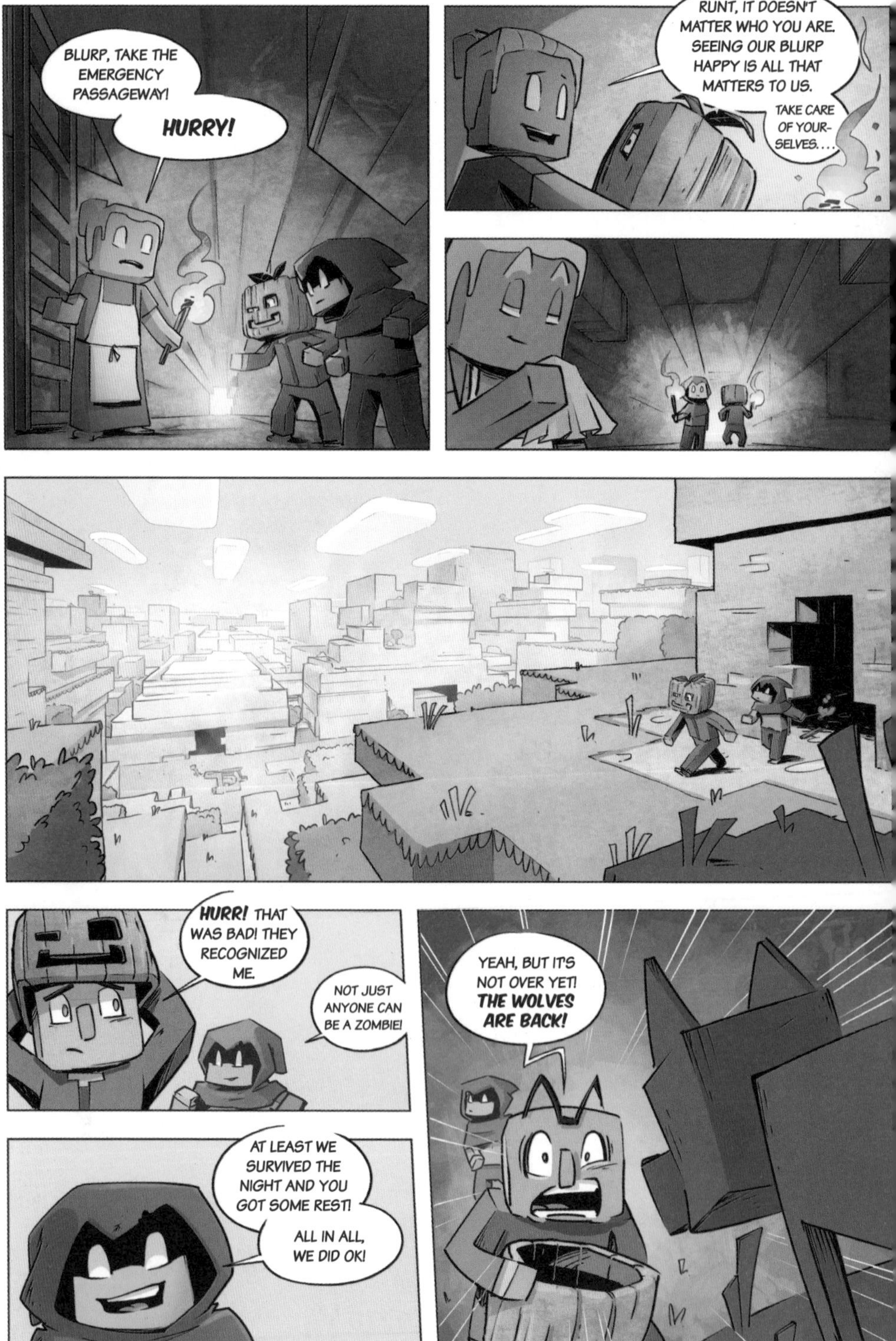
BLURP, TAKE THE EMERGENCY PASSAGEWAY!
HURRY!
RUNT, IT DOESN'T MATTER WHO YOU ARE. SEEING OUR BLURP HAPPY IS ALL THAT MATTERS TO US.
TAKE CARE OF YOUR-SELVES. . . .
HURR! THAT WAS BAD! THEY RECOGNIZED ME.
NOT JUST ANYONE CAN BE A ZOMBIE!
AT LEAST WE SURVIVED THE NIGHT AND YOU GOT SOME REST!
ALL IN ALL, WE DID OK!
YEAH, BUT IT'S NOT OVER YET! THE WOLVES ARE BACK!

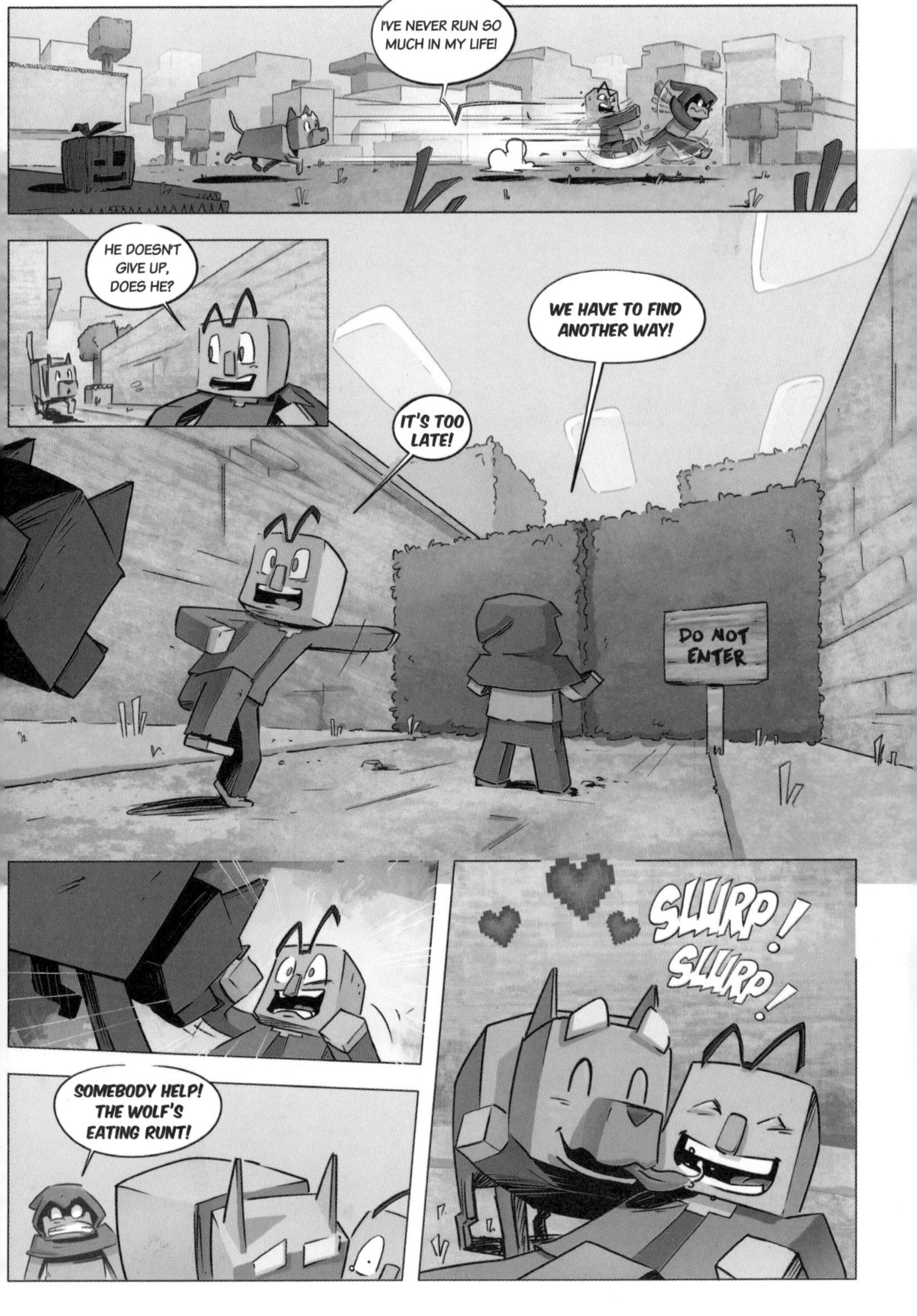
I'VE NEVER RUN SO MUCH IN MY LIFE!
HE DOESN'T GIVE UP, DOES HE?
WE HAVE TO FIND ANOTHER WAY!
IT'S TOO LATE!
DO NOT ENTER
SOMEBODY HELP! THE WOLF'S EATING RUNT!
SLURP! SLURP!

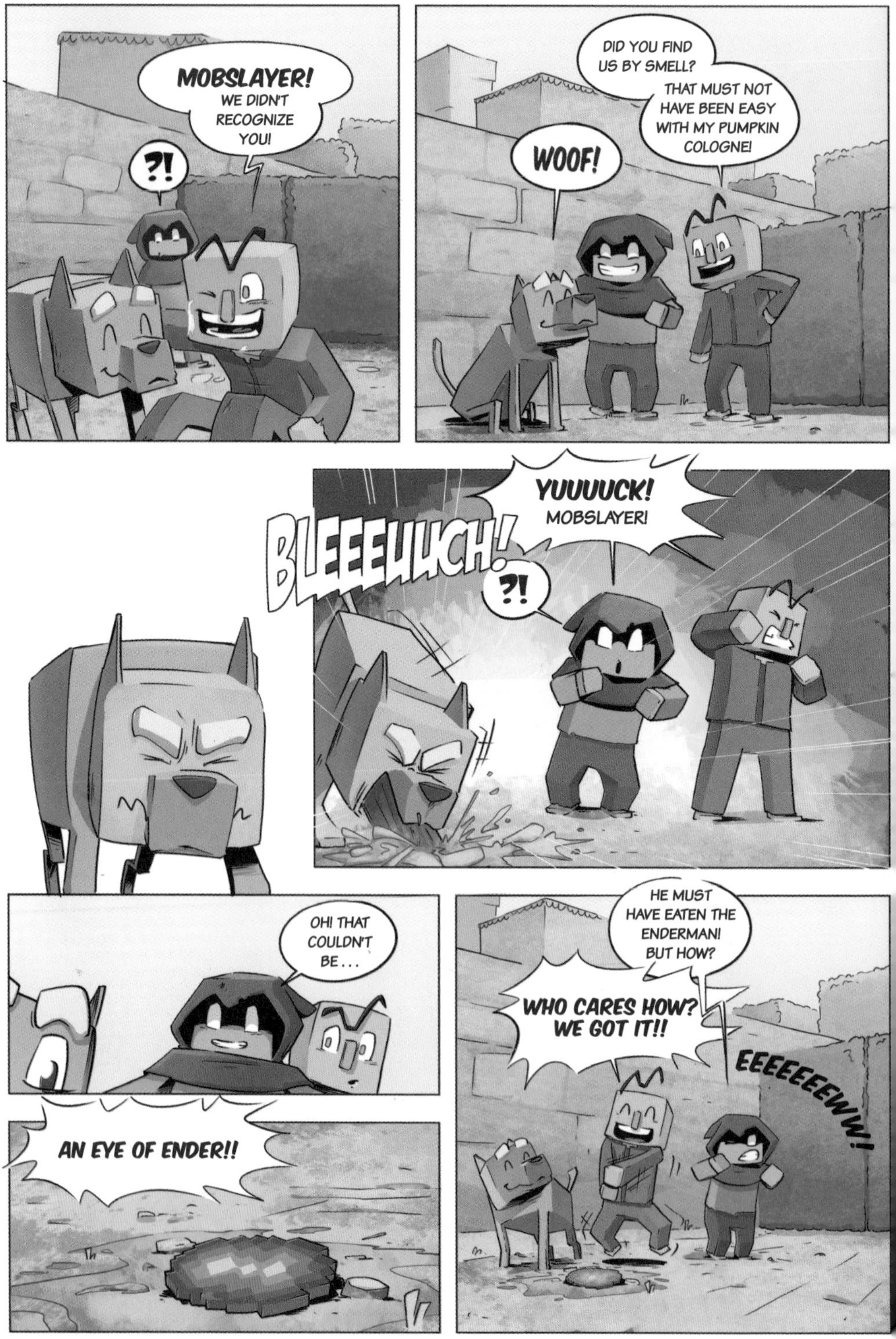
MOBSLAYER! WE DIDN'T RECOGNIZE YOU!
?!
DID YOU FIND US BY SMELL?
THAT MUST NOT HAVE BEEN EASY WITH MY PUMPKIN COLOGNE!
WOOF!
BLEEEUUCH!
YUUUUCK! MOBSLAYER!
?!
OH! THAT COULDN'T BE . . .
AN EYE OF ENDER!!
HE MUST HAVE EATEN THE ENDERMAN! BUT HOW?
WHO CARES HOW? WE GOT IT!!
EEEEEEEWW!

[redacted]

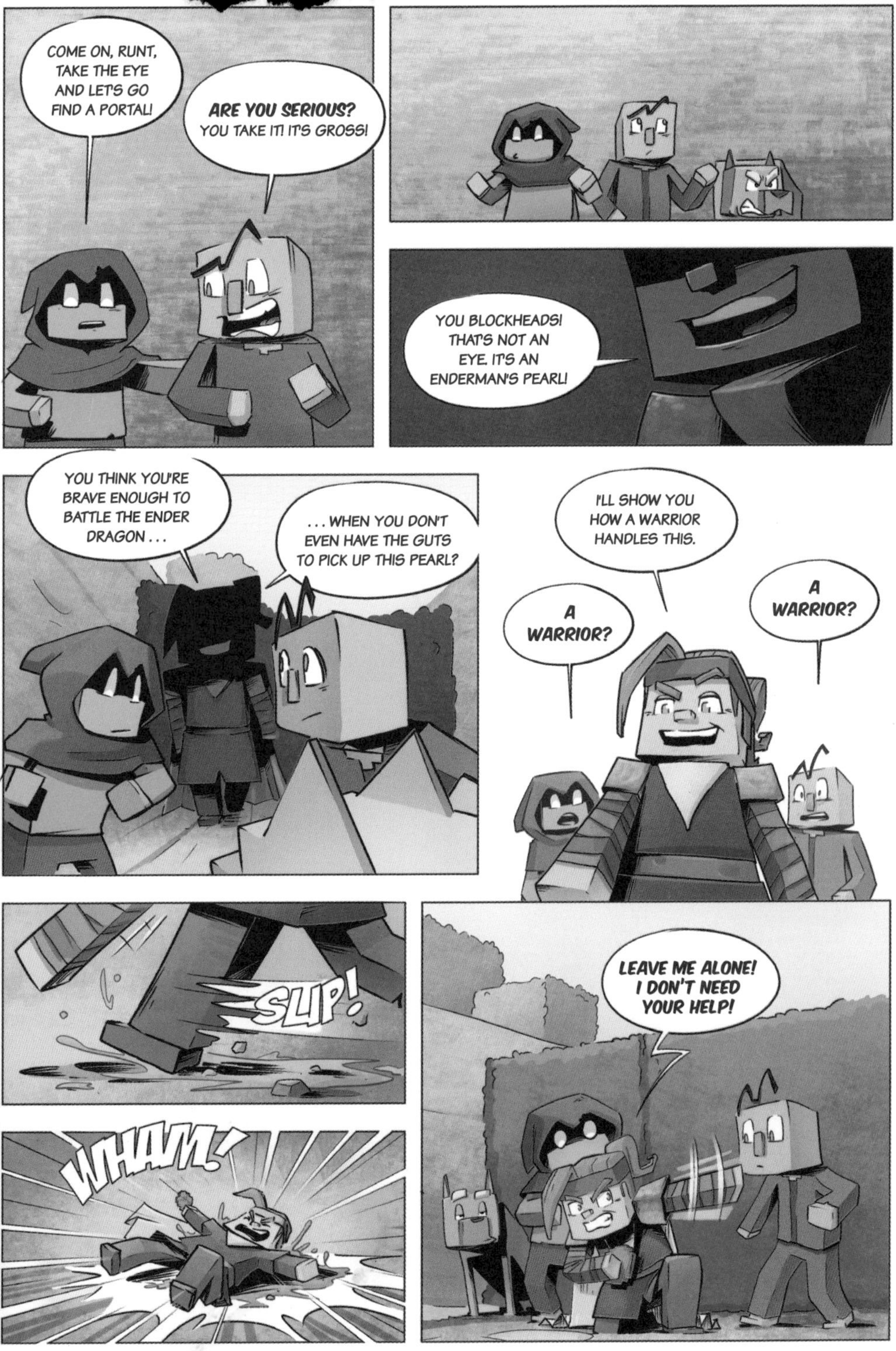
COME ON, RUNT, TAKE THE EYE AND LET'S GO FIND A PORTAL!
ARE YOU SERIOUS? YOU TAKE IT! IT'S GROSS!
YOU BLOCKHEADS! THAT'S NOT AN EYE. IT'S AN ENDERMAN'S PEARL!
YOU THINK YOU'RE BRAVE ENOUGH TO BATTLE THE ENDER DRAGON . . .
. . . WHEN YOU DON'T EVEN HAVE THE GUTS TO PICK UP THIS PEARL?
I'LL SHOW YOU HOW A WARRIOR HANDLES THIS.
A WARRIOR?
A WARRIOR?
SLIP!
WHAM!
LEAVE ME ALONE! I DON'T NEED YOUR HELP!

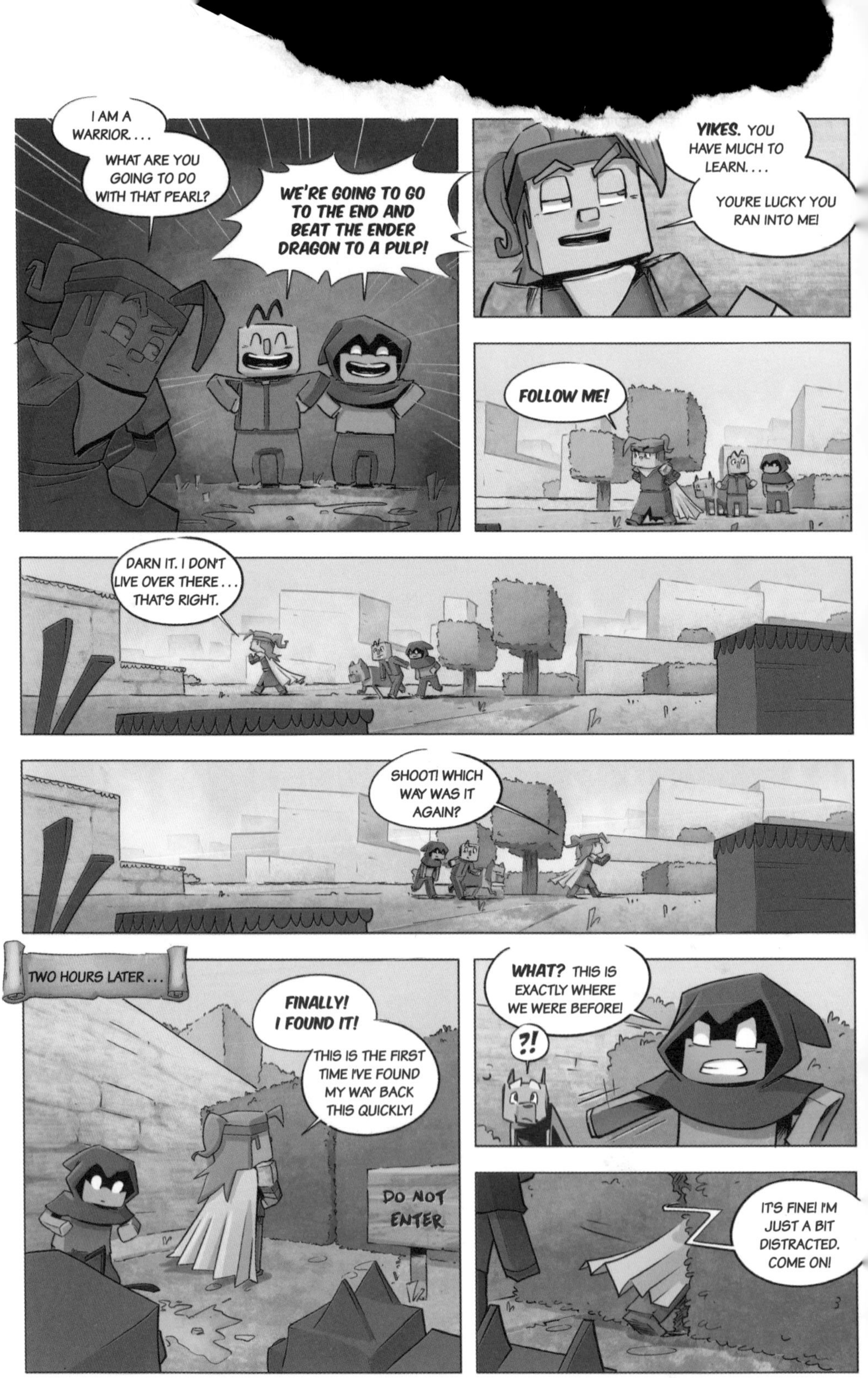
I AM A WARRIOR . . .
WHAT ARE YOU GOING TO DO WITH THAT PEARL?
WE'RE GOING TO GO TO THE END AND BEAT THE ENDER DRAGON TO A PULP!
YIKES. YOU HAVE MUCH TO LEARN. . . .
YOU'RE LUCKY YOU RAN INTO ME!
FOLLOW ME!
DARN IT. I DON'T LIVE OVER THERE . . . THAT'S RIGHT.
SHOOT! WHICH WAY WAS IT AGAIN?
TWO HOURS LATER . . .
FINALLY! I FOUND IT!
THIS IS THE FIRST TIME I'VE FOUND MY WAY BACK THIS QUICKLY!
DO NOT ENTER
WHAT? THIS IS EXACTLY WHERE WE WERE BEFORE!
?!
IT'S FINE! I'M JUST A BIT DISTRACTED. COME ON!

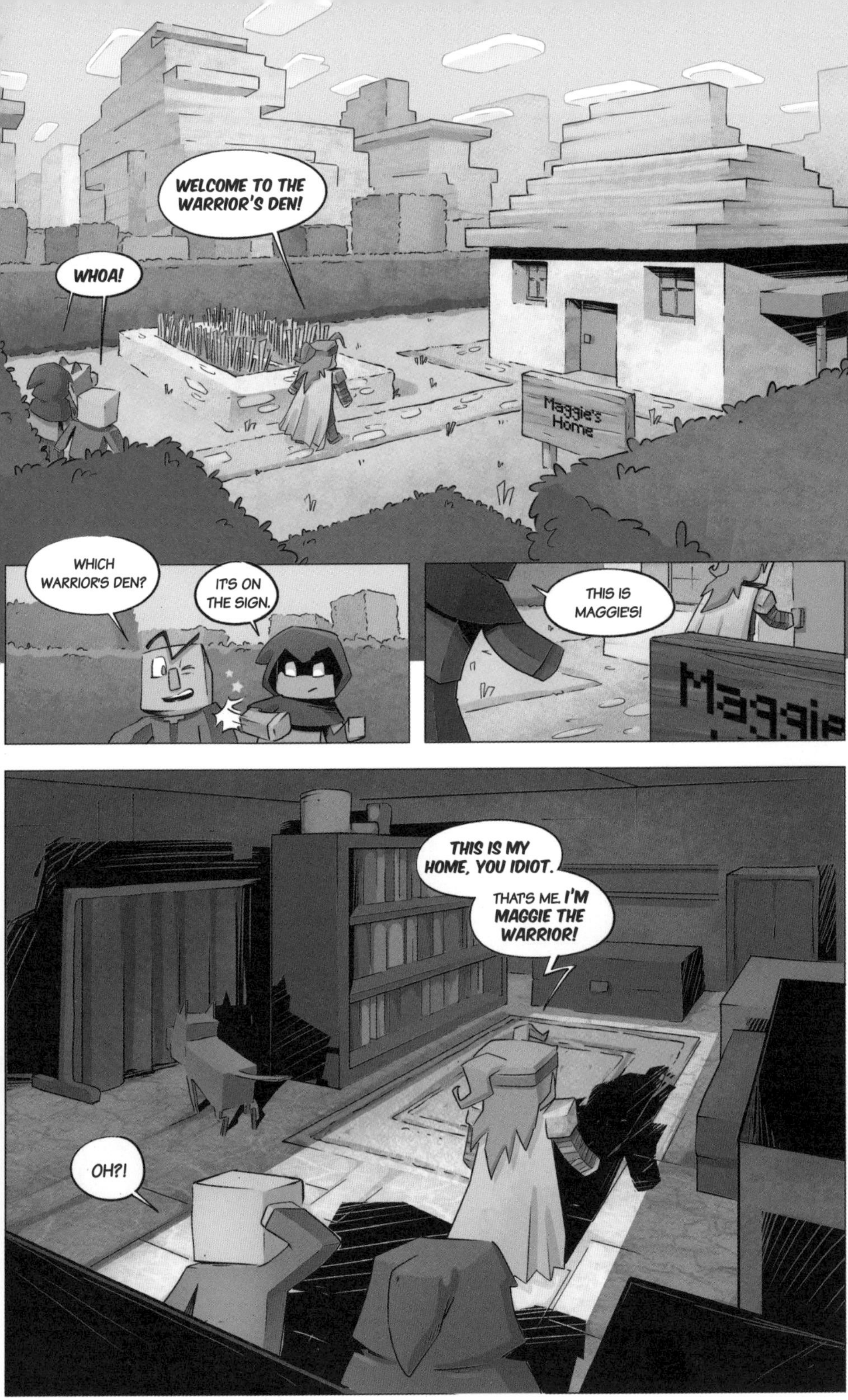
WHOA!
WELCOME TO THE WARRIOR'S DEN!
Maggie's Home
WHICH WARRIOR'S DEN?
IT'S ON THE SIGN.
THIS IS MAGGIE'S!
THIS IS MY HOME, YOU IDIOT.
THAT'S ME. I'M MAGGIE THE WARRIOR!
OH?!

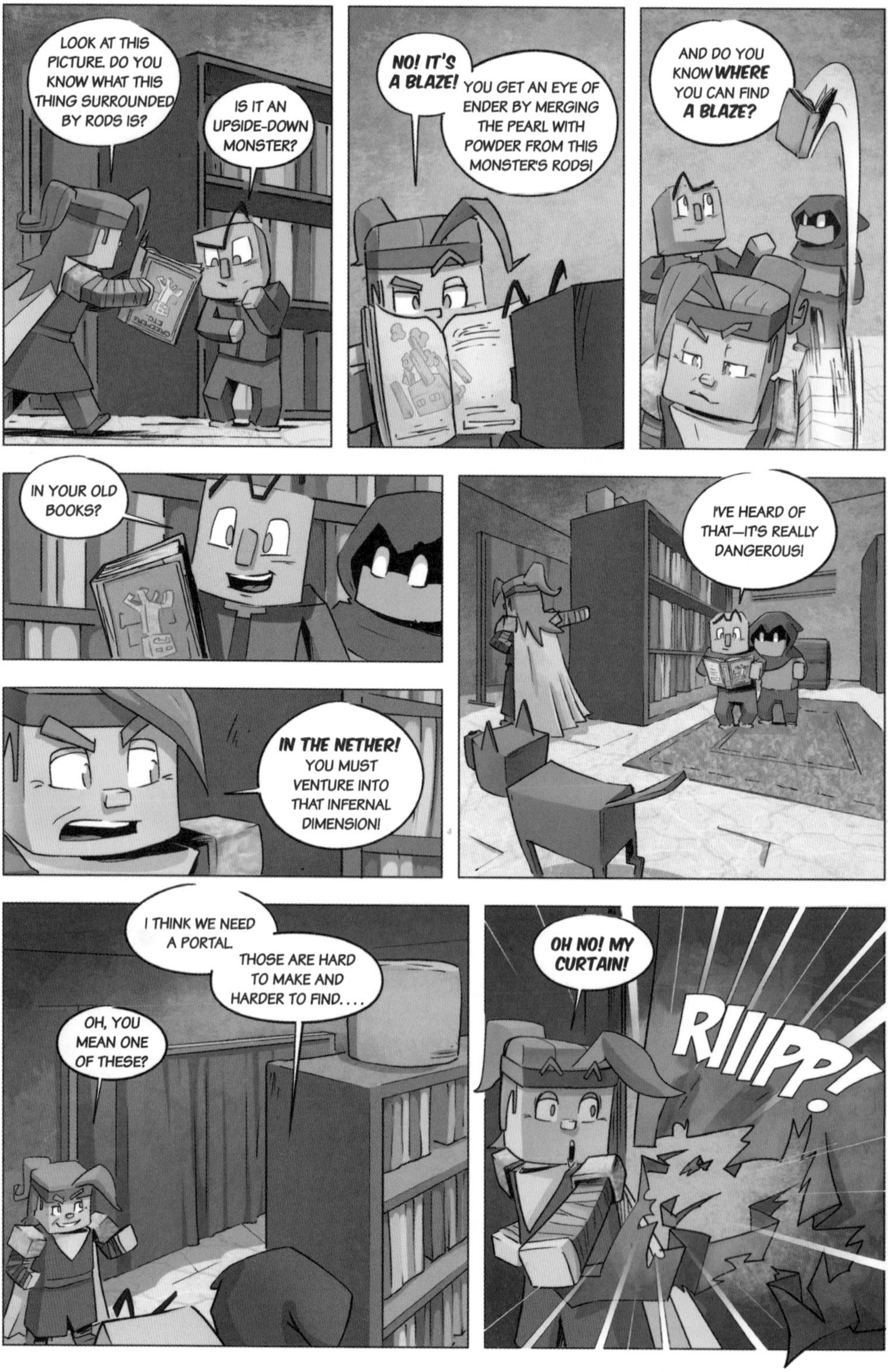
LOOK AT THIS PICTURE. DO YOU KNOW WHAT THIS THING SURROUNDED BY RODS IS?
IS IT AN UPSIDE-DOWN MONSTER?
NO! IT'S A BLAZE!
YOU GET AN EYE OF ENDER BY MERGING THE PEARL WITH POWDER FROM THIS MONSTER'S RODS!
AND DO YOU KNOW WHERE YOU CAN FIND A BLAZE?
IN YOUR OLD BOOKS?
IN THE NETHER! YOU MUST VENTURE INTO THAT INFERNAL DIMENSION!
I'VE HEARD OF THAT—IT'S REALLY DANGEROUS!
I THINK WE NEED A PORTAL.
THOSE ARE HARD TO MAKE AND HARDER TO FIND. . . .
OH, YOU MEAN ONE OF THESE?
OH NO! MY CURTAIN!
RIIIPP!

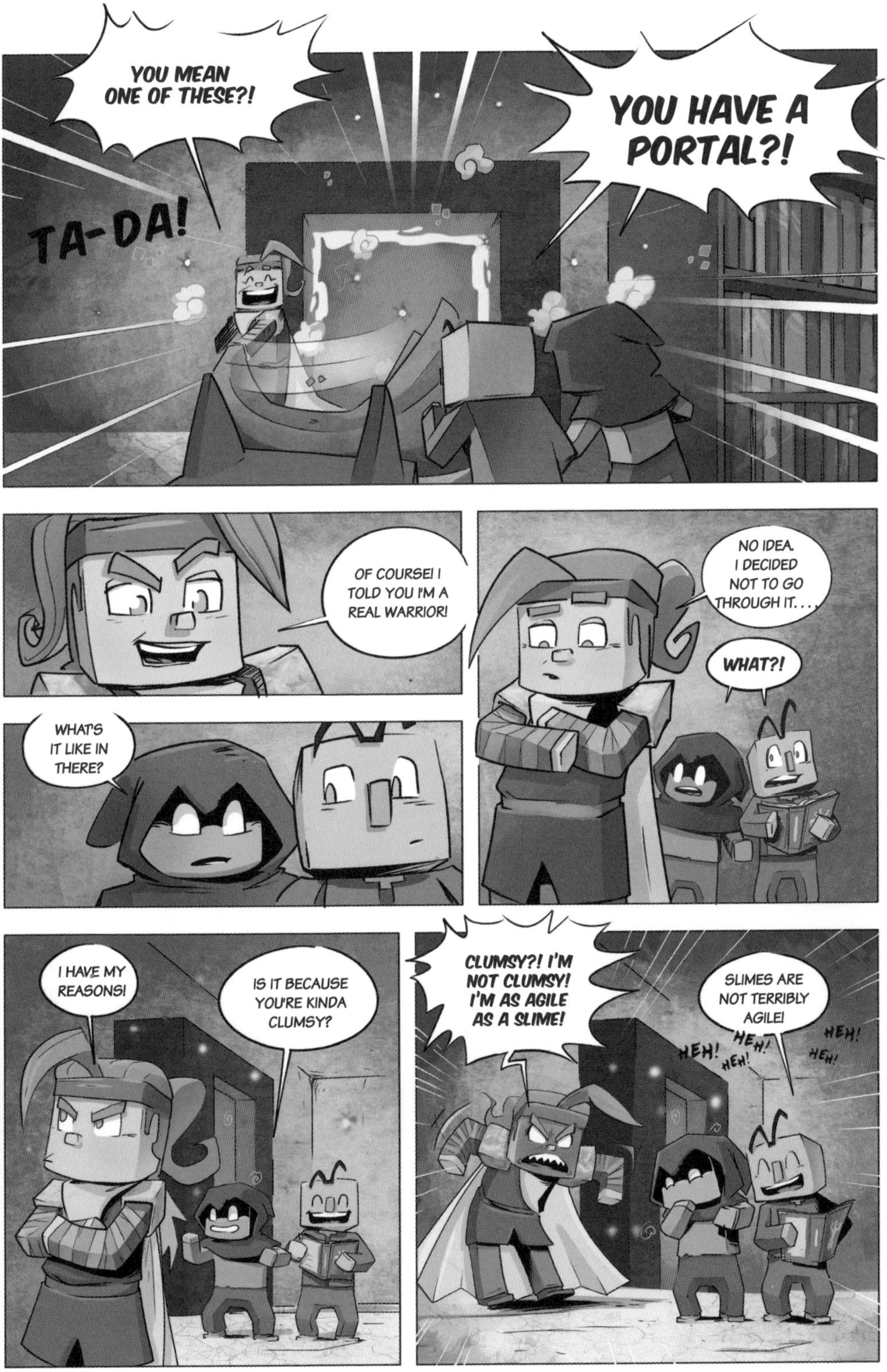
YOU MEAN ONE OF THESE?!
TA-DA!
YOU HAVE A PORTAL?!
OF COURSE! I TOLD YOU I'M A REAL WARRIOR!
WHAT'S IT LIKE IN THERE?
NO IDEA. I DECIDED NOT TO GO THROUGH IT. . . .
WHAT?!
I HAVE MY REASONS!
IS IT BECAUSE YOU'RE KINDA CLUMSY?
CLUMSY?! I'M NOT CLUMSY! I'M AS AGILE AS A SLIME!
SLIMES ARE NOT TERRIBLY AGILE!
HEH! HEH! HEH!
HEH! HEH!

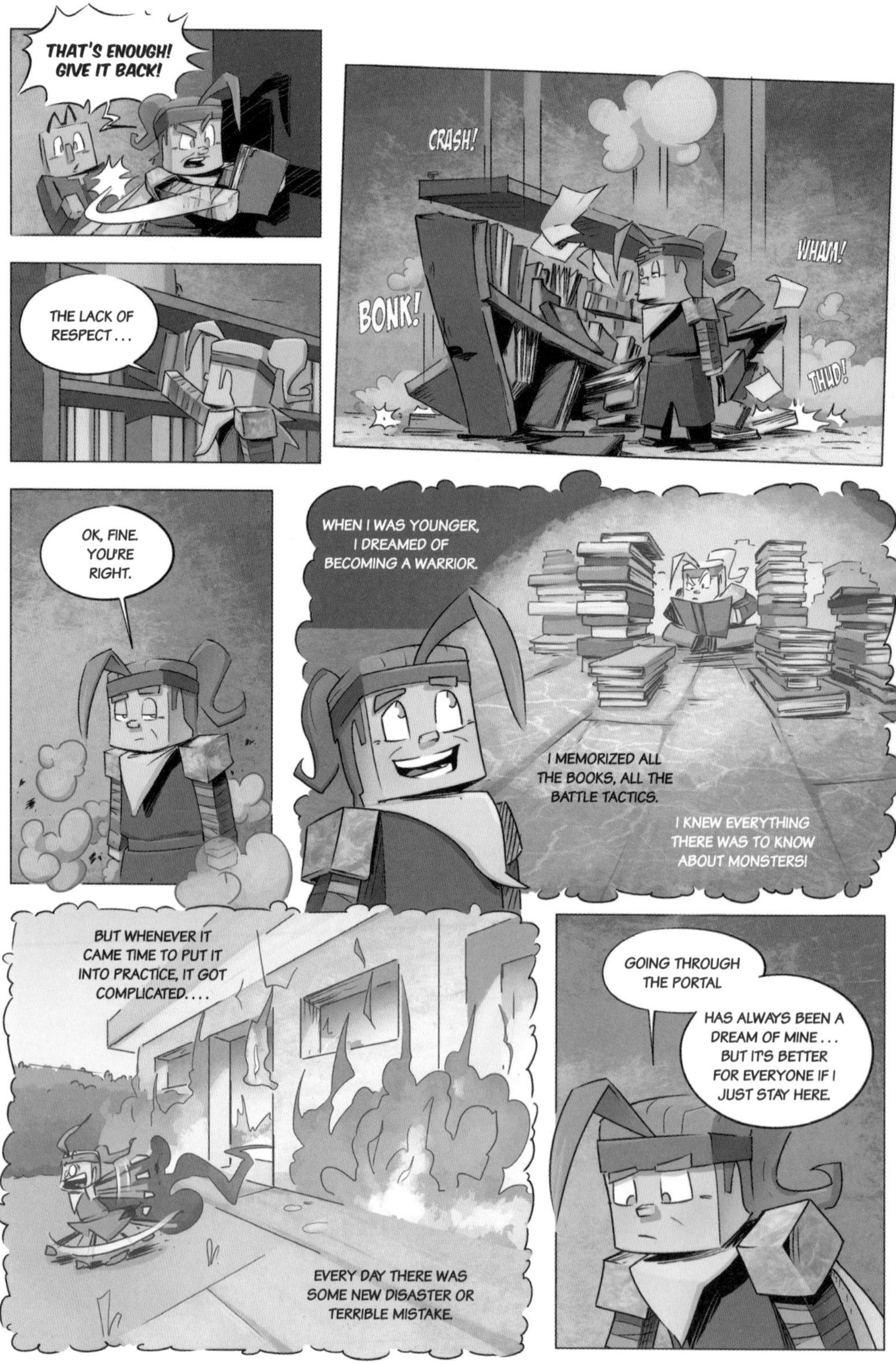
THAT'S ENOUGH! GIVE IT BACK!
CRASH!
BONK!
WHAM!
THUD!
THE LACK OF RESPECT . . .
OK, FINE. YOU'RE RIGHT.
WHEN I WAS YOUNGER, I DREAMED OF BECOMING A WARRIOR.
I MEMORIZED ALL THE BOOKS, ALL THE BATTLE TACTICS.
I KNEW EVERYTHING THERE WAS TO KNOW ABOUT MONSTERS!
BUT WHENEVER IT CAME TIME TO PUT IT INTO PRACTICE, IT GOT COMPLICATED. . . .
EVERY DAY THERE WAS SOME NEW DISASTER OR TERRIBLE MISTAKE.
GOING THROUGH THE PORTAL
HAS ALWAYS BEEN A DREAM OF MINE . . . BUT IT'S BETTER FOR EVERYONE IF I JUST STAY HERE.

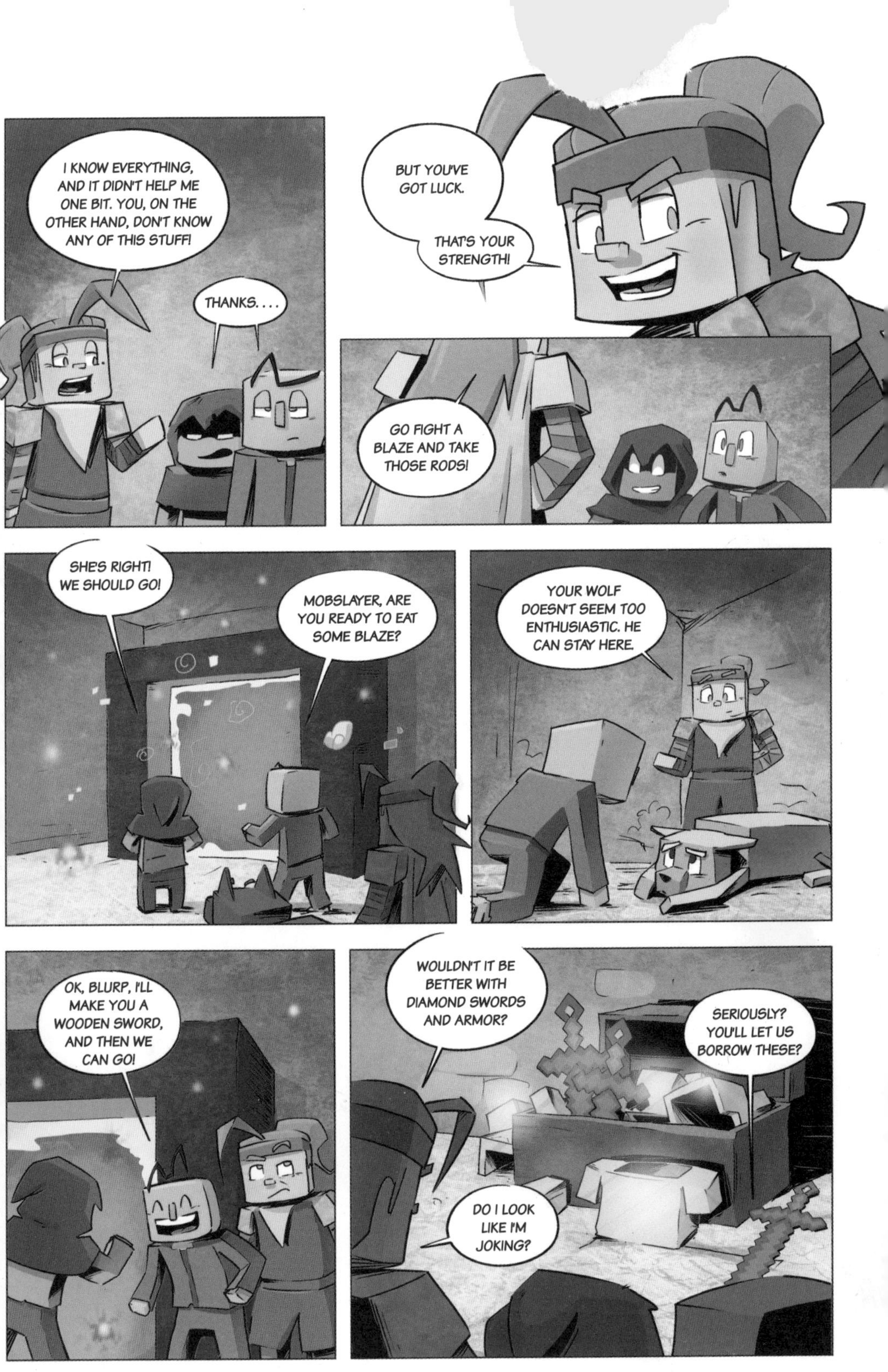
I KNOW EVERYTHING, AND IT DIDN'T HELP ME ONE BIT. YOU, ON THE OTHER HAND, DON'T KNOW ANY OF THIS STUFF!
THANKS. . . .
BUT YOU'VE GOT LUCK.
THAT'S YOUR STRENGTH!
GO FIGHT A BLAZE AND TAKE THOSE RODS!
SHE'S RIGHT! WE SHOULD GO!
MOBSLAYER, ARE YOU READY TO EAT SOME BLAZE?
YOUR WOLF DOESN'T SEEM TOO ENTHUSIASTIC. HE CAN STAY HERE.
OK, BLURP, I'LL MAKE YOU A WOODEN SWORD, AND THEN WE CAN GO!
WOULDN'T IT BE BETTER WITH DIAMOND SWORDS AND ARMOR?
SERIOUSLY? YOU'LL LET US BORROW THESE?
DO I LOOK LIKE I'M JOKING?

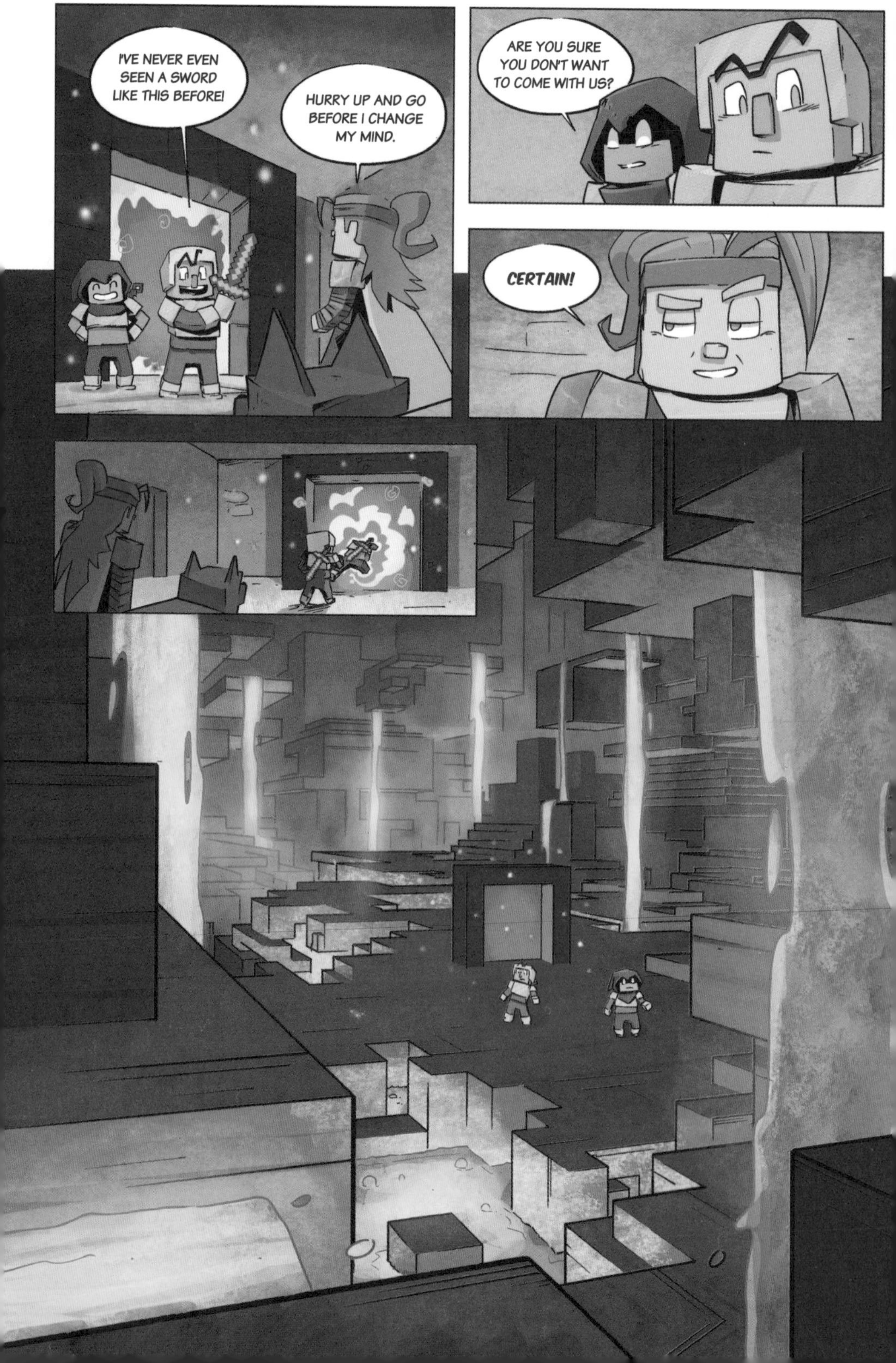
I'VE NEVER EVEN SEEN A SWORD LIKE THIS BEFORE!
HURRY UP AND GO BEFORE I CHANGE MY MIND.
ARE YOU SURE YOU DON'T WANT TO COME WITH US?
CERTAIN!

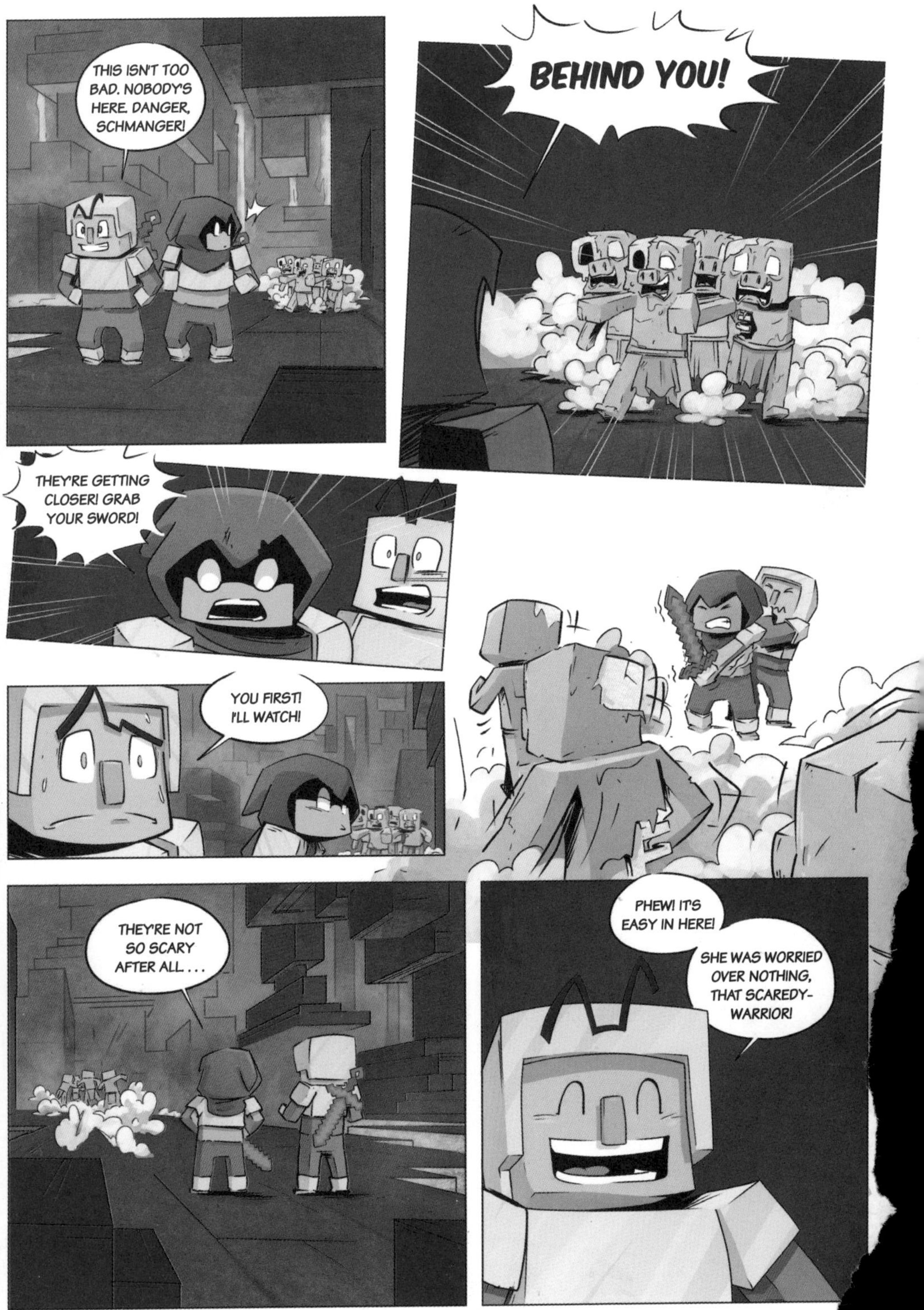
THIS ISN'T TOO BAD. NOBODY'S HERE. DANGER, SCHMANGER!
BEHIND YOU!
THEY'RE GETTING CLOSER! GRAB YOUR SWORD!
YOU FIRST! I'LL WATCH!
THEY'RE NOT SO SCARY AFTER ALL . . .
PHEW! IT'S EASY IN HERE!
SHE WAS WORRIED OVER NOTHING, THAT SCAREDY-WARRIOR!

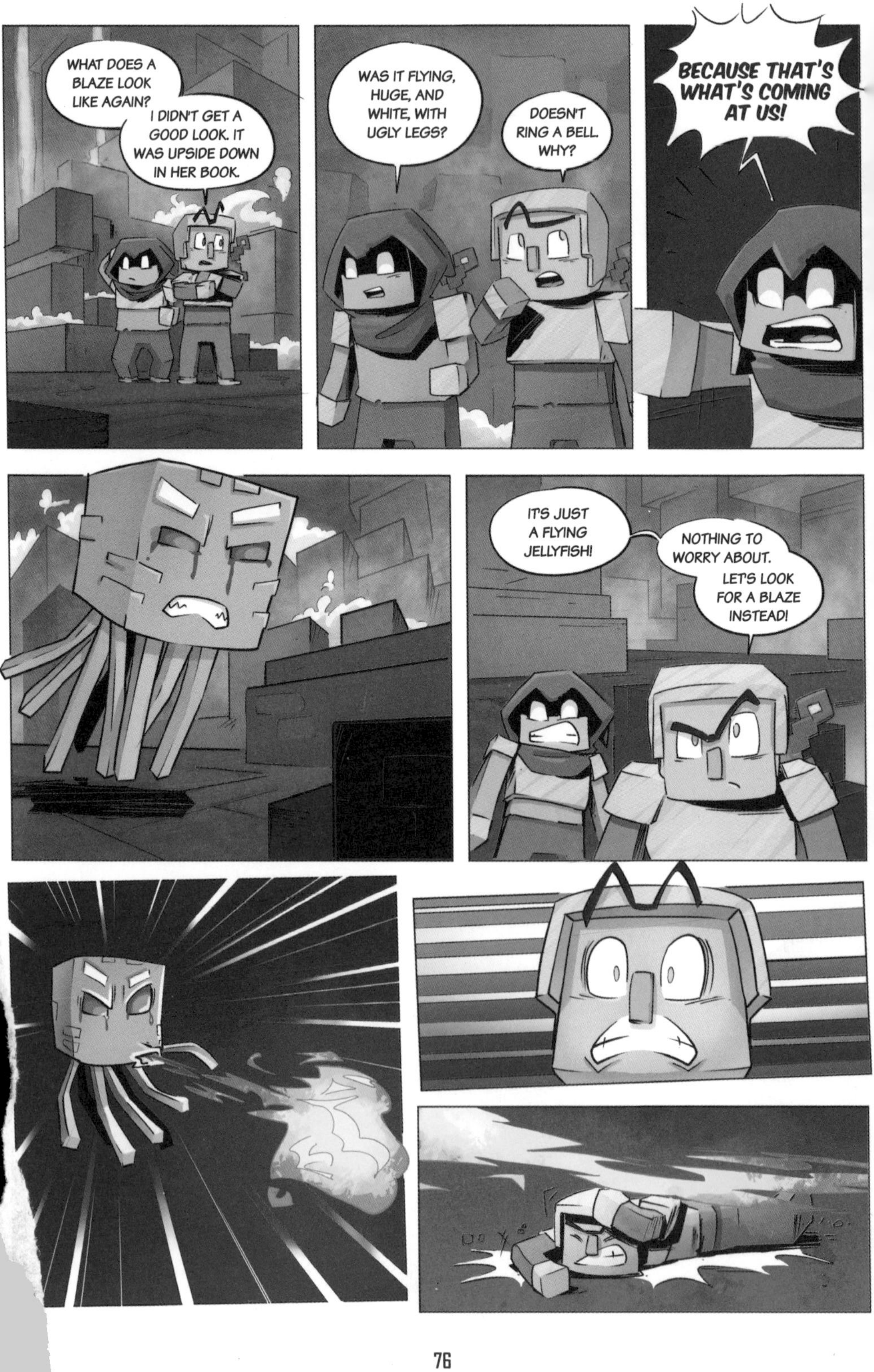
WHAT DOES A BLAZE LOOK LIKE AGAIN?
I DIDN'T GET A GOOD LOOK. IT WAS UPSIDE DOWN IN HER BOOK.
WAS IT FLYING, HUGE, AND WHITE, WITH UGLY LEGS?
DOESN'T RING A BELL. WHY?
BECAUSE THAT'S WHAT'S COMING AT US!
IT'S JUST A FLYING JELLYFISH!
NOTHING TO WORRY ABOUT.
LET'S LOOK FOR A BLAZE INSTEAD!

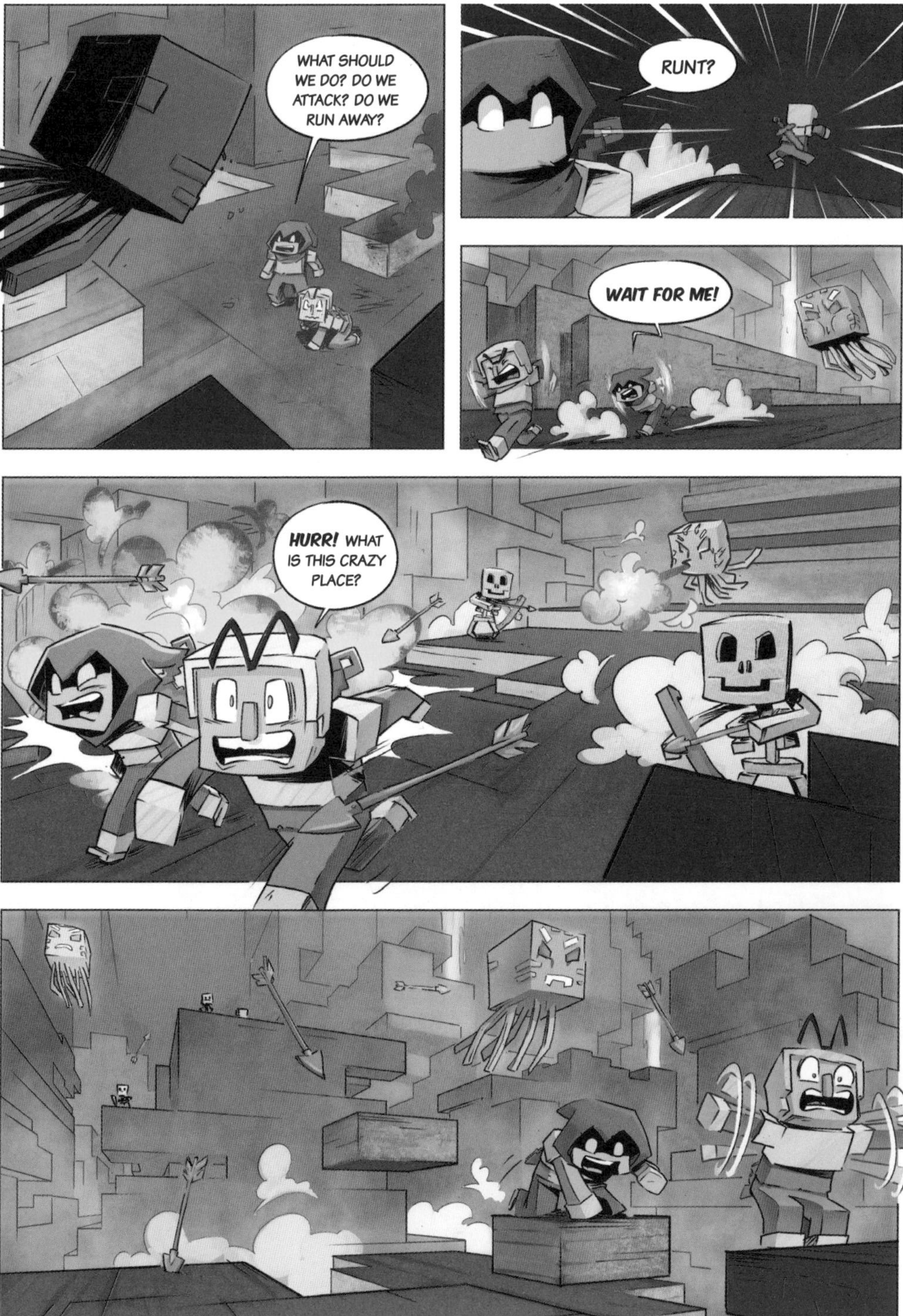
WHAT SHOULD WE DO? DO WE ATTACK? DO WE RUN AWAY?
RUNT?
WAIT FOR ME!
HURR! WHAT IS THIS CRAZY PLACE?

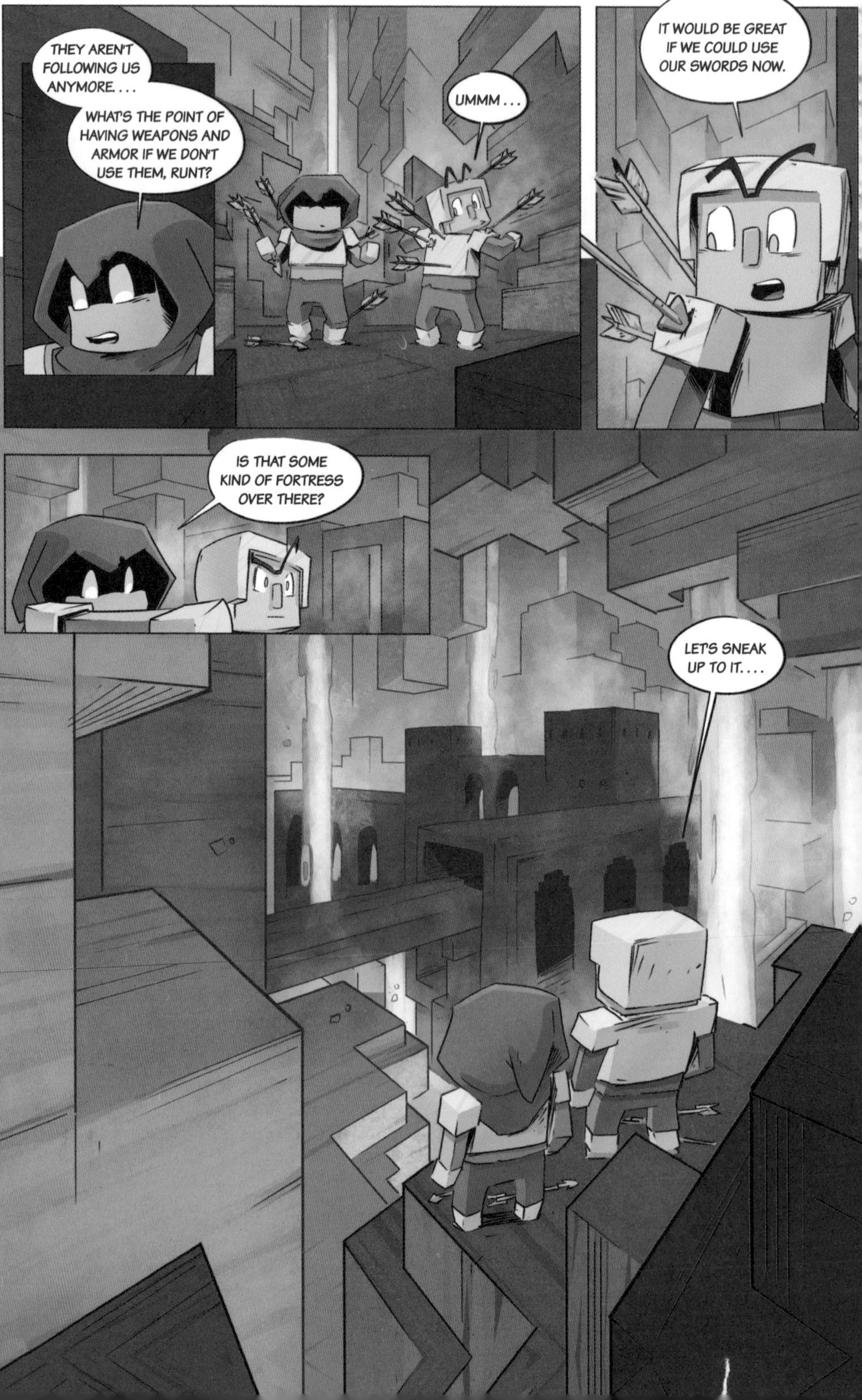
THEY AREN'T FOLLOWING US ANYMORE. . . .
WHAT'S THE POINT OF HAVING WEAPONS AND ARMOR IF WE DON'T USE THEM, RUNT?
UMMM . . .
IT WOULD BE GREAT IF WE COULD USE OUR SWORDS NOW.
IS THAT SOME KIND OF FORTRESS OVER THERE?
LET'S SNEAK UP TO IT. . . .

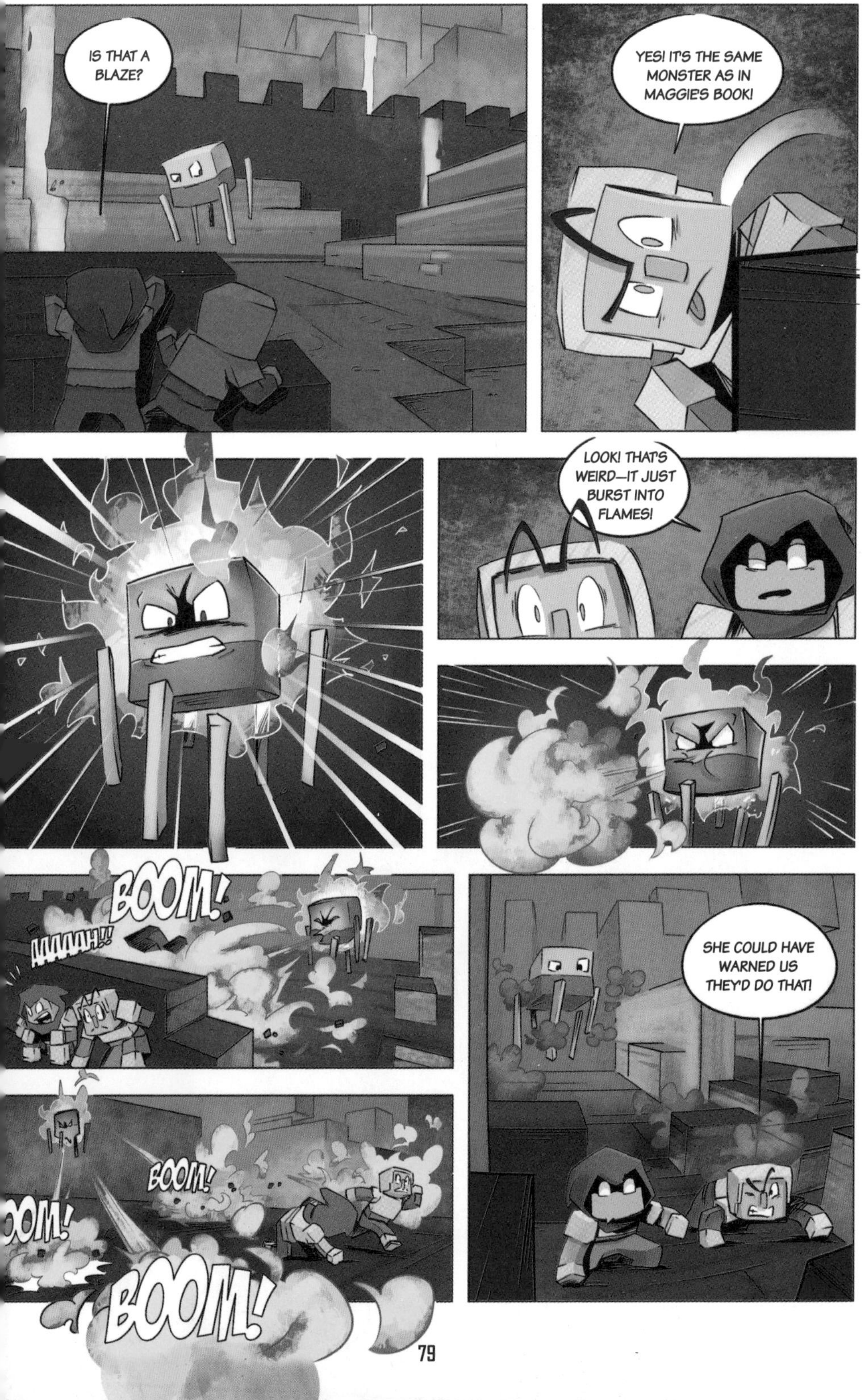

IS THAT A BLAZE?
YES! IT'S THE SAME MONSTER AS IN MAGGIE'S BOOK!
LOOK! THAT'S WEIRD—IT JUST BURST INTO FLAMES!
BOOM!
AAAAAH!!
BOOM!
OOM!
BOOM!
SHE COULD HAVE WARNED US THEY'D DO THAT!

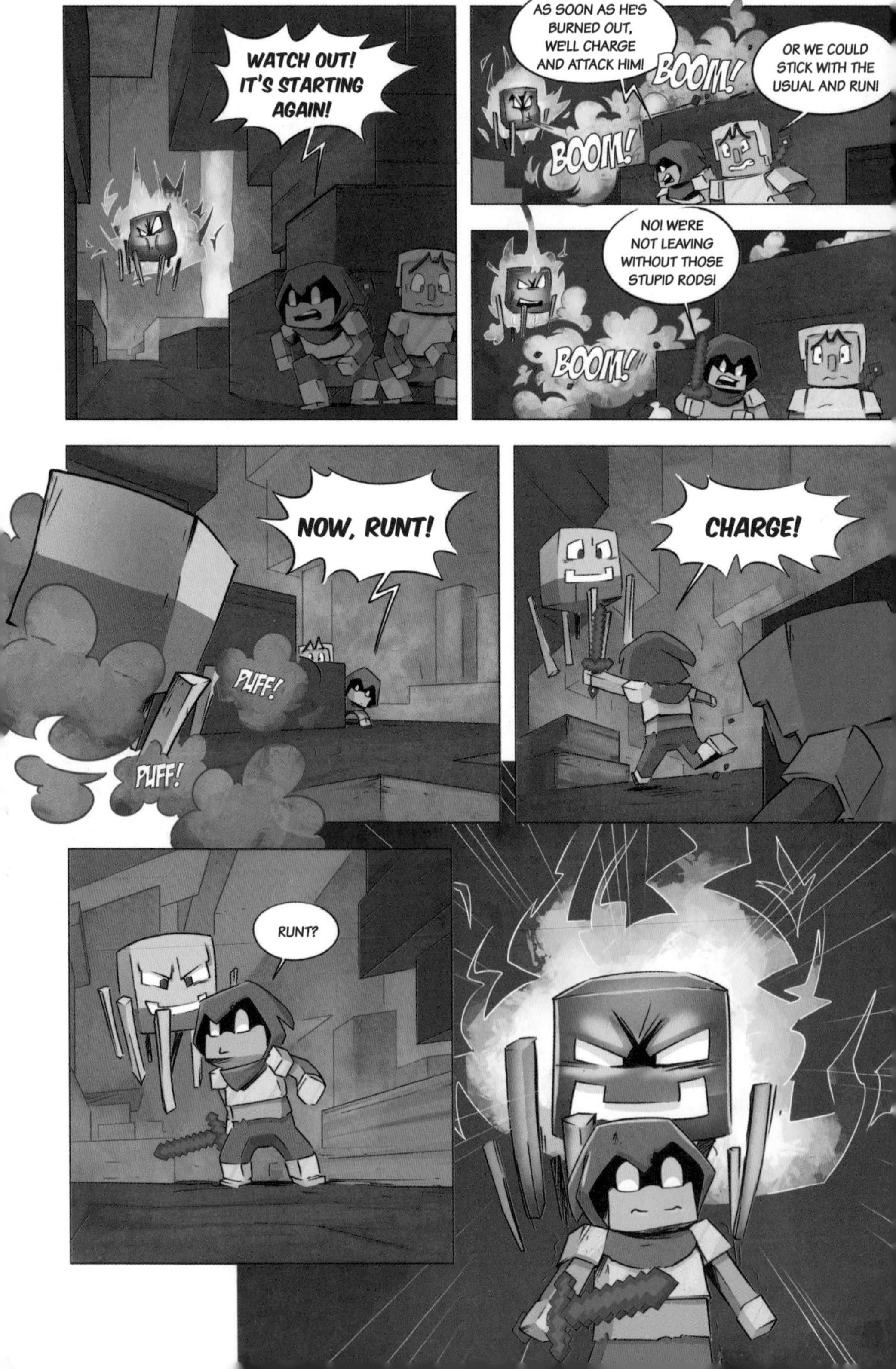
WATCH OUT! IT'S STARTING AGAIN!
AS SOON AS HE'S BURNED OUT, WE'LL CHARGE AND ATTACK HIM!
BOOM!
BOOM!
OR WE COULD STICK WITH THE USUAL AND RUN!
NO! WE'RE NOT LEAVING WITHOUT THOSE STUPID RODS!
BOOM!
NOW, RUNT!
PUFF!
PUFF!
CHARGE!
RUNT?

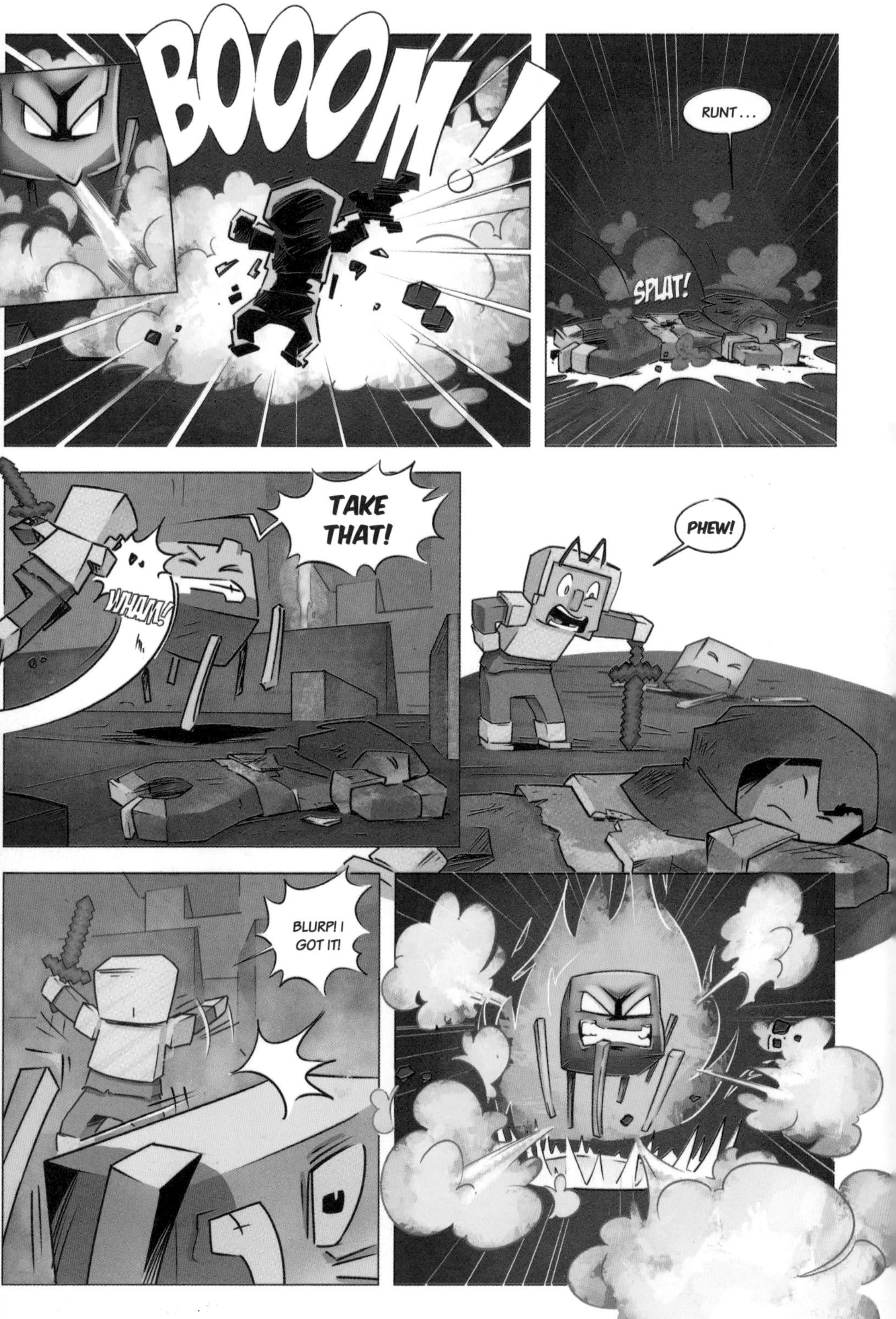
BOOOM!
RUNT...
SPLAT!
WHAM!
TAKE THAT!
PHEW!
BLURP! I GOT IT!

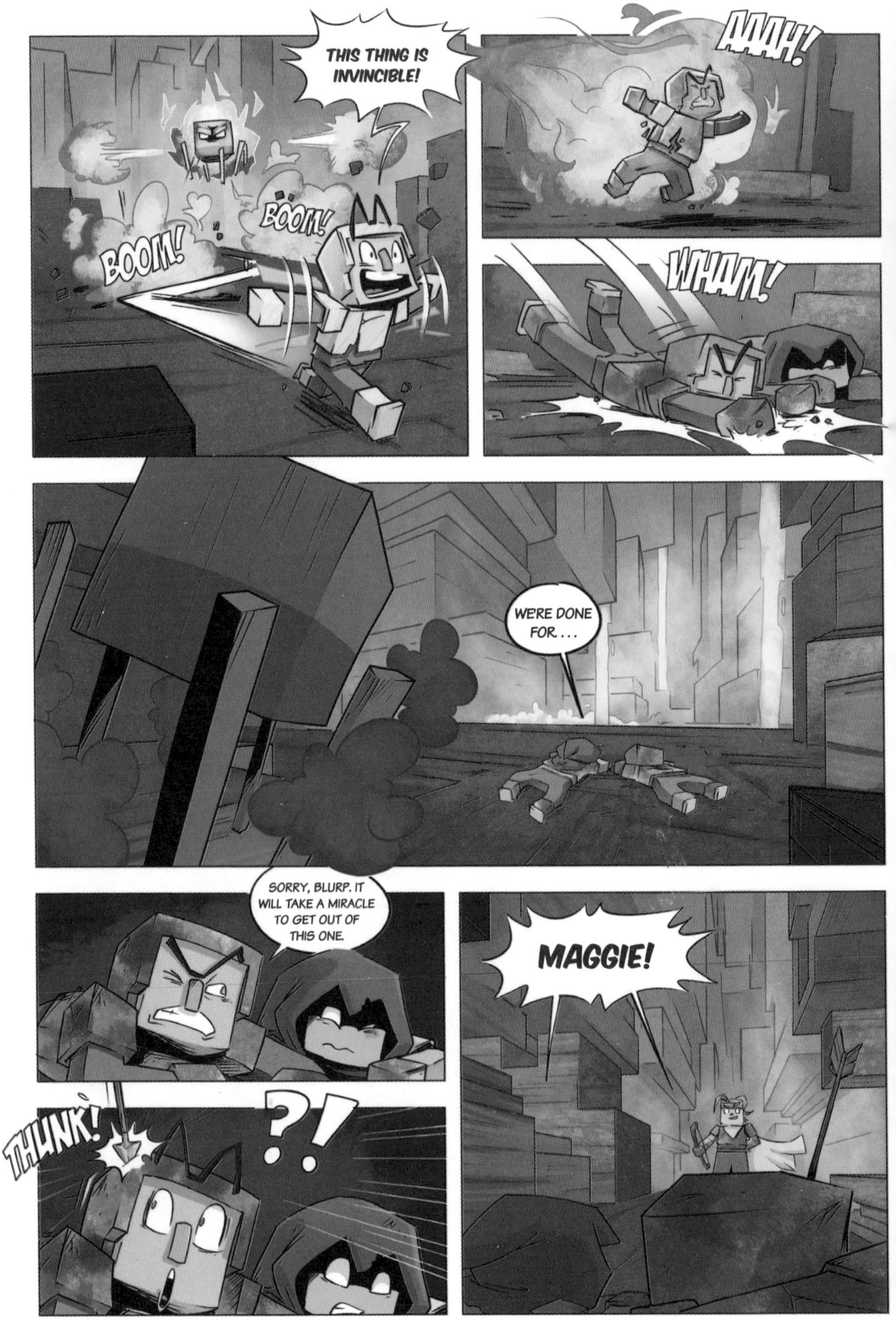
THIS THING IS INVINCIBLE!
BOOM!
BOOM!
AAAH!
WHAM!
WE'RE DONE FOR . . .
SORRY, BLURP. IT WILL TAKE A MIRACLE TO GET OUT OF THIS ONE.
MAGGIE!
THUNK!
?!

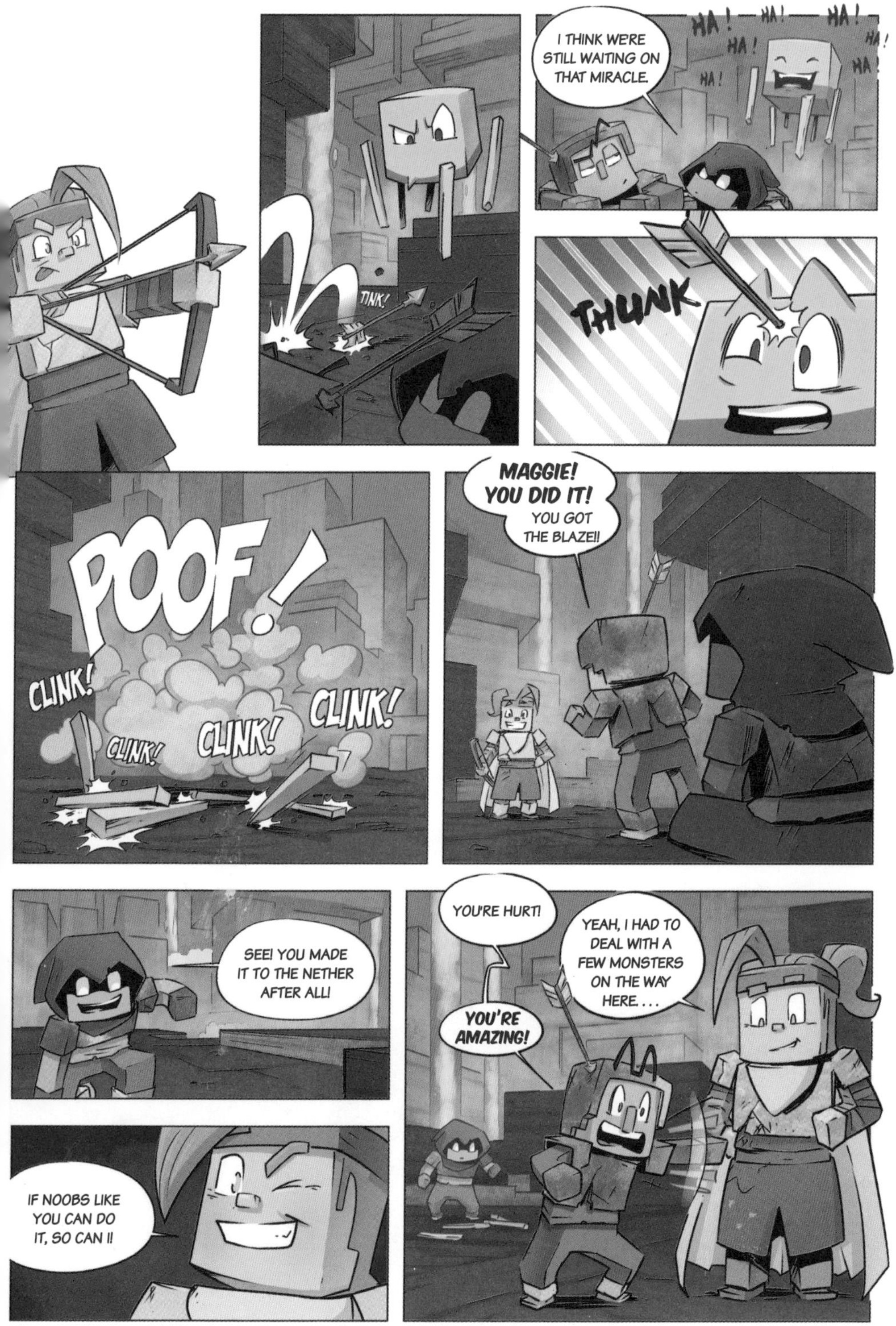
TINK!
I THINK WE'RE STILL WAITING ON THAT MIRACLE.
HA! HA! HA! HA! HA! HA! HA!
THUNK
POOF!
CLINK!
CLINK!
CLINK!
CLINK!
MAGGIE! YOU DID IT!
YOU GOT THE BLAZE!!
SEE! YOU MADE IT TO THE NETHER AFTER ALL!
IF NOOBS LIKE YOU CAN DO IT, SO CAN I!
YOU'RE HURT!
YEAH, I HAD TO DEAL WITH A FEW MONSTERS ON THE WAY HERE. . .
YOU'RE AMAZING!

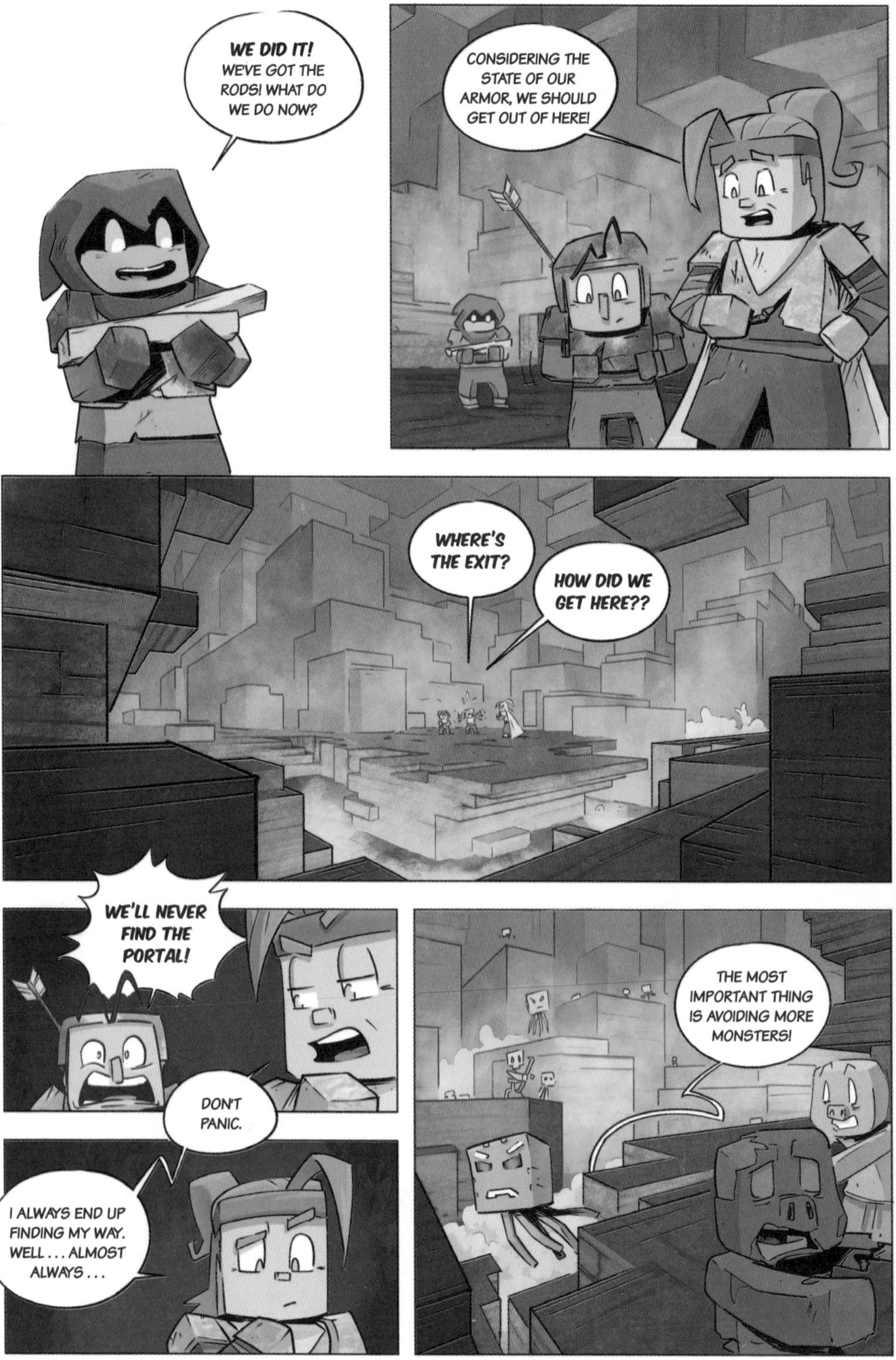
WE DID IT! WE'VE GOT THE RODS! WHAT DO WE DO NOW?
CONSIDERING THE STATE OF OUR ARMOR, WE SHOULD GET OUT OF HERE!
WHERE'S THE EXIT?
HOW DID WE GET HERE??
WE'LL NEVER FIND THE PORTAL!
DON'T PANIC.
I ALWAYS END UP FINDING MY WAY. WELL . . . ALMOST ALWAYS . . .
THE MOST IMPORTANT THING IS AVOIDING MORE MONSTERS!

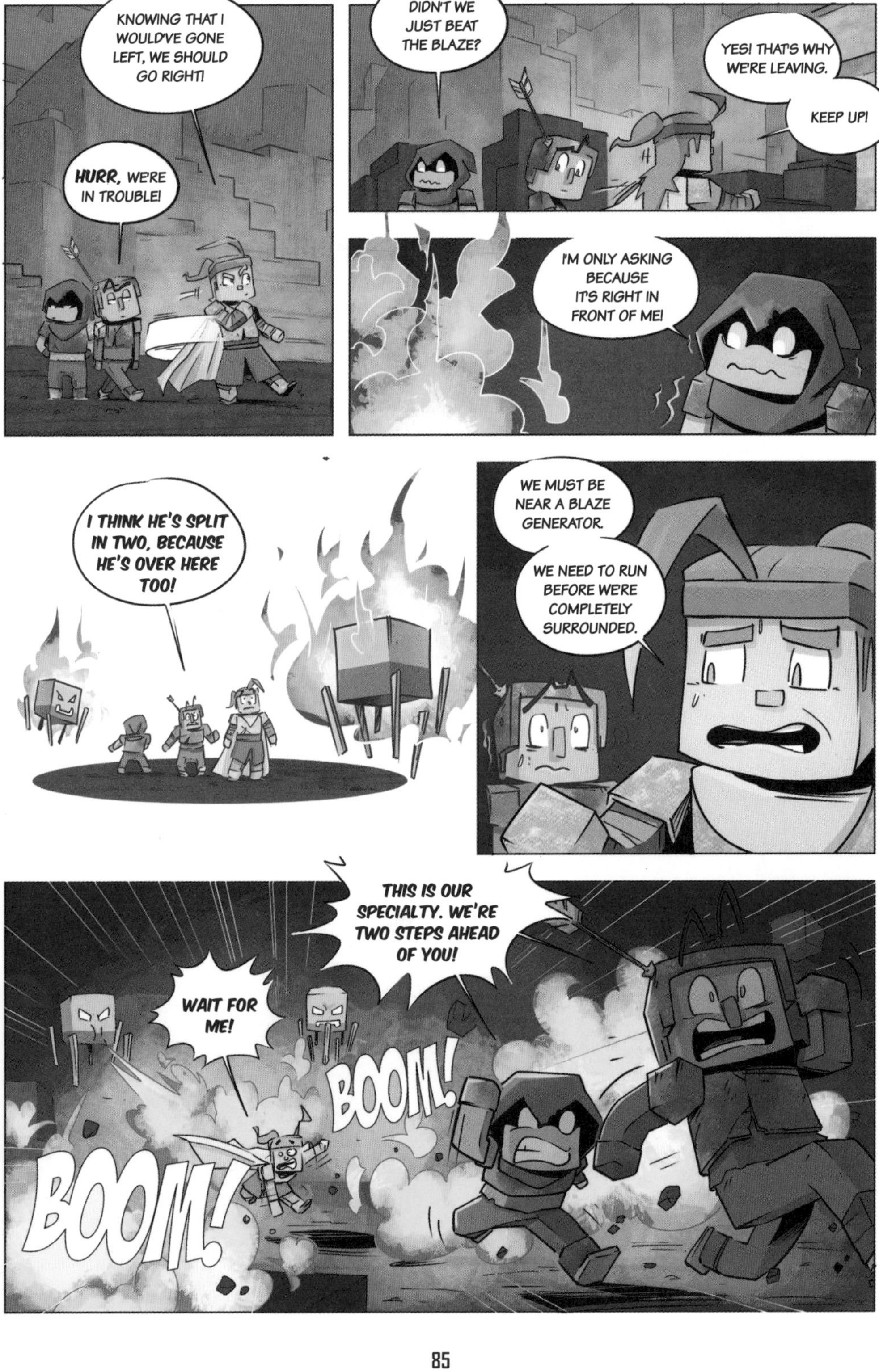
KNOWING THAT I WOULD'VE GONE LEFT, WE SHOULD GO RIGHT!
HURR, WE'RE IN TROUBLE!
DIDN'T WE JUST BEAT THE BLAZE?
YES! THAT'S WHY WE'RE LEAVING.
KEEP UP!
I'M ONLY ASKING BECAUSE IT'S RIGHT IN FRONT OF ME!
I THINK HE'S SPLIT IN TWO, BECAUSE HE'S OVER HERE TOO!
WE MUST BE NEAR A BLAZE GENERATOR.
WE NEED TO RUN BEFORE WE'RE COMPLETELY SURROUNDED.
THIS IS OUR SPECIALTY. WE'RE TWO STEPS AHEAD OF YOU!
WAIT FOR ME!
BOOM!
BOOM!

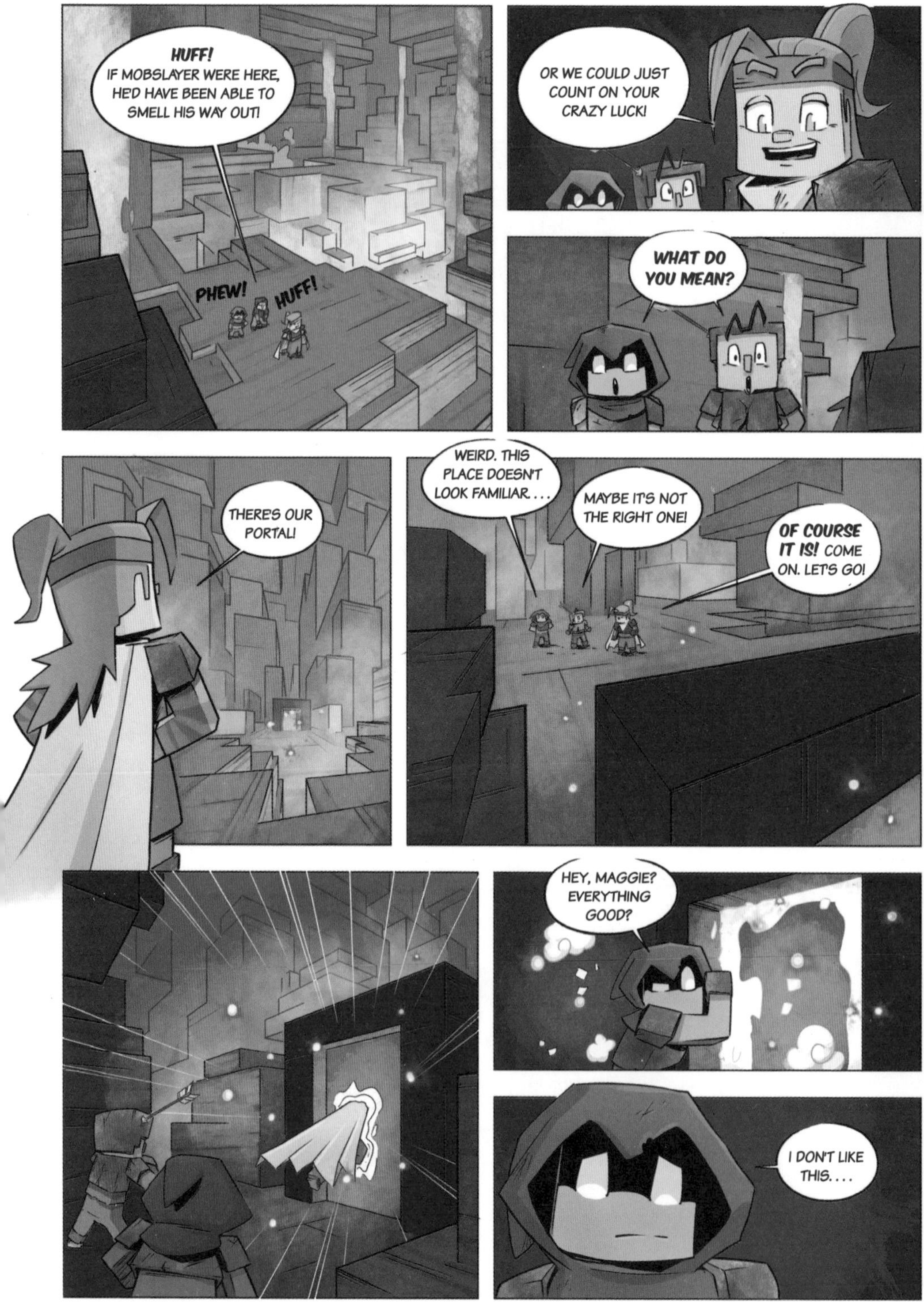
HUFF!
IF MOBSLAYER WERE HERE, HE'D HAVE BEEN ABLE TO SMELL HIS WAY OUT!
PHEW!
HUFF!
OR WE COULD JUST COUNT ON YOUR CRAZY LUCK!
WHAT DO YOU MEAN?
THERE'S OUR PORTAL!
WEIRD. THIS PLACE DOESN'T LOOK FAMILIAR. . . .
MAYBE IT'S NOT THE RIGHT ONE!
OF COURSE IT IS! COME ON. LET'S GO!
HEY, MAGGIE? EVERYTHING GOOD?
I DON'T LIKE THIS. . . .

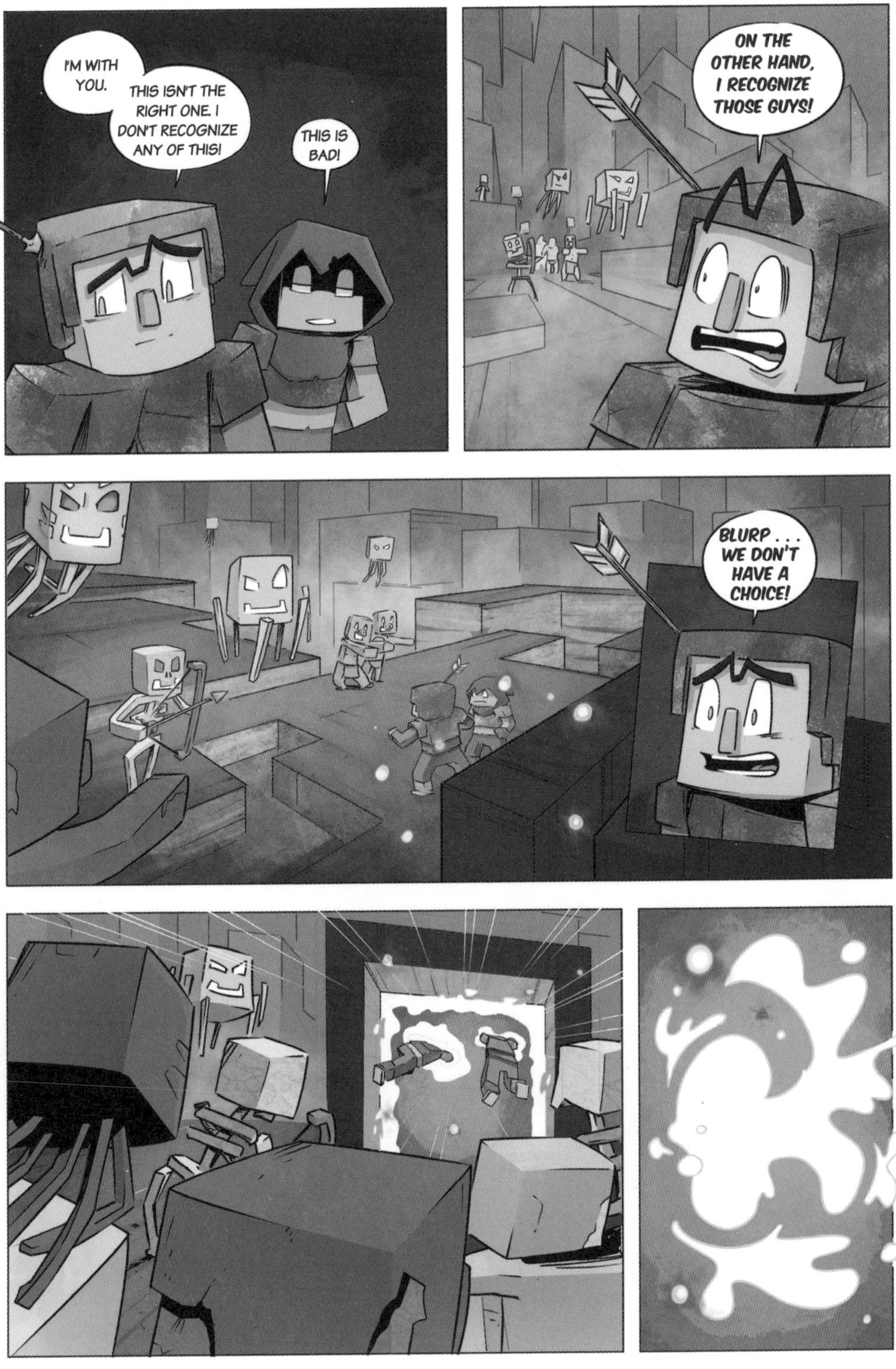
I'M WITH YOU.
THIS ISN'T THE RIGHT ONE. I DON'T RECOGNIZE ANY OF THIS!
THIS IS BAD!
ON THE OTHER HAND, I RECOGNIZE THOSE GUYS!
BLURP . . . WE DON'T HAVE A CHOICE!

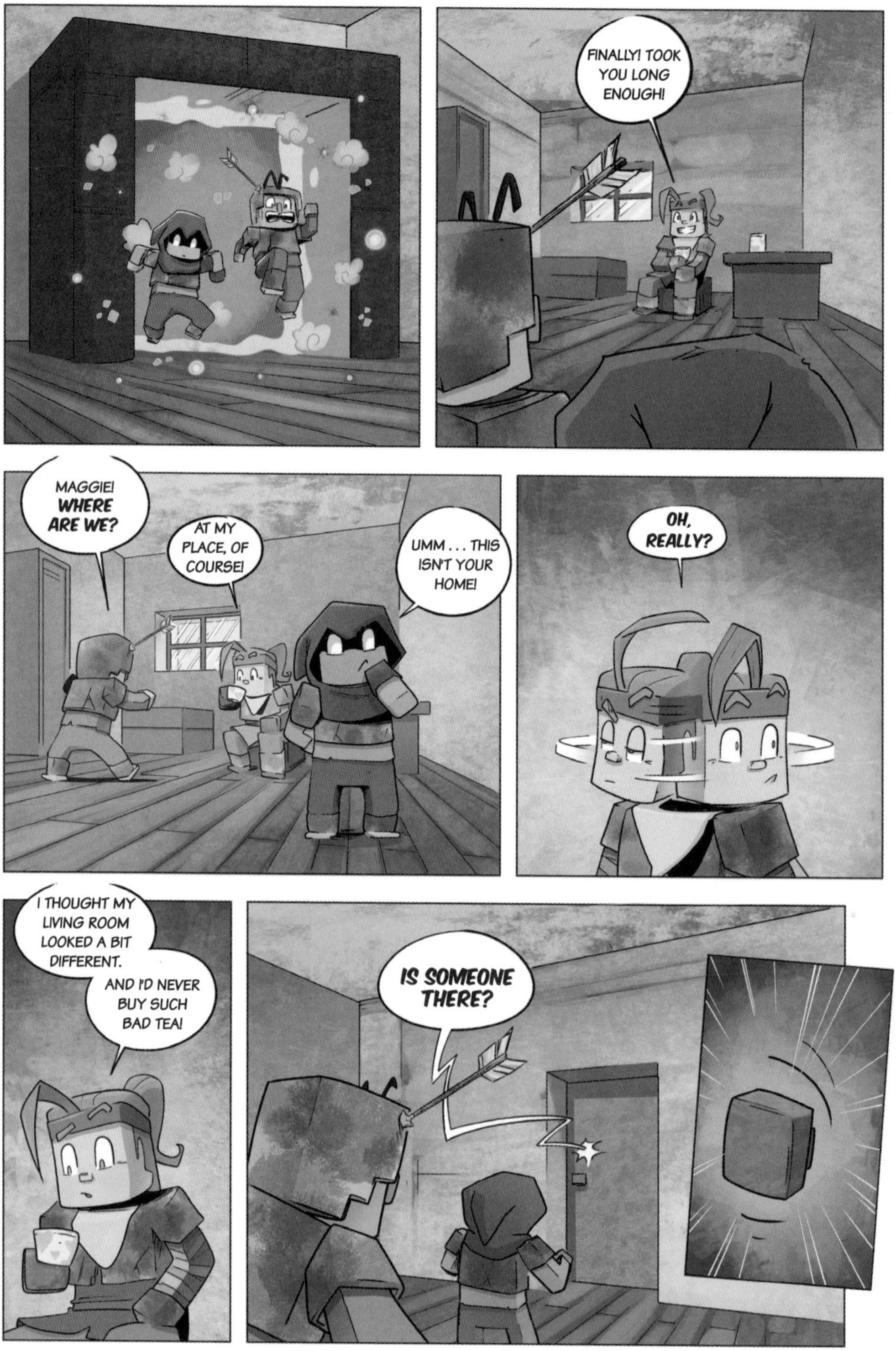
FINALLY! TOOK YOU LONG ENOUGH!
MAGGIE! **WHERE ARE WE?**
AT MY PLACE, OF COURSE!
UMM . . . THIS ISN'T YOUR HOME!
OH, REALLY?
I THOUGHT MY LIVING ROOM LOOKED A BIT DIFFERENT.
AND I'D NEVER BUY SUCH BAD TEA!
IS SOMEONE THERE?

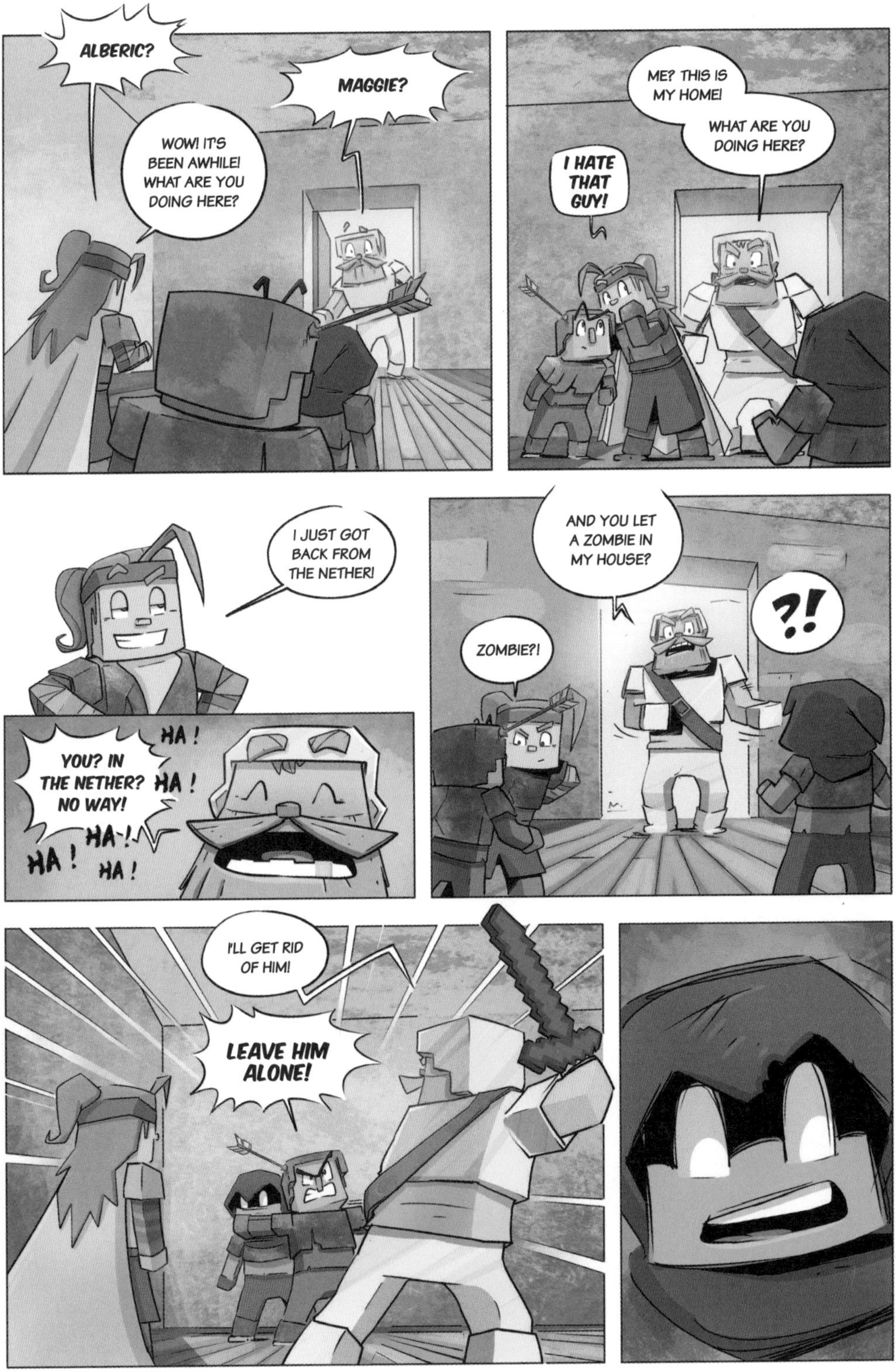
ALBERIC?
MAGGIE?
WOW! IT'S BEEN AWHILE! WHAT ARE YOU DOING HERE?
ME? THIS IS MY HOME!
WHAT ARE YOU DOING HERE?
I HATE THAT GUY!
I JUST GOT BACK FROM THE NETHER!
YOU? IN THE NETHER? NO WAY!
HA! HA! HA-! HA! HA!
AND YOU LET A ZOMBIE IN MY HOUSE?
?!
ZOMBIE?!
I'LL GET RID OF HIM!
LEAVE HIM ALONE!

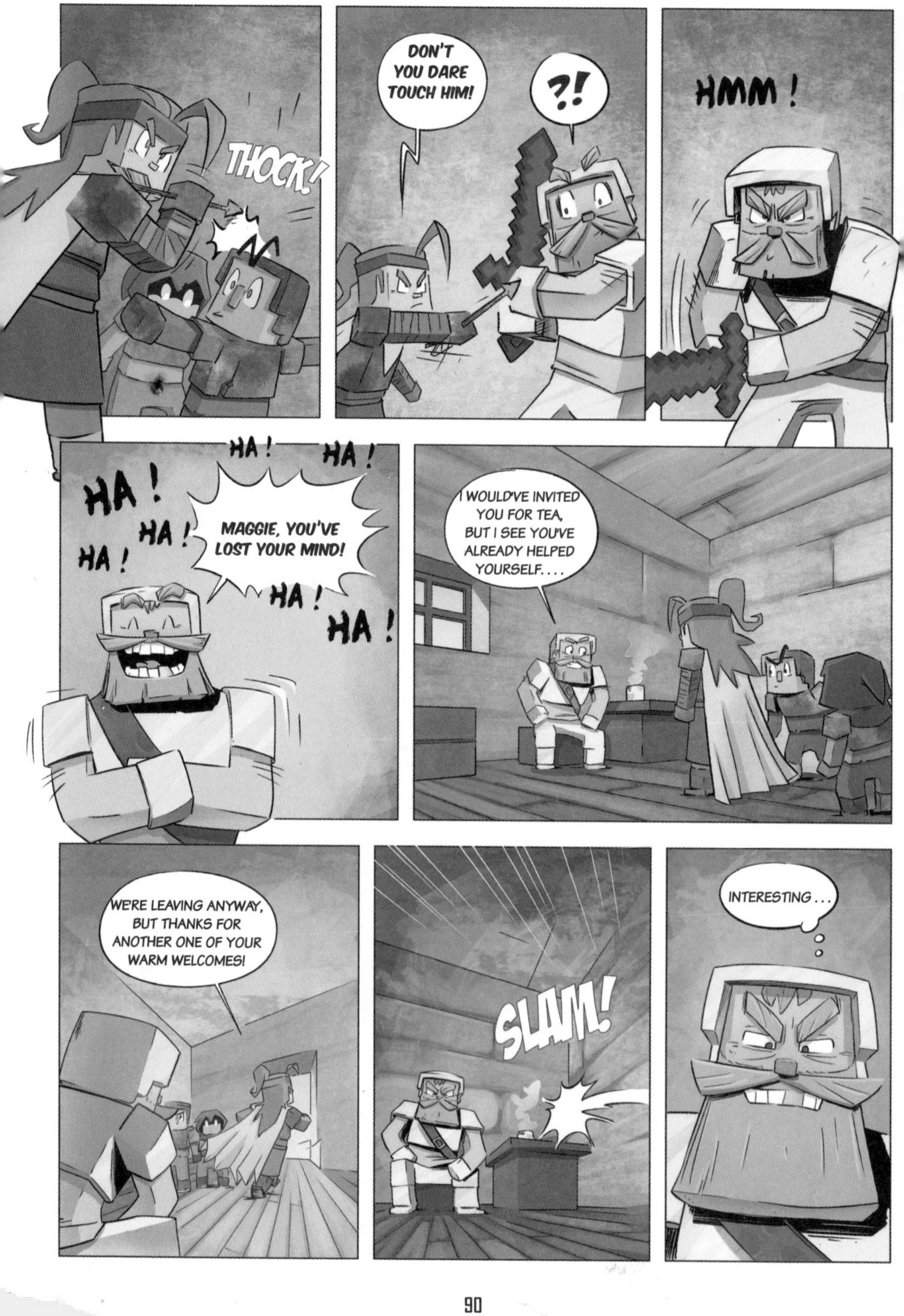
THOCK!
DON'T YOU DARE TOUCH HIM!
?!
HMM!
HA! HA! HA! HA! HA!
MAGGIE, YOU'VE LOST YOUR MIND!
HA! HA!
I WOULD'VE INVITED YOU FOR TEA, BUT I SEE YOU'VE ALREADY HELPED YOURSELF. . . .
WE'RE LEAVING ANYWAY, BUT THANKS FOR ANOTHER ONE OF YOUR WARM WELCOMES!
SLAM!
INTERESTING . . .

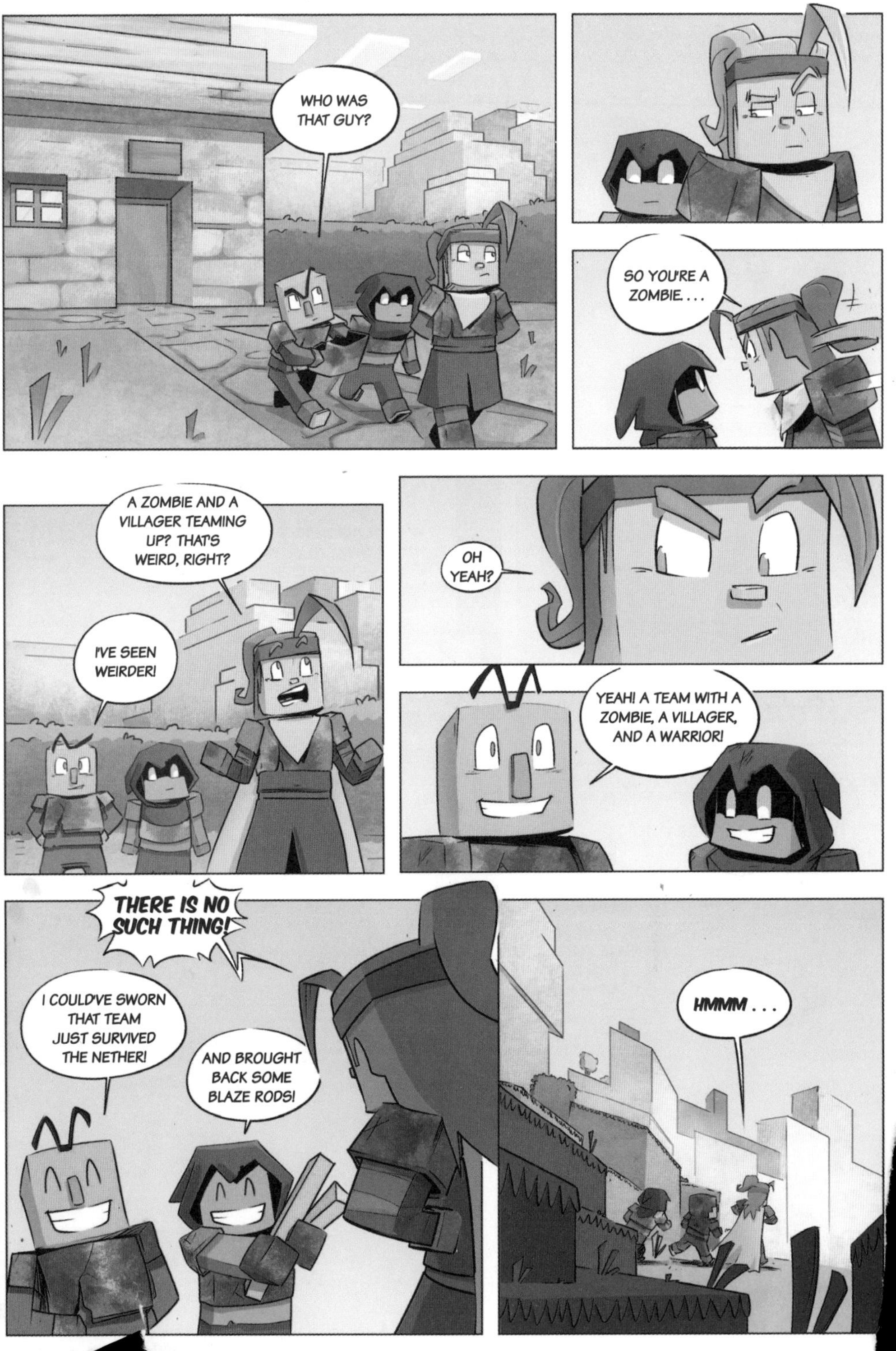
WHO WAS THAT GUY?
SO YOU'RE A ZOMBIE. . . .
A ZOMBIE AND A VILLAGER TEAMING UP? THAT'S WEIRD, RIGHT?
I'VE SEEN WEIRDER!
OH YEAH?
YEAH! A TEAM WITH A ZOMBIE, A VILLAGER, AND A WARRIOR!
THERE IS NO SUCH THING!
I COULD'VE SWORN THAT TEAM JUST SURVIVED THE NETHER!
AND BROUGHT BACK SOME BLAZE RODS!
HMMM . . .

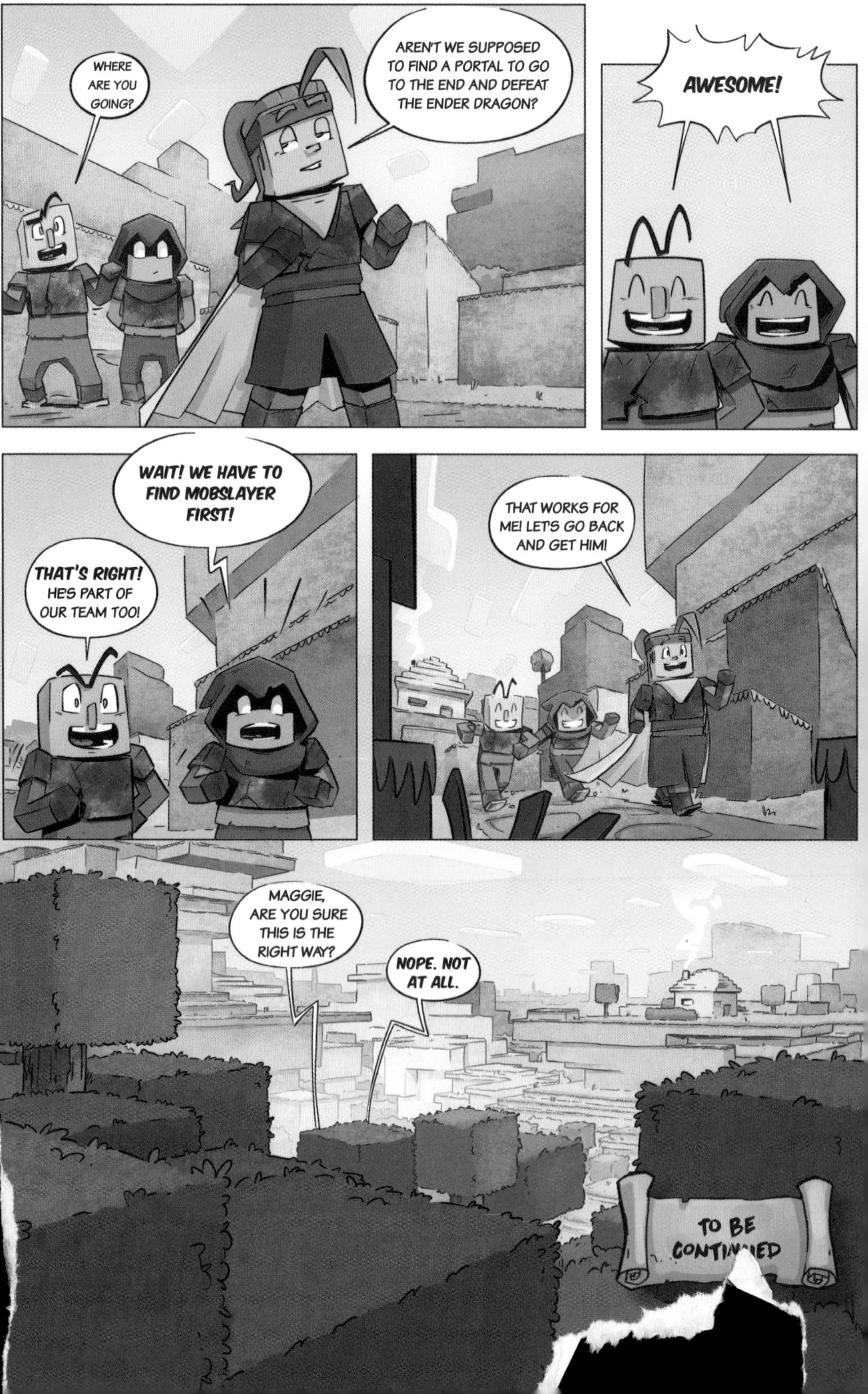
WHERE ARE YOU GOING?
AREN'T WE SUPPOSED TO FIND A PORTAL TO GO TO THE END AND DEFEAT THE ENDER DRAGON?
AWESOME!
WAIT! WE HAVE TO FIND MOBSLAYER FIRST!
THAT'S RIGHT! HE'S PART OF OUR TEAM TOO!
THAT WORKS FOR ME! LET'S GO BACK AND GET HIM!
MAGGIE, ARE YOU SURE THIS IS THE RIGHT WAY?
NOPE. NOT AT ALL.
TO BE
CONTIN ED

ABOUT THE AUTHORS

PIRATE SOURCIL is a comic book author known for his blog and his comic series *Le Joueur du grenier*, published by Hugo BD. He is also a fan of geek literature and passionate about the world of gaming.

After studying carpentry, *JEZ* turned to drawing and graphic design and decided to make a career out of it.

ODONE is a French illustrator and specializes in adding color to many comic books.